Miracle in East Texas

A Very Tall Tale Inspired by an
Absolutely True Story

Dan Gordon

Adapted from the original motion picture screenplay
Miracle in East Texas by Dan Gordon

BroadStreet
PUBLISHING

BroadStreet Publishing® Group, LLC
Savage, Minnesota, USA
BroadStreetPublishing.com

Miracle in East Texas: A Very Tall Tale Inspired by an Absolutely True Story

9781424558827 (softcover)
9781424558834 (ebook)

Stock or custom editions of BroadStreet Publishing titles may be purchased in bulk for educational, business, ministry, fundraising, or sales promotional use. For information, please email orders@broadstreetpublishing.com.

Cover and interior by Garborg Design Works | garborgdesign.com

Cover design adapted from movie poster created by Barbara Marquis-Adesanya in conjunction with Obviously Creative | barbara@obviouslycreative.com

Printed in the United States of America

23 24 25 26 27 5 4 3 2 1

For Sam Cohen:
Cattleman, pioneering aviator, sailor, geologist,
and master of all matters petroliferous.
The world is a much duller place without him.

Foreword

When Denzel Washington was interviewed on the *Charlie Rose* show about his now-classic movie *The Hurricane*, he said, "They presented that script to me, Dan Gordon's script…And I said let's go. Let's go!"

Some of the best actors in the business have had that same reaction when reading a script by Dan Gordon: Kevin Costner, Gene Hackman, Sir Ben Kingsley, James Earl Jones, Forest Whitaker, Kevin Bacon, Gary Oldman, James Garner, Michael Landon, Dennis Quaid, and yours truly, to name a few.

There's a reason for that. Dan Gordon is a storyteller who creates characters who are not only real but almost always involved in an existential struggle between the better and worse angels of themselves. They are not cardboard heroes. They are flawed. In other words, they are like most of us. They are struggling to find or resist faith and, like us all, are in need of grace.

Whether it's Kevin Costner's brooding portrayal of Wyatt Earp or Denzel Washington's rage-filled Rubin "Hurricane" Carter, who ultimately realizes, "Hate put me in prison. Love's gonna bust me out," Gordon's characters are in search of their better selves. They are all, at one point or another, going to reach out for God's redemptive love—sometimes despite their best efforts not only to avoid that love but also to deny it or, like Jonah in the Bible, run away from it if they can.

And that brings us to *Miracle in East Texas*, the movie based on Dan's screenplay, which I had the pleasure of directing, and its protagonist, Doc Boyd, whom I had the equal pleasure of portraying.

Miracle in East Texas is the story of two fast-talking hucksters: Dr. Horatio Daedalus Boyd and Dad Everett. These two hard-luck con men make their living swindling widows during the height of the Great Depression. That puts them certainly in the bottom half of the moral barrel. But then, by what can only be described as the grace of God, every lie they tell begins to come true. What follows is funny and poignant, romantic and inspiring.

It is the story of two scalawags who, despite their best or worst intentions, find those better angels inside them. It is the rollicking story of a time of miracles: the East Texas oil boom of the early 1930s, a time when bums became billionaires and sinners became saints. It is a tall tale inspired by an absolutely true story. If you enjoy the read half as much as we enjoyed making the movie, you're in for a good time!

Kevin Sorbo

Actor, director, producer

Chapter 1

The only thing they knew about Tanner Irving Jr. was that he was an old Black man and one of the only living people who actually remembered what had happened in Cornville, Texas, in the year of our Lord 1930.

"Is he in a home or somethin'? I mean, like, does he drool? I mean, do we even know if the guy can talk?" asked young Matt Ingersol.

Not that he actually cared. For him, there were only two important things about this school assignment. One was that, even though he had just turned sixteen and had recently gotten his license, he was actually getting to drive not the family Subaru but what seemed to him like an oddly majestic Ford Econovan, which contained all their video and sound equipment. The second thing was the fact that, since he was an AP sophomore taking a senior class in state history, he had been teamed up with Denise Waters, a stunning almost eighteen-year-old senior with a smile that could light up ten rooms. Her mother had been a former Miss Puerto Rico in the Miss Universe contest, and her father was a movie star–handsome sports commentator who had played six seasons in the NBA. She was the veritable "Girl from Ipanema"—tall and tan and young and lovely—and every boy at Marcus Hill Christian Academy had a crush on her. And he, Matt Ingersol, was the guy who got to sit beside her, cruising in the Econovan.

There were only a few slight impediments standing in the way of Matt Ingersol's courtship of Denise Waters.

First, Matt had recently experienced two physiological changes. He had grown from five foot ten to six foot three in less than half a year. His shoe size had gone from a nine and a half to a thirteen. He was not used to the size of his new feet and, therefore, continuously tripped over them. He also tripped over furniture, electrical wires, garden hoses, and any of the other seemingly ordinary accoutrements of everyday life that, for Matt, had become the equivalent of a Navy SEAL's obstacle course.

The second thing that had occurred was that his voice had suddenly dropped from an almost castrato-like, high-pitched teenage squeak to a Johnny Cash basso profundo, and his vocal cords had not yet become accustomed to their new and lower-pitched tuning. Thus, he would occasionally and uncontrollably emit a sound not unlike that of a duck with irritable bowel syndrome.

Put the two physiological changes together and you had a sixteen-year-old Barnum and Bailey clown in floppy shoes three sizes too big and a honker Harpo Marx would have envied, except that it was located in his throat, not attached to a squeeze bulb on his hip.

Thus, the possibility of actually impressing Denise Waters, upon whom he, like every other boy at school, had a crush, was almost nonexistent.

Chapter 1

Unfortunately for young Matt, when he asked, "Do we even know if this guy can talk?" he honked instead of pronouncing the last word of the sentence.

"Do we even know if he can *what?*" Denise asked.

"Taaalk!" Matt said, honking once again.

"Talk?" Denise asked. "Were you trying to pronounce the word *talk?*"

"Speak," Matt said, searching for any other set of phonetics that would not produce the dreaded sound.

"Ah," said Denise. "Do we know if he can *speak*. Well, whether he can or he can't, my guess is he doesn't honk."

When they arrived at Tanner Irving's farm, Matt navigated the long and elegant driveway leading up to the equally elegant home that sat atop a small hill, surveying the lush farmland below. It fell to Matt to manfully stride up to the front door and make the introductions.

He rang the doorbell and waited for what he assumed would be a live-in caregiver to greet them and invite them in. Instead, the door opened, revealing Tanner Irving Jr. He had a corncob pipe clenched between his teeth. Mr. Irving opened the door just the tiniest bit, only seeing Matt and not Denise, who stood off to the side.

"Yes?" he asked, looking impatiently at Matt, as if the boy had come to sell him unwanted magazines or cheap chocolate for a high school fundraiser.

"Uh. Uh, Mr. Irving?" Matt said, honking on the last syllable.

"Boy, did you just honk at me?"

Matt's face reddened. He cleared his throat. "Are you Mr. Irving?"

"That's me," said the cantankerous centenarian. "And who are you?"

"Um, I'm Matt Ingersol. I'm from Marcus Hill Christian Academy."

"Not interested. Good day." He closed the door unceremoniously in Matt's face.

Matt looked down at his shoes as if they somehow could instruct him as to what to do next. Alas, they were just shoes and provided him no counsel. Thus abandoned by his footwear, he rang the doorbell again.

After a few moments the door opened, and Irving once again appeared, smoking his corncob pipe like an angry locomotive belching clouds into a pristine sky. Even at close to one hundred years old, he was still strikingly handsome.

"I'm Mr. Irving, and you're from the Marcus Hill Christian Academy. We've established that. We've also established that whatever you're selling, I'm not buying."

"Uh, Mr. Irving," said Matt, beginning to feel flop sweat beading up on his forehead and dripping down, staining his shirt. "I'm not selling anything."

"Well, I already donate to the University of Texas and LSU. Those are the only scholarships that I give, and all my other charitable giving is already spoken for. So I wish you well. *Vaya con Dios*, Godspeed, and adios."

He closed the door once again, for emphasis.

Matt looked at Denise.

Denise looked at Matt and, with an unmistakable expression that gave an unmistakable message, said, "Ring the doorbell again, you wuss."

Matt rang the doorbell again.

Once again, the door opened, and Tanner Irving Jr. appeared, clouds of smoke swirling about his head like that of a sacrifice recently made to a pagan god. Mr. Irving had clearly had enough of this boy.

"Son, I'm trying to watch a ball game. Some people might admire your persistence, but I just find it annoying. Now, you ring this door one more time, and I'm coming out with a shotgun."

So saying, Tanner Irving Jr. turned on his heel and, one might even say sprightly for a man of his advanced years, prepared to withdraw into the inner sanctum of the home he considered not only his castle but, during football season, the very sanctum sanctorum of his big-screen plasma temple to southern collegiate gridiron.

"Mr. Irving, please," said Denise, stepping forward into Tanner Irving's line of sight with the same honeyed charm with which she, to that day, wrapped her six-foot, six-inch former NBA star father around her finger. "My name is Denise Waters."

She let a little more southern drip into her accent, with just the proper hint of girlish flirtation, like a subtle scent of perfume in a veritable ocean of respect. "We're here to film the interview with you for the documentary we're making for our Texas history class."

Tanner Irving, if not mollified, at least slowed the tactical retreat in which he was previously engaged. With his eyebrows raised, his look was that of a man his age who was trying to mask the fact that he may have temporarily forgotten not only who you are but also what he was just about to do before you interrupted him.

Denise Waters recognized the look. It was the same expression she had seen many times on her own grandfather's face, the one that both broke and touched her heart to know what the passing of time can do to the mental acuity of those you love the most. She decided that the only way to break through to the once razor-sharp mind of Tanner Irving Jr. was to deck it with southern charm.

"We've driven all the way from Dallas, sir," she said, almost blushing with modesty.

Tanner Irving looked from her to the gawky teenage boy standing beside her.

"Your classmate's a lot sharper than you are, son." He looked at Denise, then shot a not-so-kindly word of advice back to Matt. "You should have let her do the talking from the get-go."

With that, he dismissed young Matt entirely and turned to Denise, who reminded him so much of his own granddaughter.

"What documentary?" he asked, with as stern an attitude as he could muster, all the while feeling himself being wrapped, ever so subtly, around that little finger.

"It's about Doc Boyd and Dad Everett," said Denise, "and everything that happened out in Cornville back in the thirties."

Those words brought a snap of electricity to the air, shattering the mist around the thoughts of a man who had outlived even his own memories. It brought Tanner Irving back in an instant, with a clarity that startled him, to his own youth, to days when no one on earth was as strong as his father or as fleet of foot as that man's ten-year-old son running across the endless flatland for the sheer joy of running.

"Cornville? East Texas?" he said, turning back to Matt accusingly. "Why didn't you say so? You're late, aren't ya? Weren't you supposed to be out here this morning?"

Now it was Matt's turn to be lost in the fog of the old man's jumbled thoughts. "Ah…" he stuttered. "No, we were supposed to—"

Chapter 1

But Denise, yet again, came to the rescue. She was no stranger to the kaleidoscope of memory and illusion that tumbled through an old man's thoughts. "Yes, we were," she murmured, opening the tap of southern molasses just a wee bit more. "And we're terribly sorry for the inconvenience, but we got stuck in traffic on the interstate."

Tanner Irving Jr. smiled at the young girl. She was the spitting image of his great-granddaughter, the apple of his eye, now finishing her final year of law school, which he had happily paid for with his part of the bounty that remained from that legendary time when, in the midst of the hopelessness and despair of the Depression and dust bowl, it seemed as if giants roamed the earth.

"You gotta learn how to stretch the truth, son," he said to the boy. "This girl has a talent for it." The last part he said with no small amount of appreciation. For, in truth, no one had more admiration for one who could test the elasticity of fact than Tanner Irving Jr. He had the privilege of seeing the two best flimflam men who ever bamboozled the locals of Oklahoma and East Texas, clinging as these two men did to each impossible test of the fine line between fact and fiction, as children believe that Santa is a plate of cookies away from leaving them ponies.

"Doc Boyd and Dad Everett. Sure. You bet. Where we gonna do this…Hollywood opus?"

Victory! young Matt thought. He was now young Spielberg, about to turn a point-of-view shot into a killer shark rising menacingly from the depths toward a girl innocently swimming across the surface of the water. "Well," he said, "we thought maybe in your living room, with all your memorabilia and stuff."

And as he said the words, he was lighting the scene in his mind, adding a sepia tone here and a Depression-era black-and-white filter there.

Tanner Irving Jr. had not heard a word he said. "How about right here on the front porch. In this rocker." So saying, he planted his tall and lanky frame into his beloved rocker, from which vantage point he often gazed not only across the endless stretch of farmland but also at the dimly lit memories that flickered across his mind like the film reel in the picture shows of his youth.

"What a wonderful idea!" Denise Waters said.

But young Matt was not going to surrender his Oscar that easily. "Uh, sir?" he said, as respectfully as a budding auteur could manage. "It's a little," he struggled for a word that would not insult the man, "bland, you know? The white backdrop with the white front porch. It needs something to make it pop."

"Make it pop," Irving said evenly. It wasn't a question when he said it. It was a judgment.

"Yes, sir," said Matt.

"On my porch?" said Irving.

Matt dutifully nodded. "Yes, sir."

"I'm not big on 'popping,'" said the old man, with a surprising amount of steel in his voice. "We'll do it right here."

"You bet," said Matt.

With that, he set the Sony α6500 camera on the tripod, put an LED light panel on a stand, pulled out a white pop-up bounce board, and began to toy with the notion of racking focus, anything, anything at all to put his fingerprints as a director upon the frame.

"Ready when you are, Cecil B.," Irving said.

Chapter 1

Matt pressed the record button on the camera and said, "Rolling!" only too aware of the crack in his voice, which he had meant to sound so decisive for Denise's benefit and which instead came out as more of a mallard in heat.

Denise smiled, the kind of smile that dashes the hopes of young boys with crushes on older girls. She put the slate in front of the camera and said, authoritatively, "Cornville documentary. Tanner Irving Jr. interview. Take one."

She clicked the slate and moved out of frame. Then, she picked up the yellow legal pad filled with questions she had assiduously assembled from all the written research material at her disposal when suddenly, Mr. Irving said, "We gonna be at this for very long? More than an hour?" He looked back and forth between Matt and Denise.

Matt cleared his throat, hoping to preempt any further croaking noises. "Probably, sir."

With that, Tanner Irving rose from the rocking chair that creaked along with the floorboards of the porch. "Well," said Irving, "I'd better hit the john first. Pay my water tax."

And without another word, he walked back into his house and closed the door, leaving Matt with nothing to do but say, "Cut."

Chapter 2

"Cornville documentary. Tanner Irving Jr. interview. Take two," Denise said and snapped the clapboard shut.

"I assume you're going to ask me the questions, young lady."

It was not a question. A Tanner Irving Jr. assumption was a statement of fact.

"Yes, sir," said Denise, dripping honeyed southern charm.

"Good," said Mr. Irving. "You seem to have a certain"—he waved his hand, searching for the right word—"je ne sais quoi about you I find lacking in young Matt here. What is your name again?"

"Denise, sir," said young Ms. Waters, looking Mr. Irving straight in the eye, all journalist all the time.

"Okay, Denise, give me your best shot," said Irving, taking a long draw on his corncob pipe and puffing out a cloud that encompassed him like he was an ebony Vesuvius.

Denise glanced down at her yellow legal pad, carefully engraved with each of the questions she had fashioned the night before. But before she could ask the first one, Tanner Irving Jr. beat her to the punch with, almost word for word, the first question on her list.

Chapter 2

"How old was I when I first laid eyes on Dad Everett and Dr. Boyd?"

"Uh, yes!" said Denise. "How old were you when..."

"I got it, baby sister." He nodded his head, took another draw on the tobacco, and eased himself down into a comfortable memory, which he visited often in the late afternoons while gazing out across the beauty of the farm that had come to be his as a result of that first meeting.

But he wasn't going to give it up that easily. Let this young journalist think he was searching for it.

"Oh, let's see. That was more than eighty years ago. I must have been, maybe, nine or ten."

The truth was, it was more like ninety years ago, but an older gentleman can be excused for shaving a decade or two off his résumé for a comely, young southern girl. "But Boyd wasn't any doctor."

"He wasn't?" Denise asked, in true dismay. In her research, she had found mention of a university degree from a European institution of some repute.

"Not even close," said Irving. "And his name wasn't Boyd either. And he wasn't any kind of geologist. He was eking out a living swindling widows with worthless oil scams. I expect he couldn't have been much better at that if he had been a real doctor."

With that, Irving drifted back in his mind's eye to the first time he had seen Doc Boyd and Dad Everett driving up the country lane in their brand-new, shiny black 1929 Model A Ford convertible. He had never seen a vehicle more magnificent. The spoked chrome wheels caught the glint of the sun and reflected it like mirrors, highlighting the whitewall tires and cream-colored rims. And behind the spare tire, there was a custom-made luggage rack that held Doc and Dad's trunk like a prized treasure borne aloft by imperial servants. It was a chariot truly worthy of, if not a king, then at least a renowned professor of geology.

When he alighted from the vehicle, Boyd cut a dashing figure in his high-topped, buckled boots that clung to his calves like those of a spit-and-polish Queen's Own British officer and gentleman. The flared, white, cavalry-like riding breeches highlighted the military effect. Boyd wore a white dress shirt, buttoned up to the top button, and a crushed gray velvet blazer that contrasted the military air with one of an accomplished, cultured, academic gentleman of leisure. Topping off what Tanner Irving Jr. thought was the most exotic apparel he had ever beheld was a dazzling white derby set off with a blue sweatband, around which Tanner could see not even the slightest trace of perspiration.

Dad Everett, on the other hand, created an entirely different impression. He did not so much alight from the gleaming black Model A as he did hoist his massive bulk, not unlike a paddle wheeler off-loading its cumbersome cargo onto the dock. The Model A seemed to sigh in relief, and its springs, unburdened of the weight of the aging wildcatter, rose, like a young gazelle, at least another six inches off the ground.

Dad was a workingman to his core. When he was working on the rigs, he wore brown Carhartt canvas overalls, a dark brown shirt, and a sweat-stained fedora of an indefinite color. It was neither brown nor gray; it simply looked soiled. When he would visit the aging ladies, whom he sometimes referred to as "the widders," he wore more formal attire—gray slacks, a faded gray shirt, an increasingly tight-fitting blue blazer, and the ever-present fedora. It was difficult to say that he cut a dashing figure; rather, he presented as almost Gibraltar-like, something time-tested, solid, and true.

Where Doc was flamboyant, Dad was rock steady. Where Doc was elegant, Dad had workingman's dirt under his fingernails, of which anyone could see he was proud.

Denise interrupted Irving's reverie, asking, "Mr. Irving, did you say his name wasn't really Dr. Horatio Daedalus Boyd?"

"What's that?" Tanner Irving Jr. asked, as if reluctant to leave the golden, sepia-hued memories of his childhood, which felt like a most comfortable old pair of overalls.

"Doc Boyd?" Denise asked. "Dr. Horatio Daedalus Boyd? You say that wasn't his real name?"

"No, his name was Bumstetter, as I recall. Heinrich Bumstetter," Irving said, remembering the shock he felt hearing the man's real name for the first time during the infamous trial covered by every newspaper in the land. "Boyd was an alias. And then he was P. L. Dobson, and then, I believe, Arthur Lloyd Carrington Jr. He had a French name or two, I think. Though what they were slips my mind. Peppy La Pew or something like that."

"Why did he keep changing his name?" Denise asked innocently.

"The man was a serial bigamist," Irving responded, "and he left a string of heartbroken widows all across the nation's heartland." Irving's gaze drifted upward to the clear blue sky. "I remember a story, in fact, in which Dr. Boyd, mischievous, old scalawag that he was, had to run for his life, carrying his carpetbag, while an irate, overweight husband pursued him across the horizon with a twelve-gauge shotgun, with which he had sincerely intended to ventilate Dr. Boyd's backside." He chuckled to himself, his teeth clacking against the pipe in his mouth.

"Luckily for Doc Boyd, it was not his first such encounter, and his faithful companion, Dad Everett, had their old, original cream-colored Model A coupe waiting with the door open and the engine running for a quick getaway." Irving shook his head, half in disapproval, half in admiration. "Happily for Dr. Boyd and unhappily for the irate husband, the latter, while giving chase, caught his foot in a prairie dog hole that brought his bulk crashing down to Mother Earth and harmlessly discharging the buckshot into the prairie grassland."

He removed a handkerchief from the pocket of his pants and wiped his eyes, still grinning at the memory.

"Horatio Daedalus Boyd was simply the latest in a long line of aliases meant to keep creditors, husbands, and jilted inamoratas from filling his backside with the aforementioned double-aught buckshot."

Irving leaned forward, looking into Denise's eyes. "Course, he didn't start out with the oil scam. He began by selling Dr. Enrique Alonzo's Miracle Elixir of Life. Much later, in my teenaged years, Doc Boyd showed me photographs of that incarnation. He would stand on a loading dock or train station platform in a white smock, complete with a stethoscope around his neck and a doctor's reflector around his head. He repeated for me his patter and one particularly amorous adventure."

Irving cleared his throat and proclaimed, "'Ladies and gentlemen, boys and girls,' he would say, gathering the crowd around him. 'You've heard it said many a time you can't put a price on your health. Well, tonight, my good friends, let me tell you right here and now—you can! For only one dollar, one greenback, a mere buck, a screaming eagle, a trifling one hundred pence, you will have the cure for every ailment under the sun, A to Z. Arthritis, bursitis, conjunctivitis, diverticulitis, fibrositis, gastritis, hepatitis, laryngitis, meningitis, nymphitis, and otitis. As a matter of fact, any -*itis* under the sun will more than meet its match with Dr. Enrique Alonzo's Miracle Elixir of Life.'

"At that point," Irving continued, delighted to have an audience, "a not-unattractive, middle-aged housewife piped up and said, 'Dr. Alonzo? Will the elixir…Well, my husband's a traveling salesman, and he gets home awful tired. It just seems like he doesn't have any of the old vim and vigor anymore.'

"At which point Doc Boyd smiled at her and responded, 'My dear, did you say a *traveling* salesman?'

"The upshot of which found 'Dr. Enrique Alonzo' once again hightailing it across the prairie land, carpetbag in hand, pursued by yet another irate husband armed with a scattergun and the full intent of putting it to use against the good doctor.

"After a number of run-ins with irate customers—and some of their husbands—he was reborn as Dr. Horatio Daedalus Boyd: petroleum engineer, geologist, and world-renowned authority on all matters petroliferous. He and Dad Everett had already been working together for a bit in the Dr. Alonzo years, so it was a natural fit when he left 'medicine' for petroleum.'"

"But," said Denise, "I thought you said Dad Everett was a wildcatter and driller."

"He was," said Irving. "But he was the unluckiest wild-catter that ever lived. His name was David Henry Everett. But everyone said that the D. H. actually stood for 'dry hole.' In late 1900 he was drilling in a little town called Gladys City, Texas. He was sure there was oil there. But after three dry holes, the money to drill a fourth dried up as well. He had to gather round all the roughnecks and say, 'I'm sorry, boys. But I'm flat busted. And I can't squeeze another dime out of anyone around here. Pack it in. We're finished.' They walked off broken men.

"Two months later, a fellow named Lucas drilled a well less than a football field away from Dad Everett's. He struck oil at eleven hundred feet. Hit a gusher that blew a hundred and fifty feet in the air and brought in a well that flowed at a hundred thousand barrels a day, in a place called Spindletop.

"After that, Dad drilled at a place called Burkburnett. But the drill bit stuck and broke. It would cost a thousand dollars to get it out. Might as well have been a million. So Dad packed it in. That was 1918. And wouldn't you know it, a fella came in right behind Dad Everett, fished out the broken bit, drilled down another thousand feet, and hit one of the biggest oil fields in Texas. After that, ol' Dry Hole Everett was pretty much a joke.

"Well, these two hard-luck stories, Doc Boyd and Dad Everett, teamed up, first with the medicine show and then with the worthless oil wells."

Denise jotted down notes furiously. During the pause, Matt took the time to rack focus. There was a potted geranium plant on the porch and a bit of wisteria dangling down at the right edge of the frame. He blurred his focus on Tanner Irving Jr. and brought the two flowering plants into sharp focus, thinking how he would highlight the color when he photoshopped the image. But even the budding Spielberg was beginning to get caught up in the magic of the old man's memories. After all, he wasn't talking about things he had read in a book. He had actually been there, lived through them, known these men who had so boldly conned their way across the country a century before.

Mr. Irving began to speak again, not so much to the two youngsters as simply reminiscing aloud.

"You cannot imagine," he said, "not only the physical toll but also the emotional toll of the wildcatter's life. My father knew them all. And I met them. Doc and Dad were pretty much the last of that breed. Some of my earliest memories were of my father hauling wood out to some wildcatter's rig. They were all steam powered, and he supplied the fuel for their boilers.

"The physical work was tough, pretty much harder than anything you can imagine. It wasn't just dawn to dusk. Sometimes it was twenty hours a day. And dangerous too. A drill bit could break loose and go straight through a man working down in the shaft, like Ahab's harpoon going through a whale. And if you brought a well in, the slightest spark could set off a conflagration like hellfire itself. The explosion would rock the earth, and the flames would seem to reach up into the heavens, and sometimes it took weeks to put out a real oil fire. And there was no small danger in that either. Because usually you did it with dynamite. There were ropes and cables like snakes that could slip loose, catch a man's leg, or lash him across the face so hard it would almost take his head off.

"But I do believe the emotional toll was even worse. The wildcatter never had a big company behind him. He usually staked everything he knew on nothin' more than a hunch. Geologists could survey all they liked, but those old wildcatters, they were almost like prophets in the Bible.

"Old Dad Everett used a divining rod. It was a forked stick. And I know he put on a pretty good show for the widders, but he actually claimed to me that that old divining rod would dip when there was oil beneath the earth. A time or two, he said, it nearly yanked him off his feet. I don't know how much of that was embellishment. Doc claimed to put no stock in it, called him a primitive.

"But that's what a wildcatter was: part gambler, part diviner, part dreamer, and always a loner, with no place to stay and no one to come home to.

"They'd roll out some rickety old rig sure that this time, they were gonna strike it rich. Sure that this time, the good Lord would smile on them, that one of these days, they'd feel the earth rumble and hear a sound like a volcano about to blow its top off and then see the black gold spout up out of the earth like ol' Moby Dick himself rising up out of the ocean, blowing not seawater out of his spout but thick, black crude that you could dip a stick into, light up, and burn all night.

"They lived on hopes and dreams, cans of corned beef and cold beans. I don't believe even cowboys had as tough a life. I know that sodbusters didn't. After all, if you were a farmer, you had a decent piece of land, you worked hard, planted your seed. With any luck, there was a little bit of rain, and you were sure of a harvest. The only variable was how good a harvest it would be.

"But the earth wasn't like Lady Luck. Lady Luck was harder than the toughest saloon girl you ever saw in your life. If you had two bucks, you could be sure of a saloon girl's fidelity for at least an hour. But Lady Luck didn't care if you had two bucks or two million. She didn't care if you were Rockefeller or Dad Everett. She bestowed her favors in the most capricious manner imaginable. Whether she'd bear her treasure or not had nothing to do with how hard you worked, how much you prayed or hoped, what you risked, or how you courted her. You could miss her by a foot, and it was as good as a mile.

"And each time, the wildcatter, more than anything else, more than how much he sweat or how much he bet, *believed*. Believed that, this time, it would all fall into place and he'd finally get it right and hit just that spot where the earth would explode and bathe him, shower him, in good fortune.

Chapter 2

"It wasn't just drill bits that got broke, nor legs, nor arms either. It was men's hearts and spirits that broke, and that was the saddest thing of all. A man could get by with a bum leg. Broken arms heal. But you break a man's spirit, and it pretty much doesn't matter what his body can do after that.

"So old Dry Hole Everett, I guess, after Spindletop and Burkburnett, just gave it up. Gave up hoping and took to being nothin' but a two-bit, tinhorn flimflam man. That was a step down for him and a mighty steep one to boot.

"But I do believe Doc Boyd reveled in it. I think he may have believed half the lies that he told. I don't know that he rightly swindled those widows as much as he convinced himself that maybe he *did* love 'em. That maybe, somewhere in the back of his mind, he bought his own snake oil and took a swig, thinkin' it would cure what ailed him too."

Both of the teens listened without making a sound, as if they'd been eavesdropping on a private, perhaps sacred conversation. The old man grew quiet as well. The only sound was his rocker and the boards creaking on his front porch and the occasional sucking sound as he took another draw on the pipe.

Finally, Denise broke the silence and said, simply because she couldn't think of anything else to say, "So Doc Boyd didn't have a degree of any kind?"

"What's that?" Tanner asked, still lost in the reverie of memories of the flimflam men, who were fools or heroes or both, who more often than not had nothing but torn overalls and blackened faces from woodburning boilers that never seemed to wash completely away.

"Dr. Boyd," Denise repeated. "I read that he had a degree from the University of Heidelberg."

"He *did* have a degree. It was a beautiful diploma. I remember seeing it myself. The only problem was it wasn't issued by any university, let alone the University of Heidelberg, though it was quite beautiful to behold, bedecked with ribbons and sealing wax. And as worthless as anything else connected with Doc and Dad.

"See, what these two old rascals realized is that while they weren't much good at actually finding or drilling for oil, they both possessed an unusual facility for convincing people that they could do just that.

"Their Model A would pull up in front of a clapboard farmhouse. Doc and Dad would pile out. Doc cut the romantic figure in those beautiful, shining, high-top brown boots with the buckles on the sides and those flared cavalry pants. I'll swear, the only thing he lacked was a riding crop to smack against those boots, like one of those German silent flicker movie directors. You probably never saw one of them, but when I was a boy, they looked like the most glamorous creatures on earth. Smacked that riding crop against their boots, and men jumped! That's how Doc looked, like something out of a silent movie. He was a tall man and, as the Good Book says, 'ruddy and handsome in appearance.'

"He had, as I recall, a long leather map case. You don't see those anymore. But beautiful craftsmanship. Hand-tooled leather. Brass brads down the side and a leather cap that strapped down to it. And when he unfastened that strap and lifted the cap, he'd pull out the most magnificent things you ever did see: charts and petroleum reports. Geological surveys.

"And ol' Dad, well, he would haul himself out of that Model A with a grunt and a groan and take that old divining rod. He wouldn't pay any mind to Doc and his charts. He'd

Chapter 2

just set off across some stranger's dirt-poor farm or ranch, holding that divining rod out in front of him, waiting for the 'earth's magnetism' to overcome him like the Holy Spirit at a Pentecostal tent revival.

"Now the first thing you needed in this kind of a scam was some farmer who sat on a dusty, worthless, hardscrabble farm from which even the most diligent hand could barely scratch out an existence. And folks listened because what Doc and Dad were selling wasn't oil. It was hope.

"They started off in Oklahoma. I remember Doc Boyd telling me about it in later years, regaling me with stories so convincing that it was as if I had been there myself and seen it all…"

Chapter 3

There was a spinster of a certain age, Miss Classafay Vaudine. She stepped out of the ranch house wearing pants like a man and a Stetson to keep the sun off. She worked that place, just her and one ranch hand, all by herself. She was tough as nails, her skin browned and dried out like cracked leather from sun and wind and dust. She lived a hard life. You kids never saw anything like it, but I surely did. Lived it too.

I could tell she had been what men called a handsome woman in her youth, but that youth had been short-lived and worn away by the elements of a country that didn't allow for youth, that turned folks old before their time.

"You! You, there!" she shouted at Doc and Dad.

Now Dad looked as if he were in a kind of trance, concentrating on the vibrations welling up from the earth through his divining rod and into his very bones. As for Doc, he looked like a silent movie star with that beautifully leather-booted foot up on the running board and his geological chart spread out on the hood.

"With you momentarily, my good woman," he said, his eyes glued to the geological survey, as if he had seen something as rare as eggs laid by tigers.

Chapter 3

"First of all," said the mistress of the house, "I am not your good woman!"

"I beg your pardon, madam," Doc replied, touching his fingers politely to the rim of his white derby.

"I'm not a madam neither. I'm a miss, if it's all the same to you."

Doc glanced up from the chart, then gazed upon her as if she were Aphrodite herself, risen from the sea. "Unmarried?" he declared. "Is there some ocular affliction in the male species of these parts of which medical science is unaware?"

"In English," the spinster demanded.

Doc Boyd boldly took a step toward her and said, "Are all the men in these parts blind to leave such a blushing rose as this unplucked?"

"Mister, you see that outhouse over there?" she said, pointing at the slat-boarded outbuilding with the half-moon delicately carved into its door that hung by one rusty hinge.

"Yes, ma'am. I mean, miss. I do."

"There's a Sears and Roebuck catalog in there, and I get everything I need for this place from them. So whatever you're selling, I ain't in the market."

"My good madam…I apologize. Miss…"

"Vaudine. Miss Classafay Vaudine."

"Miss Vaudine," replied the dashing figure in the flared riding breeches, who gallantly doffed his white derby as a sign of respect for the fairer species, "I am not here to sell anything. I am here simply in the interest of science."

Just then, Dad shouted out, in a kind of reverie, "It's here, Doc. I swear it!"

Dad's massive bulk seemed as if it were being yanked in one direction and then another by a kind of uncontrollable magnetism emanating from the core of the earth itself.

"What's up with him?" Classafay asked, dry as an Oklahoma dust storm.

"Pay him no mind, madam. I mean, miss. The man is a mystic," he said dismissively. "I put no stock in such primitivism, Miss Vaudine. I am a scientist, pure and simple."

Classafay Vaudine looked Doc Boyd up and down, taking in all six foot, four inches of him, and with the smile of a young girl and a voice that was all woman, she said, "I doubt that there is much about you that is simple. Or pure."

The leathery visage softened, and, if nothing else, Doc Boyd was the first piece of entertainment—and the first good-looking man—she had beheld in some time.

"Ah," said Doc. "The tongue of the righteous is choice silver. Proverbs 10:20."

"Even the devil himself can quote Scripture," Classafay said. But she said it with a smile that meant she was enjoying every second of it.

Doc Boyd knew the look as well as he knew anything else in life. It was the crack in a ripe fig, ready to be opened.

"Miss Classafay, if I may be so bold, on this very property on which now we stand, I believe there is..."

"Oil!" Dad Everett shouted, like a Holy Roller about to speak in tongues. "Oh my, I never felt it so strong in all my life! Dr. Boyd, I'd bet my life, my very soul, that right here, on this land, there is a treasure trove all the kings of earth might covet. Oh Lordy, it's too strong for me!"

So saying, the forked stick plunged into the ground and vibrated so violently that Dad Everett swooned into a faint, being careful to break the downward trajectory of his bulk with a well-practiced elbow.

"We'd better get him out of the sun," Classafay said.

Once they had succeeded in moving the portly wildcatter into the shade and shelter of her ranch house and Dad had been revived with a glass of lemonade, he turned to his benefactress and said, "I'm mortified, madam. Mortified."

"She's not a madam," Doc corrected him. "She's a miss."

"What? A woman as beautiful as this?" Dad exclaimed. "Are the men here too blind to…"

"Already covered that," Doc informed him, sotto voce.

"Well, in that case," Dad took another sip of Classafay's lemonade, composed himself, and then declared, "Miss Vaudine, I don't think of myself as a weak man, but I've never felt the divining rod shake like that in all my life, and I have to admit, whether it was with emotion at the magnitude of the fortune to be found here or the earth's very magnetism, I was simply overcome."

"You were," said Miss Vaudine, in the same tone she had used when referring to the outhouse.

"I were," Dad said solemnly.

"Miss Vaudine," said Doc, "this is about opportunity and redemption. It's about just reward for the righteous."

"It's about the Lord's bounty," said Dad.

"Oil," said Doc.

"Black gold!" exclaimed the old wildcatter.

"You think there's oil? On this land?" said Classafay Vaudine. It was not so much of a question as it was a challenge.

"Think it?" said Doc Boyd. "Nay! I know it, as surely as I know my own name."

"Which is?"

"Dr. Horatio Daedalus Boyd." With that, he fished an elegant silver card case out of his breast pocket, withdrew from it one of his business cards, and presented it to the mistress of the house as if he were calling on royalty. "Geologist and petroleum engineer, at your service. And this gentleman is D. H. Everett."

Classafay looked at Dad. "You a doctor too?"

"I'm not a doctor, ma'am, uh, miss. I'm a wildcatter. A workingman. A driller."

"He is too modest, Miss Vaudine," Doc said, his voice dropping down an octave, as if sharing with the spinster a great confidence. "Do the names Spindletop and Burkburnett ring a bell?"

Classafay just looked at him. Obviously, they did not. Doc Boyd continued, unfazed.

"This man, whose name will be emblazoned forever along with the likes of Columbus and Marco Polo, a modern-day explorer, was the first to discover both of those sleeping black giants."

Miss Vaudine crossed her arms and looked from one to the other. "Then how come you aren't driving a Pierce-Arrow instead of a beat-up Model A?"

"Simply put," Dad responded, "I lacked the capital to bring up out of the earth the black gold that I knew was there. And those finds were nothing—dare I say it—nothing compared to the bubbling pool of petroleum that sits at this very instant beneath our feet."

Doc Boyd produced his beautiful, hand-tooled leather map case with the brass brads lining its side. He unfastened the leather cap and pulled out his reports and charts.

"Miss Vaudine," he said with a flourish, "I am holding a geological topographical and petroliferous survey of this fair county." So saying, he spread out the rolled-up reports across her coffee table. "I'll leave this with you to peruse at your leisure. What it describes is a salt dome."

"A salt dome?" she said.

"Just so."

Dad Everett's fingertip began to trace some of the markings on the survey as he added, "And anticlines, faults, the Sabine Uplift, and the Rusk Depression."

"It discusses," Doc said, "in some detail the Yegua and Cook Mountain formations. Names familiar, I assure you, to every geologist worth his salt west of the Mississippi."

"Miss Vaudine," said Dad, looking around as if to make sure that no unwanted ears could hear what he had to say, "Humble Oil has carried out thousands of seismic registrations, very quietly."

"*Very* quietly," Doc added for emphasis.

Dad Everett leaned in conspiratorially and continued. "They have leased, in a fashion which I can only describe as sub rosa, thousands of acres."

"And have paid unusual prices for some."

"All of which means…"

"In a word," said Doc, "oil."

"Gushers," said Dad.

"And you want me to invest in your venture?" said Classafay dubiously.

"No, ma'am! I mean, miss," said Dad.

Doc quickly interjected. "We want to invest in *your* venture. We'll supply the capital, the drilling equipment, the expertise, the know-how, and the manpower. You'll receive a one-eighth share, which you'll find is standard remuneration. But one-eighth of a fortune is still a fortune. We will assume all the risk, and you, dear lady, shall reap the just reward."

Classafay had softened now, considerably. She looked from one man to the other, her eyes burrowing deep into their souls as she asked, "Are you men…religious?"

Whereupon, Doc Boyd reached out one hand to Miss Vaudine and the other to Dad Everett, who immediately joined hands, forming a prayer circle with the mistress of the house.

"O Lord," Doc intoned in humble piety, "we ask your blessings on this, your venture, and these, your servants, that all the works of our hands may glorify your holy name. In Jesus' name, we pray. Amen."

And two minutes later, Miss Classafay Vaudine affixed her signature to a lease, granting all petroleum rights on her land to Horatio Daedalus Boyd, PhD in petroleum engineering, geology, and all matters petroliferous.

Chapter 4

Now, what you have to understand is that widows were the mother's milk of the petroleum hustle. Thus, each morning, Doc and Dad, over cups of coffee flavored with chicory and perhaps a fine cigar and even, on occasion, a shot of liquid courage, would peruse the morning papers for likely business prospects. Dad leaned toward rye whiskey, whereas Doc was a bourbon-sipping man; he considered it more of a gentleman's drink. The fact that it was Prohibition prevented neither from getting either.

The Longbranch Saloon, since Carrie Nation had begun wielding her axe against all libations, had been rechristened the Dugan's Family Restaurant. The Dugan in question made sure that the sheriff got his share of Dugan's finest private stock, and no one in recent memory had ever seen a federal man in these parts. All the same, Dugan kept the bottles discreetly out of sight. And, as long as one was ordering a proper cup of coffee, no one objected to the addition of a shot of that which had always ensured conviviality and a general feeling of warmth and optimism during what were increasingly trying times.

It was bad enough to face the thought of the Depression and dust bowl when you were sober. But to deprive a man of drink while he was facing both agricultural and financial ruin was, in general, deemed cruel and unusual in those parts, especially where oilmen were concerned. Men who risked everything on instinct, hard work, or, in Doc and Dad's case, pure chicanery could hardly be expected to do so without the occasional pick-me-up.

Dugan's Family Restaurant, in which no one could recall ever having seen an actual family dining, was a kind of oilman's gentlemen's club on the Oklahoma frontier. The leather-backed chairs were comfortable, the spittoons plentiful, and the service never dawdling.

Doc and Dad pored over the morning papers like fortune tellers examining tea leaves. They were not concerned with news, neither national nor local. Sporting events held little interest, if any. And Wall Street was a far-off place that played no part in their plans. Indeed, the only parts of the daily gazette that were of interest to them were the obituary pages, for they yielded up the names and circumstances of the newly minted crop of widows.

Doc Boyd perched his spectacles on the end of his nose and read aloud to Dad Everett, who jotted down the pertinent information. Doc wet his thumb, turned the page, and, with an index finger, traced his way down the death notices until he came to one that caught his interest.

"Carl Fred Simms," he read, "of Lathrope died after a lingering illness, leaving behind his wife of thirty-five years, Flora May Simms."

"Ah," said Dad, "the Widow Simms." He noted with his pencil both her name and town of residence as well as the full name of her deceased husband.

Chapter 4

"Clarence Albert Jones," Doc declared, "passed on to paradise after a short illness, leaving behind a wife of twenty-nine years, the lovely Therma Lou Jones."

Dad perked up. "I'll take the Widow Jones."

Doc put the paper down, removed his spectacles, and looked his partner straight in the eye. "I thought I'd take the Widow Jones."

Dad, as if responding to an unspoken challenge, removed his own spectacles, leaned forward, and, in a reasonable tone, stated, "She was only married twenty-nine years. She's bound to be younger."

Doc leaned in closer to his business partner. "That's kinda why I had my eye on her. You don't want to add cradle robbing to your list of felonious activities. I'm doing you a favor."

Dad took a noisy slurp from his well-fortified coffee, smacked his lips, leaned back luxuriously, and, with a smile of maturity and wisdom, declared, "The older the violin, the sweeter the music."

"I'll flip you for her," Doc said.

"Whose coin?"

"Not yours, that's for sure!"

Doc may have been the snake-oil salesman, but he'd never seen a man better at cheating at games of chance than Dad Everett. His stubby, tar-stained, weathered fingers were like a virtuoso violinist's when it came to working a deck of cards or palming a genuine coin for one guaranteed to come up heads with every flip.

The two business partners amiably settled the terms of the barter for the Widow Jones by agreeing to throw down rock, paper, scissors.

Dad threw rock while Doc threw down scissors, losing the match.

"Very well," said Doc. "I shall console the Widow Simms. But I get the car."

"It's my car!"

"But," Doc pointed out, "you get the nubile Widow Jones."

"So what am I gonna do for transportation?"

Later that evening, Doc Boyd pulled up at the home of the Widow Simms in Dad's worn-out Model A. He got out, approvingly checked his visage in the side mirror by the fading light of day, adjusted his derby to a jaunty angle, buttoned his crushed velvet blazer, and strode purposefully—map case in hand—toward the front door. He knocked three times with a devil-may-care air so as not to startle the widow within, and he was truly impressed when the door opened to reveal a tall, slim, and undeniably handsome woman.

She looked to be in her early fifties and was properly dressed in black, which he thought to be an appealing color for her. Chestnut locks framed her delicate face. She was by far the handsomest widow he could recall ever having seen.

He gave her his business card and stated that he was shocked to learn of the passing of her beloved husband and that he had a matter of some importance to discuss with her in light of her beloved's recent and tragic demise.

At roughly the same time, Dad Everett alighted from the mule he had procured for the evening from Hawkins' Livery. He hiked up his trousers, buttoned his blazer, adjusted his fedora, blew into his hand to check his breath, which had just been freshened with a stick of Beemans, and knocked on the door of the nubile Widow Jones. She, too, he reckoned, was a good deal fairer than your average, run-of-the-mill widder.

Chapter 4

Like Doc, he expressed his shock to learn of the passing of her dearly departed husband, Clarence.

As he did so, Doc was already ensconced on the love seat of the Widow Simms's parlor, extolling the virtues of her late husband, Carl Fred.

"He was a good man," Doc intoned, with the proper mix of respect and admiration.

"You knew my late husband?" the Widow Flora May Simms inquired, brushing away a chestnut lock that had fallen loose across her forehead in what Doc thought of as a beguiling fashion.

"Oh yes, indeed," he said. "In fact, that's why I'm here. Because although the law of the land gives me every legal right to do so, I have come to tell you, I will not hold you to the agreement I made with your late husband regarding his investment in a particular business venture."

"A business venture?" Flora May said, startled to learn of her late husband's heretofore unbeknownst financial dabblings. "What kind of business venture?"

"An oil well, to be exact. And not just any well but something known in geological circles as the apex of the apex."

"Why," said the Widow Jones, "whatever is that?"

For Dad Everett, in a remarkable synchronicity, had just mentioned that exact phrase—"apex of the apex"—to her.

"My dear," Dad explained, "it is something that occurs among the shifting geological plates that make up the earth's layers of crusts only once every 457,200 years."

"Give or take," said Doc Boyd, quoting a similar figure to Flora May Simms.

"What is it that happens every 457,200 years?" Flora May inquired.

"What happens, madam?" said Doc. "How shall I explain? In the mysterious depths of Mother Earth…"

"Pressure builds up," Dad said. "Indeed, it has been building up for ages upon ages, as if the earth were waiting to loose her bounds and burst forth in a—"

The Widow Jones kept her eyes fixed on Dad in unguarded anticipation.

"Fountain of abundance, a river of shining gold—black gold, that is—an unequivocal stream of unending riches," declared Dad Everett.

"Oh my stars and garters!" said the Widow Jones.

"It bursts," Dad continued, "in an almost, some might even say violent, explosion. As if Mother Earth herself took pity on us, her unwieldy children, and decided to baptize us in a veritable Niagara of glorious fortune."

"How exciting!" exclaimed the Widow Jones.

Doc had just described a similar eruption from the mysterious depths of Mother Earth, eliciting oohs and aahs from the Widow Simms.

"Your beloved late husband, Calvin," Doc said.

"Carl."

"Just so. Carl recognized the potential of this investment."

"Oh, he was shrewd."

"Sharp as a tack!" Doc responded, with admiration.

At the Widow Jones's, the conversation had progressed to the point where she had granted Dad Everett permission to call her by her Christian name, Therma Lou.

"Therma Lou," Dad Everett intoned in a mellifluous baritone voice. "Therma Lou. Like a church bell ringing softly in the distance. Therma Lou. Therma Lou, though I have every legal right to do so, I will not hold you to the agreement I made with your late, beloved husband. You are too laden down with the burden of your grief and the sudden loneliness of widowhood. Bereft of the companionship of your lover and friend, your comforter and provider, the source of poetry and beauty in your life..."

It was not long before both Doc and Dad were each holding their respective widow's hands, consoling them for their loss.

Now the late Misters Jones and Simms may have been many things, but they were, neither of them, the sources of poetry and beauty in the lives of these women for whom the long, flat, unending road of widowhood stretched gloomily out before them. Moreover, the knowledge of geology and petroleum engineering were among the least important attributes that a flimflam man hustling a widow needed to possess. Both Doc and Dad had two far more important attributes. Both could quote the Scriptures at will, and both had memorized all of Shakespeare's sonnets. Now, you might not think that would have much to do with petroleum exploration, but when it came to widows, you would be wrong.

"Love's not Time's fool," Doc recited beautifully, "though rosy lips and cheeks within his bending sickle's compass come."

"Love alters not with his brief hours and weeks," Dad quoted, in his mellifluous baritone, "but bears it out even to the edge of doom."

Well, a sonnet here and a slice of homemade pie there and by the end of the evening, both Doc and Dad pulled checks from each of their widows in the amount of five hundred dollars, making each of them the proud owners of twenty-five percent of the Cherokee Petroleum Company.

"And," said Doc Boyd, pocketing the check from the Widow Simms, "may the good Lord smile upon our endeavors."

Then, in the ensuing days, Dad Everett rolled out the cheapest, most broken-down, sorriest excuse for a drilling rig anyone had ever seen. With local farmers pitching in on this truly poor-boy drilling operation, a well spudded in on the dirt-poor ranch of Miss Classafay Vaudine. With great fanfare, Doc and Dad lit the fire in the boiler of the rig, tossed in a few logs, and set the steam gauges. And slowly but surely, the canvas belt began rotating the flywheel, which began transferring the rotational energy to the drill bit. Then, with even greater fanfare, Doc and Dad took turns with sledgehammers, hammering in the hand-painted wooden sign which proudly proclaimed:

The Classafay Vaudine Number One Well

Then, on a moonless night, usually betwixt midnight and one, when no one was looking, Dad Everett carefully salted the well with quart after quart of Quaker State oil.

The following day, Dad and Doc were at the drill site. The purpose of their visit was to take a core sample and examine the cuttings bucket. The drama was high, the stakes even higher, as the cuttings bucket was hauled out, with Miss Classafay Vaudine, as one-eighth owner of the enterprise, dutifully in attendance.

Dad stuck his stubby fingers into the cuttings bucket after the core sample had been taken. And, dramatically, he held up those same stubby fingers, now besmirched with sand and the black, tarlike substance, and exclaimed, with the same religious fervor of a penitent who had seen the light of his Lord and Savior, the words which were music to any oilman's ears:

"Woodbine sand!"

"Woodbine sand?" Miss Vaudine inquired, clearly not understanding the import.

Chapter 4

"Oh Lord!" exclaimed a passionate Dad Everett. "We done hit the Woodbine!"

Miss Vaudine tugged at his sleeve and asked again, "Is that good?"

"Ma'am," said Dad Everett. "I mean, Miss…" At a total loss for words at their good fortune, he simply said, "It's *pshooom!*" He pantomimed an unbridled, petroliferous release to the heavens.

"Thank you, Jesus!" Doc Boyd proclaimed. "I want to thank you, Jesus!"

"Amen!" Dad Everett ecstatically joined in.

"Oh my sweet Lord!" said Classafay Vaudine. "Amen! *Amen!*" She peered over at the cuttings bucket. "Can I touch it?"

This course of events ushered in a new, feverish round of activity with the widows.

"It was like a miracle," Doc Boyd told the Widow Simms as they strolled through the meadow of her ranch in the golden, fading light of the setting sun. "Woodbine sand! Now all we need is a few thousand more to bring this well in, and we'll be sittin' in high clover and finally I'll be able to ask for your hand in marriage."

Flora May Simms threw her arms around Doc Boyd and, in a girlish fashion, kicked up her heel and sighed, "Oh Horatio!"

At the Jones ranch, Therma Lou was likewise overcome by not only Dad Everett's good fortune but his proposal as well.

As for Doc Boyd, he would later admit, much to his surprise if not chagrin, that he had felt a sudden rush of joy when Flora May Simms had said, "Oh Horatio!" and thrown her arms around him, accepting what, heretofore for him, had been his standard, flimflam proposal. Indeed, he did not recognize his own emotions, so foreign were they to everything in what one could only call his checkered experience.

He not only felt as if he had truly proposed matrimony to the Widow Simms but also felt delighted, in a way he had not been since boyhood, that she had accepted. He was under no illusion that everything he had said to the Widow Simms was anything but the same well-worn, well-scripted lie he had said to every other widow, indeed to countless other widows, across the prairie. But this was palpably different, if not somewhat frightening.

For, this time, he felt as if he believed every word of his own lie.

There was, he knew well, no more dangerous thing that a flimflam man could do than believe his own malarkey. But it was undeniable that he felt an affection, which he had never known before, stirring in his own bosom for Flora May Simms and his delight at her acceptance of his proposal buoyed him up, made him feel light as a feather and want to kick his heels up in joy.

In addition, there was that ticklish feeling in his throat. And whether it was from an abundance of fried chicken combined with advancing years or genuine emotion, he could have sworn that his heart began to flutter, like the wings of a thousand butterflies beating within his breast.

That Flora May Simms was comely was beyond doubt. She may well have been the handsomest woman he could recall. But there was something in her touch that transcended mere beauty. When her arms wrapped around him and he felt her heart beat next to his, he marveled at the fact that every studied line, uttered a thousand times before, that he had spoken to her regarding the depths of his affections was, somehow, amazingly true.

Chapter 4

That thought, at one and the same time, thrilled and terrified him. And it opened a door of insight into his own soul and psyche, which he had long suspected was true of him. Namely, that no one wants to believe in a con man's lies more than the con man himself, who holds out the same hope as a child waiting for fairies to trade coins for canine teeth left under the pillow.

Could it possibly be that, just as the words of his affections were somehow true, this time, miraculously, when they drilled down into the bosom of Mother Earth, she would yield up her treasure as well?

Indeed, Doc had to admit, the thought was there every time they spudded in a new well. That maybe, this time, the Rusk Depression and the Sabine Incline, the salt dome and the apex of the apex, would turn out to be right beneath their feet. That, this time, they would be not con men but oilmen, tapping into a sleeping black giant waiting to be awakened like a fairy-tale princess longing for Prince Charming's kiss to rouse her from her slumber.

"What're you thinking?" Dad said to Doc as he saw the wistful look in his business partner's eye.

"There *is* oil in these parts, Dad. It's not all just a con. There really is oil out there somewhere."

"Doc," said Dad, "that is of no concern to us. Because we're not in the oil business. We're in the widder business. I thought you knew that by now. After all, you're the one who taught it to me."

"Nonetheless," said Doc, "this is oil country. I'd stake my reputation on it."

"Well, that and a nickel will buy you a sarsaparilla."

A silence hung in the air between the two gentlemen. Dad leaned in toward the younger man. He was at least fifteen years older than Doc and wiser, he thought. Or if not wiser, at least less of a romantic.

"Son," he said, "don't let yourself think like that. The oil business is the cruelest one on the face of the earth. It'll break your heart quicker than any gal, and the worst thing you or I can do is fall for our own con. We've set the traps. They're takin' the bait. Now all we have to do is the same thing we've always done, and we'll be just fine."

But there was something in Dad's voice that told Doc he was trying to convince himself as much as he was offering sage advice to his younger partner.

Whether it was the fact that the Widow Jones, Therma Lou, whose name was like a distant church bell, had gotten under *his* skin as well or that he allowed himself to return to the reverie he had known at Spindletop just before he had run out of money or at Burkburnett just before the bit broke and dashed all his hopes and dreams, he, too, wished, like a child, that maybe, this time…

Happily for their cause, Doc had already snapped out of his reverie. "Yeah. You're right. Worst thing a con man can do is fall for his own con. Time to get back to business."

And so, Dad and Doc hit all the widows in the area a second time, increasing the size of the investments and the intake of endless slices of pecan pie from their ladyloves, as they had done countless times before, selling about a thousand percent of the fraudulent shares while waiting for the exact moment when they had milked every last drop that their scam could yield before it was time for them to make their getaway and relay to the widows the devastating news.

"Oh, cruelest of fates…" Doc said in anguish.

Chapter 4

"What do you mean?" the Widow Flora May Simms inquired as she watched the tall, handsome man beat his fist against the wall in frustration at the tragic turn of events that seemed to have dashed his carefully laid plans for their marital bliss. She touched his arm gently, and he turned to her with a look of despair that Valentino himself might have envied.

"Despite our best efforts and all our hopes and prayers," he said, "we have hit a dry hole."

"A dry hole?" replied Flora May.

Doc looked up to the heavens, as if imploring the Almighty to stay the evil decree. But alas, their fates were sealed.

"It is completely worthless," he said, a broken man.

And this time, yet again, he was shocked at the true bitterness of his words, even though they were key to his con and, more importantly, to his getaway.

His anguish over the fact that they had not struck oil was not simply part of the scam; it was real. It was concrete, as if a hole had been blown through his heart. His daydreams—and those he had dared to dream at night against his will and better judgment of an end to his wanderings and a new life built around hearth and home with Flora May Simms—had suddenly come crashing down around him. In true anguish, he felt tears of frustration well up. The con was still a con, and no matter how many cookies or glasses of milk he left out, there would be no rocking horse in the gleaming light of dawn. And far worse than that, he knew he would no longer know the joy of the warmth of Flora May's hand on his shoulder.

They had walked through her meadow on a golden afternoon, the sun's rays bathing her face in a light the great masters of Amsterdam and Paris might have envied. She linked her arm through his, and they daydreamed aloud in wonderment at their good fortune at having found life's true treasure in each other's embrace.

For once, that was not a con.

For once, it was true.

He dared not whisper even to himself the words he longed to say: *I love you, Flora May.* Yet again, he slammed into his own reality, as solidly built as a prison-yard wall. There would be no future with Flora May Simms. No warm comforter. No urgent prayer. The flutter in his heart would be nothing more than gas pains. For their entire relationship was built, he knew, on nothing but the lies he had told a thousand times before and that he had no choice but to tell yet again to Flora May.

"And to make matters worse," he said, "my dear, because of my affection for you and my determination to secure your financial future, Dad Everett and I have incurred debts to bring in the well, which we cannot possibly pay off. And unfortunately, that is not the end of it."

There was more bad news to come.

At the home of the Widow Jones, Dad Everett was likewise, to his surprise as well, in the depths of despair as he explained their predicament.

"Tragically, my dear, because you are a shareholder, the creditors may seek relief from you as well. Indeed, I am mortified to admit it, but face the truth we must. If I do not take prompt and certain action, you could lose your home."

Of course, that was paraphrasing the truth just a tad. Because if Doc and Dad did not take prompt and certain action, they could end up behind bars. But that would remain Doc and Dad's secret. Instead, they informed the widows that unnamed creditors might seek relief by seizing their homesteads.

Chapter 4

Therma Lou gasped at the very thought of it, as did Flora May Simms.

"But fear not!" Doc Boyd proclaimed like a knight-errant, a paladin of the plains. "I would sooner lose my life than allow that ever to happen."

Once more, Doc knew the strange sensation that the well-rehearsed speech was, this time, the truth. But he could not indulge such feelings. And so he continued.

"You have but to sign over all your worthless shares to me, and I will assume full responsibility. They'll never be able to touch you. Of course, it means that I will have to flee or be incarcerated." And that, for sure, he knew *was* the truth. "But I will gladly sacrifice myself in order to protect the woman I have come to care for so dearly."

With that, the manly lovers stole off into the night as the widows wept tears of gratitude and clutched to their bosoms the love letters written to them over the last few months.

"Adieu, *mi amore!*" Doc Boyd called out from the running board of the Model A as Dad Everett, who had already bid farewell to his ladylove, stuck it in gear and pulled on the gas lever. The two men disappeared into the distance, fugitives forever, in order to protect the women who, only days before, had dreamt of being their wives.

It worked every time.

But this time, for whatever reason, though neither of them spoke of it, Doc and Dad felt as if their hearts had broken as well.

They had, by now, bilked every widow in Oklahoma. And thus, they decided it was time to go to Texas.

Chapter 5

The train was a vintage 1880s steam engine, lovingly maintained and, miraculously, still in service. The hardwood seats had no cushion or padding. Hand straps hung from the ceiling for those not fortunate enough to obtain a seat. There were only five cars where once there had been fifteen. The stock market crash had already taken its toll, and the drought before that had exacted its measure of pain from the endless stretch of flatland and the sinewy, country-strong folk who stubbornly continued to eke out a living from the now-parched earth.

Two conductors and one Pullman porter worked the cars. Two boxcars carried more hard-luck, rail-riding bums than marketable goods. The caboose contained a potbellied stove that provided the only warmth in winter, but in summer, there was no relief from the stifling, dry heat that held no mercy for man nor beast nor growing things struggling to survive.

The train station in Irving was little more than a squat building with neither hustle nor bustle. Everything seemed to move more slowly in the heat of the noonday sun. It was not merely the temperature that dictated the languorous tempo of the little town on the outskirts of Dallas. It was, quite simply, that there was no place to hurry to and no cause for rush. Time stood still here, as if conserving its energy against the chance for a better day.

The engine let off a long, loud blast as the train belched black smoke into an endless, cloudless firmament. There was neither tree, nor shrub, nor scrub bush, nor even cacti.

Doc and Dad alighted from the train carrying their carpetbags, which contained the divining stick, the leather case for bogus charts emblazoned with imaginary domes of salt, inclines, and depressions that were whimsy instead of science, and Doc Boyd's "diploma" from the University of Heidelberg, proclaiming him a PhD in petroleum engineering, geology, and all matters petroliferous.

Stepping out onto the platform, Doc and Dad beheld the long stretch of terrain, uninterrupted by mountain, hill, incline, or depression.

"So this is Texas," said Dad Everett.

"Very flat," Doc said. "And, from appearances, those may be the kindest words I can say."

Doc and Dad walked down the middle of the street. There was no fear of being run over by beast or machine. A general store on the corner, Dave Cohen's Dry Goods, beckoned the two new arrivals.

Doc turned to Dad and said, "I don't know about you, but I've always found that general stores with well-swept porches are inevitably well-stocked with all the provisions any man could desire." So saying, the two strangers in town entered the enterprising Mr. Cohen's emporium.

Indeed, Doc's instincts proved, yet again, to be infallible. The store had in stock all the bounty a frontier town could provide: bolts of cloth and sacks of beans, flour, coffee, sugar, cornmeal, and grits. There was hardtack and hardware, even the odd bit of livery. A man could buy a new suit of clothes, and a child could obtain a chunk of rock candy. There was a neat rack with gazettes of the day and an ice chest promising liquid refreshment and relief from the dry and dusty thoroughfare that shimmered with waves of heat from which they had just escaped.

"I'll take a Dr. Pepper and a Moon Pie," Doc said.

"Sarsaparilla for me," said Dad Everett.

And, almost as an afterthought, Doc added, "And a copy of the *Dallas Morning News.*"

The soda pop was to slake their thirst, the Moon Pie an indulgence for Doc's sweet tooth. But the *Dallas Morning News* was the road map of their trade.

Doc and Dad gulped their soda pop. Doc offered Dad a bite of the Moon Pie, and the portly, older gentleman readily accepted more than a bite. More than half, actually.

"You know," said Doc, "you could buy your own, instead of eating mine."

To which Dad simply replied, "Mmm."

Doc turned to the proprietor. "And two of your finest nickel cigars, if you please."

Soft drinks and Moon Pie consumed, cigars stored in Doc's breast pocket, to be enjoyed with a libation once the sun had set, the two men stepped onto the wooden, raised sidewalk outside the dry goods store and opened the paper to the obituaries page. With a practiced eye, Doc scanned like a falcon circling its prey.

"Well, here's a likely prospect," he said. "Town called Cornville."

"Cornville? Where's that?"

"It appears to be next to a little town called Mule Chute."

Chapter 5

"Mule Chute?" Dad said, enunciating each word.

"An onomatopoetic little burg if ever there was one," Doc replied. "Here's an interesting item."

"What's that?" Dad asked, wiping the last bit of chocolate from his lips with his sleeve.

"'Thurman Dial declared dead today,'" Doc read.

"What do you mean, declared dead?"

"Seems he went missing in Juarez, Mexico, prospecting five years ago, never to return. And his lovely bride of thirty years, Junipera Sue Dial, has had to declare him dead to collect the insurance, which probably didn't amount to a hill of beans."

"A likely prospect," said Dad.

"Just so," said Doc.

Just then, a seemingly brand-new, gleaming black Model A with a shining chrome radiator and whitewall tires pulled up majestically beside the dry goods store. In its window, a sign proclaimed, almost with despair, For Sale.

For Doc, it was love at first sight. And, perhaps to assuage feelings of a broken heart over the loss of the Widow Simms as much as to provide them with a much-needed means of transportation, Doc decided to buy it. It was, he admitted, an extravagance, but the black leather seats and chromium dashboard were, quite simply, irresistible and far superior to their last vehicle, which had been little more than a farm car.

The owner was a fellow wildcatter, an oilman who had fallen, as all oilmen had, on hard times. Doc offered two hundred fifty dollars. The wildcatter protested like a stuck pig that it had cost him $500 when brand-new, to which Doc retorted, "Then that's what you should sell it for, if you can find someone foolish enough to buy it. I'll make it three hundred dollars, cold cash."

"Four hundred," said the hard-luck oilman.

"Three fifty," Doc retorted.

"You might as well be holding a gun up to my head! Four hundred, not a penny less!"

Doc just smiled and said, "My friend, if you listen carefully, you'll hear the pitter-pat of three hundred fifty dollars walkin' out of here on its little green feet."

"You drive a hard bargain."

"It's the only kind I know," said Doc. "Going once. Going twice…"

"I'll take it," said the hard-luck story.

Doc wet his thumb, pulled out the bounty of the Oklahoma widows, peeled off three hundred fifty dollars, and tossed his carpetbag and petroliferous chart case into the rumble seat. Dad added his luggage, and the two men rode off toward the little town of Cornville and the newly minted widow, Junipera Sue Dial.

Chapter 6

The Dial Ranch was a handsome spread that sat on a seemingly endless stretch of prairie land. There was a sturdily built log home, far too large to be called a cabin. The size of it, in fact, seemed to both Doc and Dad to be almost baronial.

Whereas Doc, at six foot four, many a time had to stoop to enter a farmer's doorway, he was positively dwarfed by the massive portal that formed the entryway to the main ranch house.

The door itself was plain, standing out of the ordinary neither in color nor design. But where size was concerned, it spoke of grandeur.

Everything about the place spoke of craftsmanship. Whoever had built it was not only a carpenter but also a true artisan. And the place, even in hard times, showed a hard-fought pride of ownership, the kind of place you had to save up for, not something built out of an inheritance. It was as hand-crafted as an Englishman's bespoke suit. The steps leading up to the front door were sound and sturdy enough, it seemed, to hold not only guests or cowboys but also a visiting army.

With a house like this, Doc suspected that the Widow Dial would strike a stately figure, if not stout. She would be a large, bare-boned woman who could birth a cow and break a horse as easily as she could knead and proof a loaf of home-baked bread. Indeed, the smells of home cooking wafted toward them from within.

Now if Doc had been on his game, he would have thought that strange. He was familiar enough with the species to know that freshly minted widows tended not to cook in the early stages of their mourning. And the Dial Ranch was far too remote for a neighbor to drop by with a consoling casserole. He reckoned the nearest ranch to the Dial spread was some twenty-plus miles away over a badly pitted road, which, he feared, might have ill effect on their newly purchased roadster.

But Doc was not on his game. He was still enthralled in the smell of new leather from their just-purchased automobile, and the day itself was a rarity in Texas; it lacked both oppressive heat and humidity. On such a day as this, the smell of fresh-baked cornbread raised no suspicion whatsoever. The Widow Dial may well have had grandchildren for whom she cared, or it may have been for hired hands. Either way, it smelled, some-how, of Sunday to him, and he thought how well it might go with a plate of fried chicken, okra, and baked beans made rich in flavor with fatback or belly bacon.

Thus, allowing his thoughts to drift to the comforts of home cooking, to which he was not accustomed and for which, at times, he longed, he knocked optimistically upon the widow's door.

At first, there was no sound from within.

"Knock louder," Dad said.

Doc threw him a disdainful glance, sighed, and said, "I know how to knock on a door, Dad."

"Well, so far, it's produced no effect. And somebody's obviously at home. I can smell the cooking."

Chapter 6

Doc rapped the mighty door with his knuckles once again and called out, "Mrs. Dial? Ma'am? Are you within?"

The two men heard footfalls approaching, but they were certainly not what Doc expected, nor was the tiny woman who opened the massive door, which served only to accentuate her lack of stature.

She stood barely five feet tall in a doorway that easily measured eight feet in height. She was pleasant looking with a ruddy complexion and reddish-brown hair to match, though it was streaked with gray, which, together with the creases on a weathered brow, marked her, indeed, as a woman of the prairie, to whom life may have been fulfilling but not necessarily kind.

"Yes?" she said tentatively, eyeing the two strangers with neither friendliness nor suspicion but simply the closely held judgment of a woman used to living more than twenty miles away from the nearest neighbor and now a widow, to boot.

Doc Boyd produced one of his business cards from his vest pocket, which contained, as well, the golden chain to a watch fob affixed to his vest, which bespoke of a golden watch to match within. In truth, however, it was all part of the scam. Doc was all sizzle and no steak. All hat and no cattle. All chain and no gold watch. But the gold chain did produce a certain air of dignity and fastidiousness, which he liked.

He eyed the petite Widow Dial and said, in his most mellifluous tones, "Dr. Horatio Daedalus Boyd at your service."

She scarcely examined the card he had handed her as she pronounced, "There must be some mistake, Doctor. There is no one in ill health, thank the Lord, in my home."

"Dear lady," said Doc Boyd, "my degree is in geology and petroleum engineering, not the art of medicine, and I assure you that the matter on which I have come is of some importance. Otherwise, I would not have dared to disturb you after you have had such a trying time."

Doc introduced Dad, and the Widow Dial said they could call her Junipera Sue. She stood on no formalities but invited them in to state their business and, indeed, offered them coffee for their trouble.

The parlor, too, was a handsome one and, in keeping with the doorway, impressive in its expansiveness. There was a large fireplace and a handsome elk head mounted above it, which, together with the craftsmanship and size of the home, indicated to the men that the late Mr. Dial must have been a large man who was as handy with a rifle as with a carpenter's tool. And someone to be reckoned with.

After the introductions and Doc and Dad complimenting the quality of the coffee, Doc launched into his usual preamble, delineating his acquaintanceship with the late Mr. Dial and tailoring his tale to the information contained in the newspaper article describing the late Thurman Dial's unfortunate demise in Old Mexico.

"And so you knew my husband?" Junipera Sue inquired, with the kind of eagerness that Doc recognized well. Widows, in their grief, were always anxious to hear tales of their late husbands, especially if they had met their untimely end far from home.

"Can't say we really knew him well, Mrs. Dial," Doc said. "We spent but an evening with him."

Junipera Sue nodded understandingly. "In Mexico?" she asked, obviously wanting to hear more of their encounter.

"Just outside of Juarez," Dad said. Then, by way of explanation, he added, "We were looking for oil down there."

"Didn't pan out," Doc said, clicking his tongue at the never-ending vexations common to the wildcatter and prospector.

Chapter 6

"But," said Dad, "that's where we met…uh…"

It was clear that the older man had forgotten their mark's husband's name. It was not the first time this had occurred, and Doc had some concern that the older man was losing his touch. The concern was not based on affection; rather, it was on the efficacy of their partnership. Each man must pull his weight. In Dad Everett's case, his weight was not inconsiderable. Now, if his memory was deserting him, his utility to their common endeavors was in question. Thus, when the older man faltered, Doc hastened to pick up the slack.

"Thurman," Doc said, casting Dad a disapproving glance.

"That's right," Dad pronounced, trying to regain a certain air of nostalgia about their encounter with the widow's late husband to cover for the fact that he had forgotten the man's name. "We met over a plate of moles and frijoles. Thurman said to us that he had a hunch—"

"More than a hunch!" Doc added with a flourish. On the spot, he decided to embellish the story with the romance of an encounter south of the border. "Thurman told us a gypsy had actually foretold his future and said that oil would be discovered on his ranch and make him and his beloved Junipera Sue wealthy beyond measure."

Junipera Sue looked from Doc to Dad in wonderment. "That's so unlike him."

"Mexico can bring that out in a fella," Dad said, nodding his head like an understanding older uncle, wise to the magical ways of nights down Mexico way.

Mrs. Dial was genuinely touched by these two men. They were fellow prospectors, really, and had come all this way to pay their condolences. But to her surprise, Doc Boyd said it was not only their sympathies that led them back to Texas.

"We came," Doc said, "to conduct several scientific experiments to see if, well, to see if what Thurman said might be true. And to our amazement, it was."

"Would you gentlemen care for some cornbread?" said the Widow Dial. "If I leave it in the oven any longer, it's going to get burnt."

"Ma'am," said Doc, with genuine enthusiasm and almost salivating at the thought, "It's been a long time since I've had a home-cooked meal. And I have to admit to a special fondness for cornbread."

"As do I," said Dad.

Indeed, in both men, the very smell evoked primal memories of childhood suppers from days long ago. They were, after all, two old bachelors mainly used to their own companionship, interrupted only by visitations to the various widows. They were all too familiar with the sound of each other's snores or the emissions of noxious gases from the endless plates of beans they consumed out on the rigs.

While the Widow Dial walked with her girlish gait toward the kitchen and the enticing smell of fresh-baked goods, Doc and Dad brought out their newly reconfigured geological charts and surveys, tailored to the names of the local townships.

By the time the Widow Dial returned with a plate of steaming cornbread and a dish of home-churned butter, Doc and Dad had the tools of their trade already laid out upon her coffee table.

The widow offered up the cornbread, which both men slathered with generous helpings of the sweet cream butter. The first bites activated salivary glands they had long since forgotten existed. The late Mr. Dial's spouse knew a thing or two about hearth and home. The cornbread tasted like cake, and with the fresh-churned butter seeping down through the golden crust, neither man could remember a flavor quite as sweet. It was the kind of taste, in fact, that could make even a confirmed bachelor turn his thoughts to matrimony, to the comforts of married life and a home instead of a blanket under the stars or rented rooms above a livery stable or saloon.

"My," said the Widow Dial. "These charts certainly look impressive!"

"Not nearly as impressive," said Doc, "as this cornbread. I can honestly say that my own sainted mother could not have matched it."

The Widow Dial blushed with a kind of matronly charm, though there was an absence of the fluttering of the heart that usually followed one of Doc's endearments to the widows with whom he had been acquainted. Again, if he was more on his game, the notion might have gnawed at him. But, truth be told, the cornbread had disarmed him.

On the other hand, man did not live by cornbread alone, and there was business to be done, and both he and Dad knew it. They carefully finished the last crumbs of their delicacies, put the saucers on the end tables, and turned their attention to the maps laid out on the coffee table.

"This," said Dad, "is a geological, topographical, and petroliferous survey of the areas composed of Mule Chute and Cornville, Texas."

"My goodness!" said the Widow Dial, impressed before they had even begun to get to the heart of the matter.

"What it describes, my dear Mrs. Dial," said Doc, "is a salt dome."

"A salt dome?"

"Just so," answered Doc with a practiced nod and an ingratiating smile.

"And anticlines, faults, the Sabine Uplift," Dad interjected.

"The Rusk Depression," added Doc.

"The Yegua and Cook Mountain formations," Dad continued.

It was as though they were chamber musicians playing a well-rehearsed duet.

"Names," said Doc, "familiar, I assure you, to every geologist worth his salt west of the Mississippi."

Junipera Sue looked from one to the other, her face lighting up in delight, as Doc and Dad described the indications on their charts of a massive field of oil beneath her ranchland.

"Well!" she said, with true religious fervor. "It is a season of miracles!"

"Praise Jesus," Doc solemnly intoned, to which Dad added, "Amen."

But Junipera Sue appeared to be in a kind of reverie, which neither man could understand. She had, after all, just lost a husband. Even the widows whose passions for their late spouses had long since dimmed had never displayed the euphoria with which the Widow Dial now spoke.

"First Thurman literally coming back from the dead, and now what this fortune teller prophesied becoming a reality!"

Doc and Dad looked at each other.

"Coming back from the dead?" Doc said. "Why, whatever do you mean, dear lady?"

"The day after I had to go down to the county office and declare Thurman dead, up the road comes the dustiest, dirtiest tramp you ever did see! I was afraid of him, and I don't mind saying so. I pulled out Thurman's shotgun, and I said, 'Git!'"

Chapter 6

She pronounced *git* with such enthusiasm that it made Doc and Dad quite literally jump. She was a feisty little woman, clearly enthralled with her own tale.

"And who do you think that tramp was?" she asked, almost giddily.

Doc and Dad looked at each other, fearing the answer.

"My very own sweet husband, Thurman! Just a modern-day Lazarus is all it was!"

Just then, there was the sound of heavy footfalls, the kind of a giant, the ones accompanied in children's stories by the words "Fee, fie, foe, fum!"

"That must be him now! You can tell him about our good fortune yourself!"

"Jesus!" Doc Boyd exclaimed.

"Yes!" exclaimed Junipera Sue, jumping to her feet and clapping her hands in joyful delight. "Praise Jesus in all his glory!"

The ominous footfalls grew louder, echoing down the hallway toward the parlor. At that moment, the sun was virtually blocked out by a giant of a man who filled the baronial entryway. He stood easily seven feet tall, if not more, and was the widest man Doc had ever seen in all his days. Over his shoulder, he carried a .30-06 Winchester lever-action rifle, which looked like a child's toy in this giant's beefy paw. The huge man squinted a look at the two strangers and brought the Winchester down off his shoulder.

"Uh," said Dad, "maybe we ought to come back another day. You know, all this good news at once..." He looked at Doc with undisguised anguish. There was only one thing to do in such circumstances, and that thing was to beat a hasty retreat.

But against all common sense and reason, Doc decided to brazen it out. He grinned from ear to ear and walked, joyously, toward the giant, as if greeting a long-lost brother, and tried to embrace him, though his arms could not encompass the redwood tree trunk-like torso of the man.

"Thurman, big fella!" he said. "How are ya?"

Thurman grunted, the kind of grunt that giants emanate right before they try to eat the bones of children in fairy tales.

"By golly," Doc stammered, trying to regain his composure. "Just a mountain of a man!"

The squint in the big man's eyes turned positively reptilian. "Who…are…you?" he growled.

Doc gulped.

Dad began to consider whether he could fling his massive bulk out the parlor window.

Junipera Sue looked, with some distress, at her recently risen from the dead beloved. "Don't you know these men, dear?" she asked. "They said they met you in Juarez."

"Actually," Dad said, verbally backtracking and eyeing the distance between himself and the window and coming to the conclusion that there was no chance for escape, "it was just outside of Juarez."

"And you told them about the fortune teller," Junipera Sue reminded her husband.

The ogre began to grind his teeth. He looked from one flimflam man to the other and said in a raspy voice, "I don't remember no fortune teller." His massive foot took a step toward them in what Doc could only consider a menacing fashion. "And I don't remember neither one of them neither."

It was as if Doc could hear a rattlesnake inside his brain, issuing out a last warning before sinking fangs into flesh, inflicting painful and certain death.

Chapter 6

Dad had the same reaction and said, "Come to think of it, it was a very dark night, and the lighting in that place was very dark. Very dark."

Thurman growled again. It seemed to be a habit of his. He growled before he spoke, as if chewing the words between his massive mandibles before allowing them to escape. He growled and leaned in toward the two con men, looking from one to the other, staring them both in the eyes.

"I don't know you two fellas. And I don't know about no fortune teller!"

"You know," Doc said, as if remembering something all of a sudden, "it could have been somebody else. Lot of large men south of the border."

But instead of pacifying this resurrected Goliath, Doc's words seemed to further aggravate him.

"I don't know what you're talkin' about, I tell ya!" he thundered, the walls vibrating with his rumbling bass voice.

"Well," said Dad, inching his way along the wall, hoping, somehow, to ease his massive girth past the ogre, "obviously a case of mistaken identity. No harm, no foul. We'll just be running along."

Just then, however, it was Junipera Sue who stepped up and blocked both Doc and Dad's escape.

"No, you won't!" she proclaimed, like a schoolmarm about to whack a wayward child's knuckle.

"Now look, ma'am," said Doc, mentally tap dancing to find any possible explanation for their bald-faced lie. "I can explain," he continued, knowing that he could not possibly.

Junipera Sue leaned in close to him and whispered, as if to hide the awful truth, "It's just the amnesia."

"Amnesia?" Doc and Dad both exclaimed, clinging to the word like survivors of the *Titanic* to a passing life vest.

But Junipera Sue's whispered diagnosis seemed only to even further agitate the giant to whom she was wed.

"I don't know them, I tell ya!" he shouted, waving his arms, as though swatting away apparitions that only he could see.

Junipera Sue stood on her tippy-toes as she reached up to gently stroke the flushed cheek of this colossus of the prairie. "Now, Thurman, you just calm down and remember what the doctor said."

"What *did* the doctor say?" Dad asked, with no small amount of relief.

Once again, Junipera Sue whispered, as though sharing some shameful secret. "Thurman got hit on the head by some banditos," she confessed, looking back and forth from Doc to Dad to see if the import of her words had sunk in. "They robbed him blind and left him to die."

Doc and Dad struggled to contain their joy at the pronouncement. Not that they wished the big fellow any harm, but these words were not a mere life vest floating by on the icy waters surrounding their sinking ship; they were, indeed, a lifeboat and an outstretched arm, blankets, and hot soup. They were a reprieve from the awful decree.

"And then," said Junipera Sue in awe and childlike wonder, "one day, one word came into Thurman's mind." She paused, what could only be described as a pregnant one, before relieving the suspense that hung in the air between them. "Cornville." She pronounced, as if it were a magical incantation.

"Cornville," the ogre uttered, equally full of awe, as if describing a mist-enshrouded Xanadu.

Chapter 6

Junipera Sue's face lit up in delight. "He knew it was home! He knew he had to get back to Cornville, and he made it back, and Della Call down at the general store recognized him and said, 'Praise Jesus! It's Thurman Dial come back from the dead.'" This last she shouted out with the religious fervor of a genuine conversion.

Junipera Sue continued, in the voice of one who had witnessed a biblical miracle come to life. "He doesn't hardly remember a thing, but he found his way home. To Cornville."

Doc Boyd looked up at the heavens and intoned, with no small amount of reverence and thanksgiving, "Oh Lord, we owe you for this one."

"Praise Jesus!" Junipera Sue said, jumping up and down and clapping her hands in childlike delight, as if possessed by the Holy Spirit.

"Amen," Dad added heartily.

Whereupon Junipera Sue turned to her husband and jumped just high enough to tweak his nose in an unmistakable gesture of love for the big fellow.

Chapter 7

Dad Everett was off in the distance, waltzing with his forked divining rod, as Doc spoke with Junipera Sue and Thurman, from whose furrowed brow the storm of agita had seemed to pass, almost magically, with the tweaking of his nose by his beloved, little Junipera Sue.

"If we do find something here," Doc said, "Dad Everett and I will need someplace to sleep, and there don't seem to be any hotels in Cornville."

"No hotels in Cornville," Thurman repeated.

It was not a statement as much as it was a kind of self-questioning, a test of memory. Were there hotels in Cornville? He seemed to be asking himself the question, as if the answer revealed one of the great mysteries of life.

And of course, the answer was no.

Life was cruel. There were no hotels in Cornville. There was, however, some comfort in the knowledge of that fact. It was a certainty. And in Thurman's muddled mind, that was a rare commodity.

Junipera Sue broke into Thurman's reverie. "Well, we own the general store in town. Mrs. Call takes care of it for us. There's a room upstairs, and you'll both be welcome to it."

Chapter 7

"No hotels in Cornville," Thurman added, as if in admonition.

"No, indeed," said Doc, struck by the profundity of Thurman's observation.

Just then, Dad seemed to swoon. And then, just as suddenly, he was yanked violently as if by the earth's magnetism. Being pulled against his will, the forked stick vibrating, pulsating in his chubby hands, he was flung like a dog hanging on to a length of rope jerked about by a playfully sadistic master. The divining stick pulled Dad hither, thither, and yon.

It was, Doc had to admit, one heck of a performance.

The three onlookers ran from the massive porch, out to where mysterious, primal forces unseen propelled the old gentleman.

"Oh Lordy!" Dad exclaimed. "I can't keep up with it!"

Dad was like a man possessed, running after a forked stick that moved, if not of its own volition, then by the same ancient powers that erected the megalith of Stonehenge and the pyramids of ancient Egypt.

"Oil!" Dad bellowed. "Why, I never felt it so strong in all my life, Dr. Boyd! That gypsy fortune teller was absolutely right! Oh Lordy, it's too strong for me!"

So saying, the forked stick plunged into the ground and vibrated with such violence that the portly, old gentleman fainted like a southern belle with a case of the vapors.

Thurman growled and then said, "We better get him out of the sun."

***

Having been revived by lemonade and, to Doc and Dad's mutual delight, treated to Junipera Sue's buttermilk-crusted fried chicken, okra, and the belly fat bacon–flavored baked beans of Doc Boyd's childhood memories, the geologist, petroleum engineer, and master of all things petroliferous and the ancient wildcatter produced, from their well-worn briefcases, letters of agreement assigning to them the mineral rights to the Dial Ranch. They promised in return one-eighth of the proceeds from the exploitation of said rights, which, Doc reminded Junipera Sue and Thurman Dial, though only one-eighth, was one-eighth of a fortune, which was a fortune itself nonetheless, especially when said fortune consisted of a pool of oil, a sleeping black giant that would yield to them a treasure all the crowned heads of Europe would envy.

"Oh well," Junipera Sue said, flustered. "We'd just be happy with enough to cover our bills and tear up the credit slips for all the folks who've bought from our general store. Seems like we're the only thing keeping half the folks in this town afloat, and I don't know how much longer the good Lord will let us do it for Cornville."

"Cornville…" Thurman repeated, nodding his head with the gravity of the word and the burden of supporting its populace with the credit they extended in their modest emporium.

Documents having been signed and sealed in triplicate—one for the Dials, one for Dad and Doc, and one to be filed, in good time, with the proper authorities—the two aging flimflam men availed themselves of the Dials' invitation to use the single room above their general store as their temporary abode.

Having bid their newfound partners adieu, Doc and Dad drove back along the rutted and pitted dusty road, back into the prairie metropolis of Cornville.

It was a modest town, which reflected the character of its denizens. This was no cow town, with bawdy houses, dens of iniquity, gambling, and such goings on. The local bourgeois eked out their livings providing services and goods to the farmers and small family ranchers scattered across the flatlands of a seemingly endless, dry horizon broken only by shimmering heat waves and the occasional dust devil dancing across the plain.

There was a restaurant that, though it served alcohol, did so discreetly, due to the Prohibition laws imposed like a wicked curse against a people in desperate need of the brace of liquid courage. Doc and Dad promptly referred to it as New Dugan's, after the similar saloon back in Lathrope.

There was a barbershop, a Chinese laundry, the Dials' general store, the local constabulary, two livery stables, and an incongruous purveyor of Hungarian sausage. There was also a millinery shop and a blacksmith and, just recently, the local *Cornville Gazette* had begun to publish a biweekly journal of what passed for news in this part of East Texas. There was also a cigar store, whose proprietor kept beneath the counter a few discreet bottles of the forbidden hooch to be served up in coffee cups, though no one could ever recall having seen a percolator on the premises.

Doc and Dad bought a couple nickel cigars from the proprietor and two cups full of what the owner purported to be Canadian whiskey, which tasted more like something made in a bathtub, with just a hint of dirty socks instead of peat moss. Thus fortified, they retrieved the key to their new abode from Della Call, the woman who ran the Dials' store.

They walked up the rickety steps leading from the alleyway behind the store to a small landing, which gave way to the single room, bearing witness to the sign in the general store's front window that read Room to Let.

The staircase seemed to have been added as an afterthought, and Doc could tell that Thurman Dial, the mountain of a man who had escaped certain death at the hands of Mexican desperadoes, had neither been its architect nor its builder, so shoddy was the workmanship thereof. The stairs creaked and groaned under Dad's not-inconsiderable weight. Some essential nails appeared to be missing, and dry rot had set in on several of the steps.

Doc wondered exactly how long it would be until a board broke through, causing Dad and his girth to become caught like an obese groundhog unable to completely come out of its hole, predicting neither winter nor spring.

Earlier that evening, the men had enjoyed a large steak dinner at New Dugan's in celebration of having closed the mineral rights deal with the Dials and thus procuring the goods which would be the basis for swindling the widows of Cornville and its environs. They headed back to the cigar store and indulged in several more porcelain coffee cups of the local moonshine.

Dad yawned, obviously depleted by the afternoon's performance with the divining rod. "Well," said Dad. "Early to bed, early to rise."

There was not much that Doc felt he could contribute to a conversation that began with that phrase, so he simply let it slide. Doc inserted the key to what would be their new home, forced open the rusty lock, and stood stunned as the handle promptly came loose in his hand.

"What a piece of…" Doc said.

He picked up the other half of the handle, which had fallen inside the room, jammed the two halves back together, and closed the door, which refused to fit back into the frame.

Chapter 7

That's when Dad pointed out the loose hinge, necessitating Doc's trip back down to the general store for a screwdriver and screws with which to refasten it.

Judas Priest! he thought to himself. *Just once, I'd like to make enough money to spend a week, not more than that, just one week in a* real *house that doesn't smell of dirty laundry and unbathed prospectors and cold cans of beans and rotted corned beef.*

Which was exactly what the room reeked of.

Having refastened the door hinge and reattached the door handle, Doc lit the lantern, which was the only source of illumination, as the room was not wired for electricity.

However, that was not the only thing it lacked. There was an outhouse out back, down the stairs and behind the alley, so the room came equipped with a chamber pot, which still retained the residue of the previous occupant. There was a washstand with a pitcher and basin, though the room had no running water.

To make matters worse, there was only one bed, and not only had Dad already laid claim to it, but he was also fast asleep, wheezing and snoring as was his wont after a large meal. The only thing left on which Doc felt he could stretch his six-foot, four-inch frame was what once had been a couch and was now denuded of its cushions. It was thus scarcely more than a frame and boasted a straw-filled mattress whose filling protruded through the blue ticking. Moreover, the straw within was moldy. This he knew by the odor that filled the room as he sat down upon it.

He pondered whether this indicated that the previous occupant had been a bed wetter. It was not a comforting thought. Then, he looked up at the ceiling and saw the stains and mildew from what was obviously a leaking roof.

"Land o' Goshen," he said to himself. "I am entering my sixth decade, and all I have to show for my labors is a room that smells like an outhouse shared with a snoring fat man in the only thing that passes for a bunk while I am myself forced to make do with a bed wetter's moldy straw mattress."

He was neither inebriated enough nor tired enough to fall asleep. Nor was he preoccupied with the details of their upcoming labors since they would be no different than those they had carried out countless times before in Oklahoma.

But at the thought of Oklahoma, his mind drifted back to the Widow Simms, for he had experienced something with her that was, he had to admit, a novelty. He had said to her the exact same words that he had said countless times before to an equally countless number of newly minted widows. He had recited the same sonnets and quoted the same passages of Scripture, confessed the same affections.

But this time, as if under the spell of Shakespearean fairies in *A Midsummer Night's Dream*, he found, to his amazement, that he himself believed every lie he had told her.

It was an alarming prospect. It was, he knew, the worst violation of a con man's code, if, indeed, any con man ever possessed anything even remotely resembling a code of either honor or conduct. The worst thing a con man could do was to believe his own con.

And yet, there it was. Undeniable. Every whispered term of endearment uttered to the Widow Simms was actually true. His affections for her were indelibly marked upon his heart, an organ to which, heretofore, he had paid little if any attention. Indeed, he would have testified on a stack of Bibles, were he a religious man, that the thing existed merely to pump blood and could not possibly be the repository of the word that remained unnamed.

Somehow, pronouncing it in a foreign language lessened its reality.

Amore.

He put no stock in it. Held no truck with it. It had no currency with him. It was something for pimple-faced adolescents who swooned at the touch of a young girl's hand beneath a harvest moon.

There had been such a girl once, in Doc's youth. He was eighteen, and she was sixteen. She was, he had believed all these years, the loveliest creature he had ever beheld. And he, who was never at a loss for words even in his adolescence, was tongue-tied in her presence. He felt a tickle in his throat, felt his heart race, at the mere thought of her. They had held hands and gone to a county fair. And he had, on the village green, on a soft summer night heavy with the scent of jasmine and honeysuckle, beneath the gracefully hanging boughs of a weeping willow, stolen a kiss. And she had kissed him back.

And on that night, long ago, he fully considered getting down on one knee and asking for her hand in matrimony. But then there stretched before him the vision of all that would entail. Debt. Responsibility. Bills to pay. And more horrifying still—solid employment.

None of that, he felt, was for him. No matter how enticing the sweet soap smell of her skin or the softness of that first kiss, marriage was for suckers. Marriage was what his parents had.

His father, Adolph Bumstetter, was a German immigrant sodbuster who married a mail-order bride for whom he had need but little affection. Bumstetter was no gentleman farmer in the south. He worked as hard as the mule behind which he plowed his row, as much a slave to the land as any of the children of Israel under Pharaoh. The mail-order bride was there to wash and cook and clean.

She must have provided some marital comfort since young Heinrich was their offspring. But he did not possess a single memory of joy in that household. Old Adolph had produced a son because he needed a cheap hand to help him on the farm.

Being the son of a German sodbuster instilled in young Heinrich a steel determination never to follow in his father's footsteps. His father was, as far as he was concerned, part of the larger class of human beings known as suckers. And young Heinrich was determined to be part of the other class of the species.

Heinrich was a smooth talker. A slick operator. With a wink and a smile, with a twinkle of his blue eyes and his athletic build, people said that he could sell ice to Eskimos.

Thus, when he stood at the fork in the road that led, on the one hand, to marriage to the young girl from whom he had stolen a kiss on the village green or, on the other hand, to a life of freedom in which he imagined he would graze off the fat of the land, off the gullibility of the chumps, the suckers, the rubes, the marks, and the pigeons, he had chosen the latter, and he never looked back. Until tonight.

He had made money, and he had lost money, and he was always one step ahead of the law, irate husbands, or brokenhearted widows. And then, before you knew it, almost in the twinkling of an eye, here he was, about to enter his sixth decade, on the verge of being an old man.

He stared over at the bed on which Dad slept, his massive belly rising and falling with each wheezy snore and then, suddenly, not breathing at all. *Sometimes,* Doc thought, *Dad did not breathe for dangerous lengths of time, only to snort like a bull moose in heat, gasp for air like a drowning man, then snore again.* He knew it would not be too long before Dad would avail himself of the chamber pot. The old man would not chance the rickety stairs in the dark. *This is what my life has become,* Doc thought.

It was the cornbread that did it, Junipera Sue's cornbread, that smell of home that started it. And then the fried chicken. But it wasn't just the meal; it was the love with which she had made it for that hulking, monosyllabic sodbuster to whom she was wed and whom she seemed to love so deeply that she would actually jump as high as she could just to tweak his nose in delight.

The afternoon spent with the Dials did not fill him with nostalgia for his home, as he believed it had done for Dad. Instead, it sent his mind a-wandering back to Oklahoma and Flora May Simms. She had made him fried chicken that was equally as good as Junipera Sue Dial's, and he felt that she had done so with equal affection.

He recalled a particular afternoon when Flora May had made a picnic for the two of them, and they had strolled through the meadow adjoining her farm, hand in hand. She had tripped, or feigned to do so, and leaned against his shoulder. And he had been quick to put his arm around her to steady her. But the feel of her hand upon his arm, the touch of her skin, the golden sunlight playing across her hair, and the look of unbridled joy in her eyes had produced within him the oddest sensation, a sweet kind of ache, that emanated, he knew, from that organ which, heretofore, he firmly believed existed only for the pumping of blood. It was simply an internal plumbing device and certainly not that thing to which suckers, chumps, pigeons, and marks referred to as the repository and, indeed, source of what they named *love*.

She smelled faintly of lilac. And whether it was from a scented soap or some long unopened bottle of perfume, he could not tell, nor did it matter. It took but the scent of her to make his heart race as rapidly as it had once on a village green, on a soft summer night heavy with the scent of jasmine and honeysuckle, beneath the gracefully hanging boughs of a weeping willow.

He had uttered words he knew to be a lie—that he harbored the fondest of affections for her and that he wished for nothing more than to be financially able to ask for her hand in marriage, that he longed for little more in life than the sweetness of her companionship.

And all of it was true! Every single lie he told! Despite that, and finding himself yet again at the forked road, he chose the path that led him farther and farther away from that which he professed was his heart's true desire.

Dad's snort and gasp and bull moose roar broke Doc out of his reflections on the *amore* he had felt for the Widow Simms. The old man groaned as he swung his chubby legs off the bed and stumbled about in search of the chamber pot. Doc feigned sleep so as not to be dragged into conversation with a man relieving himself in such close quarters. Dad finished his business, stumbled back to bed, and soon resumed the wheezy roar.

Finally, blessedly, Doc drifted off to sleep. And when he did, he found himself back in a meadow with Flora May. They opened their picnic basket as they had done on that sunlit afternoon, the golden light softly playing across her chestnut hair. In the dream, he could smell the fried chicken that they had shared, the biscuits, fresh baked and soaked in butter, the sweet corn, and pecan pie. But, more than anything, he could have sworn there was the scent of lilac.

He laid his head down in her lap. She stroked away a lock of hair that had fallen across his forehead, as a mother would do to a much-loved child. And he experienced a contentment which he knew, even as he was dreaming, was not a dream but a memory. It had actually happened.

They *had* strolled through that meadow arm in arm. She *had* fallen against him, and he *had* felt the softness of her skin. They *had* spread a picnic blanket and opened a basket she had so carefully packed with the food she had made, spiced with its secret ingredient in which only suckers, chumps, and rubes believed: love.

He knew that he was dreaming and could hear Dad's snoring intruding upon it. He was conscious of the fact that he was fighting a losing battle to remain asleep, to remain in that meadow with his head in the warm lap of the Widow Flora May Simms, who stroked a lock of hair from his forehead.

The sound of Dad relieving himself in the chamber pot once again announced the dawning of the new day and consigned Doc's reverie to what he knew could never be more than what it had been: just a dream.

"Well, Doc," said Dad. "Rise and shine."

Chapter 8

On May 7, 1930, Dad procured a poor-boy rig in the little town of Kilgore. On May 8, Dad, Doc, and Thurman began skidding the drilling rig across the Dial Ranch to the place that Dad Everett, almighty Providence, and an imaginary gypsy fortune teller had all predetermined was the site upon which their fortunes would be made. They pushed and pulled the ancient rig across the rocky ground, much, Doc imagined, as the children of Israel had done with the giant stones meant as monuments to Pharaoh's ego. Still, he realized, the efforts in which he was now engaged were more difficult than the work he had escaped doing for his German sodbuster father, pushing a plow behind a mule's rear end across the red clay earth of his father's farm.

The rig groaned and teetered, and then there was the sound of wood cracking as the spokes of the left rear wheel once and for all gave way, broke, and disintegrated, like the charred remains of a cook fire with no fuel left to burn. The derrick teetered and came crashing down on its left side, a wounded beast that would be moved no more.

"Rusted-out, two-bit piece of junk!" Dad Everett said and spit brown tobacco juice on the busted rig like an ornery camel straight out of the tales of Ali Baba.

Doc felt no less anger and resentment, not only at the rig but also at their station in life, which consigned them to labor beneath the noonday's sun with worn-out tools. But Doc was the con man's con man and possessed a facility for turning each new misfortune into but another prop upon which their house of cards would be built.

"Take it easy," he said to the red-faced, old gentleman.

But Dad would not be mollified. "Worthless thing's held together with spit and baling wire!" So saying, Dad Everett began kicking the broken rig as crueler men might treat a recalcitrant beast of burden that stubbornly refused its master's entreaties to carry its load even another step. Dad kicked and spit and swore oaths of vengeance against the rickety derrick and rusting boiler that fueled it.

Doc put a hand on his shoulder and said, "It doesn't matter, Dad."

That sentence, and Doc's smiling visage, served but to increase the chaos in the caverns of Thurman's already overtaxed mind. "But the drill site is still almost a quarter mile away," Thurman explained.

Doc tentatively put a hand on the giant's massive arm, as if trying to mollify a silverback gorilla about to pound its chest in fury. "Well, Thurman," he said, in what he hoped were calming, dulcet tones, "that's true. But that is *a* drill site. That is not *the* drill site."

The difference between *a* and *the* was a vexation for Thurman, as much as if Doc had tried to explain to him the difference between pie and pi. One was vittles and the other a mathematical formula. And the fact that the words were pronounced in exactly the same way need not be a source of confusion.

Thurman felt as if his head were about to split apart, like a giant watermelon that's fallen off the truck. It was as confounding to him as the Fibonacci sequence to the village idiot.

"What," Thurman said, feeling the blood beginning to pound in his ears, "does that mean?"

"Well," said Doc Boyd, in the voice of a kindergarten teacher, "it just seems to me like the hand of Providence has been guiding our every step."

Doc's answer provided no comfort for the confused ogre. Thurman pointed at the distant site, almost a quarter mile away, and said, "But, but, that place down yonder, where Mr. Everett swooned with the forked stick, that's where he said the oil is."

Thurman looked up to the heavens, as though for guidance, which was when Doc only added to his confusion by saying, "Yes! But this is where the cottonwood tree is."

Thurman growled his fee-fi-fo-fum growl and said, "The cottonwood tree?"

"The cottonwood tree," Doc said gently. "Thurman, don't you remember what the gypsy fortune teller told you?"

Thurman looked from Doc to Dad and then, once again, up at the heavens.

"Uh…argh! No, Dr. Boyd. I rack my brain, and I can't remember a word she said."

But Doc and Dad were now like a pair of virtuoso violinists playing *Eine kleine Nachtmusik*. Doc laid it down, and now Dad picked it up without missing a beat.

"Oh my," Dad said, "you're right, Doc! I was so bullheaded about gettin' to where I was going that I didn't see what was right in front of me. The living truth of that gypsy's prophesy. What was her name?"

Chapter 8

"Her name is of no importance, Dad," Doc admonished the older man, not wanting to add further to Thurman's confusion. He turned to Thurman and said, "Thurman, when you told us about the fortune teller, you said that she told you there was oil on your place."

Thurman had heard this so many times now that he simply answered, "Uh-huh." For him, it was an established fact. There had been a fortune teller, and she had told him that there was oil on his ranch. It had been somewhere outside of Juarez, over a plate of moles and frijoles, before the gang of banditos had laid him low with their many repeated blows to his head and the only thought left in his scrambled brain was *Cornville*.

"And you told us," Doc continued, "that she had said it was no more than fifty paces away from the cottonwood tree." He pointed to the lone cottonwood tree a short ways off, which stood like a sentry against the East Texas horizon. In a voice filled with wonder, he said, "I had forgot clean about that until that wheel broke down right here!"

"Me too, Doc!" Dad said with growing excitement.

"But I don't know nothin' about no cottonwood tree," grumbled Thurman.

"Neither did we!" said Doc. "Neither did we. Just proves my point!"

"We all forgot, Thurman, just like you," said Dad. "Now, let me just measure off and see how many paces it is to that tree. One, two, three, four…"

So saying, Doc began to pace off, with his chubby legs, the distance between the fallen rig and the lone cottonwood tree.

But Thurman, however, had not yet crossed that particular Rubicon of his mind.

"But that old divinin' stick said it was over yonder." He pointed at the spot where, only the day before, the portly, older gentleman had swooned and his divining rod seemed pulled toward the ground as if the earth itself were about to open up and swallow him whole. "It was yonder," Thurman said again, definitively.

"And," said Doc reasonably, "I'm sure there is oil over yonder. But *your* gypsy—just like *your* house—said fifty paces from the cottonwood tree, and I believe the good Lord himself saw what we were too blind to see, what was right in front of us."

"The…cottonwood tree?" Thurman said hesitantly.

"The cottonwood tree," Doc confirmed, as though saying *amen.*

Dad, meanwhile, realizing that the cottonwood tree was no more than *thirty* paces from where they stood, began shortening each step until he resembled an elephantine ballerina dancing on pointe across the prairie.

"Forty-seven, forty-eight, forty-nine, fifty!" Dad shouted out. "Fifty paces on the nose, Doc! No more, no less!"

"Well, that confirms it!" Doc said with scientific certainty. "I say we drill here, and we will hit the Woodbine sand at thirty-five hundred feet. I'd stake my reputation on it!"

Thurman looked unsure of it all. He had seen the old man swoon, and, indeed, he had never seen anything like it. He felt like one of the Levites witnessing Moses coming down from the Mount, and now he was being told that it was *a* Mount Sinai, not *the* Mount Sinai?

Dad could sense that Thurman was not yet ready to make that leap of faith.

"Mr. Dial," he said, purposely using the formal appellation. "If we're too bullheaded and turn away from the spot that the

Lord himself has revealed to us," he intoned solemnly, "then we don't deserve the treasure that he has literally laid out at our feet."

Thurman was thunderstruck at the thought. After all he had been through, after all his travels and travails, the attack of the desperadoes, the seemingly endless five years mindlessly wandering through the desert toward the beacon of Cornville, his personal lighthouse of Alexandria, his own torch of liberty stretching forth her light to all those bereft of hope, toward his beloved Junipera Sue, he might be somehow undeserving of the reward to which the Lord himself was leading him?

"Thurman," Doc said, realizing that the giant oak was about to fall and needed but one more thrust of the axe and a mighty biblical heave-ho. "Thurman, *Jesus* wants us to drill right here. And I say we trust in the Lord and leave the rest up to him."

To which Thurman and Dad intoned in humility and solemn gratitude, "Amen."

Chapter 9

So it was that Doc and Dad began spudding in what would come to be known as the Junipera Sue Number One, exactly fifty paces from the lone cottonwood tree that struggled to maintain its foothold on the arid land of this drought-inflicted region of East Texas known as Cornville, just a stone's throw from the equally dusty township of Mule Chute, a name much derided and ofttimes purposely mispronounced by the surrounding country folk who, one supposes, had to feel superior to someone, even if in name only.

They devoted the first of their labors to building the drilling platform and then to easing the rickety oil derrick atop it. Once they had accomplished that, they had to put into place the actual steam-powered drilling mechanism and boiler.

That was when Dad Everett was in his glory. This was no con. There was no room for flimflam, ballyhoo, or folderol on an oil rig. Dad Everett was one of the best cable-and-tool men to be found, and a really good one was scarce as hen's teeth.

You had to have more than just the requisite knowledge and skills. You had to have a *feel* for it. You had to be able to look at the cable and just from the way it moved, simply from the tremor or tensions, from the "cable dance," Dad called it, you had to be able to know what was happening thousands of feet beneath the earth.

You had to be a steamfitter, boilermaker, carpenter, and one heck of a good all-around mechanic and mechanical engineer. A miscalculation could result not just in a broken drill bit. It could also kill a man, rip his leg off, or his head, just as easy.

In addition to cable, you had to know your way around rope more than any cowhand and know more knots than any sailor.

Dad had been there for the birth of modern drilling, near Beaumont, at Spindletop back in late 1900. There, Dad had used the old-fashioned lift-and-drop tool bit. It was just like rock mining with a pickaxe. Then he ran out of money, and a fella came in behind him with a fishtail bit and a rotary drill, went down eleven hundred feet, and hit the biggest oil strike in the country. Dad caught on to that old fishtail bit right away.

Then he met a fella out in Shreveport, name of Granville Humason. Dad had an idea for a two-cone drill bit that could work twice as fast as that old fishtail. He and Humason shook hands and began working up drawings. Dad knew it would make 'em richer than the Queen of Sheba. It would revolutionize everything there was about oil drilling.

About that time, Dad had a sweetheart, Lou Della Havermeyer. She was a big German Swedish girl with a ruddy complexion and an easy smile, and she was a good cook to boot. Well, Dad was smitten. That was back in the day long before anyone ever called him "Dad." He was D. H. to all the wildcatters, but to Lou Della, he was her very own Davey, and he loved to hear her call him that.

Dad figured with the money he and Humason were gonna make on that two-cone drill bit, he'd finally have a steady income. He wouldn't be dependent upon whether he brought in a gusher. He and Granville would open up a real machine shop and crank out drill bits just like they were printing money. Then he figured to get down on one knee and ask for Lou Della's hand in marriage. He had a ring picked out and everything. Borrowed two months' wages on his last job to buy it.

Then Lou Della got the influenza.

D. H. nursed her day and night, and he figured you couldn't hardly get any more intimate with a human being than when they were helpless and you had to help 'em out with everything. But she coughed and coughed till she coughed up blood, and folks warned D. H. that she might be consumptive and he could get it too. But it didn't matter to him at all. Lou Della was his own true love, and he'd have laid down his life for her if he could have made that bargain with the good Lord.

But there weren't any bargains to be made. Life is short, he reckoned, shorter for some souls than others, and so it was with Lou Della Havermeyer, who succumbed to the fever.

He had left it to his partner to take out the patent, and they had a handshake deal that the two of them would split fifty-fifty the proceeds from the invention and split the expenses of setting up their tool and drill bit machine shop too. Well, Humason took the patent out in his own name, and D. H. bore no grudge against him for that. Truth be told, it was more Granville's design than his own.

But Ol' Granville had what folks called a thirst, and on the night that Dad was ministering to Lou Della's final needs, hearing the terrible sound of her raspy, labored breathing, begging her not to die, and trying to make bargains with the Lord or the devil, whoever would take him up on the offer, Ol' Granville was out slaking that thirst of his in a bar in town. And he got to blabbin' about their drill bit to a Texan named Howard.

Chapter 9

Now, this Howard wasn't anybody's fool. He knew a good deal more about drilling than he let on, and right there on the spot, he offered Granville one hundred fifty dollars, cash on the barrelhead, for a hundred percent of the rights to his patented two-cone drill bit. Howard wrote out the note and gave him the money, and Granville signed his John Henry on the dotted line, and Howard signed his: Howard Hughes Sr.

Granville must've known he might have made a mistake because he drank up fifty dollars of the hundred and fifty that Hughes gave him that night. The next day, D. H. was making funeral arrangements when Granville came and told him the news and offered him his fifty bucks.

D. H. didn't say much. Didn't take the money either. Called Granville a fool, is all.

But the truth was, when he put Lou Della in the ground, all his hopes and dreams seemed to go in with her. He didn't care that they'd lost the rights or that they wouldn't have their machine shop: Humason and Everett Tool and Drill Bit Company. The only reason he ever wanted it in the first place was so he could marry Lou Della and make her his bride. And now that she was cold and in the ground, it seemed to Dad that his heart wasn't so much broke as it was cold and dead too.

He went back to being a wildcatter. He and Granville never spoke again.

Hughes had a partner name of Walter Sharpe, and when Sharpe died in 1912, Howard took over the company and became one of the richest men in the world.

Then Dad went bust at Burkburnett. That pretty much knocked the stuffing out of D. H. His hair turned white overnight, and folks took to callin' him Dad to his face and Dry Hole behind his back. And now here he was, teamed up with

Doc, bamboozling widows and spudding in worthless oil wells to which they'd sell their even more worthless shares.

Still, there lived within him the true wildcatter's heart that maybe this time, just maybe, this would be his time. In spite of all the odds. In spite of drilling thirty-five actual paces from a lone cottonwood tree on a hardscrabble, dusty ranch in East Texas instead of the fifty he counted off for Big Thurman, that an imaginary fortune teller in Juarez, over equally imaginary moles and frijoles, had supposedly prophesied would make them all rich. In spite of knowing it was all nothing but Doc's well-rehearsed con about Rusk Depressions and Sabine Inclines. In spite of knowing everything they'd said was as much a lie as every other time they'd said the exact same words. Still, manipulating the real tools of his trade—watching the swivel make a pressure-tight seal on the drill hole, lowering the drill pipe sections that made up what they called the drill string, firing up the woodburning boiler that powered the steam engine, finally pushing the lever that started turning the drill bit, and seeing the drilling mud flush out the rock as the drill bit pushed its way down through the earth's crust—his heart beat quicker with the thought that maybe, just maybe, this time the earth would begin to tremble like a young girl kissed for the first time, and the gases released from the depths of Mother Earth would rumble up and break that pressure seal, and black gold would shoot up from the drill hole, anointing them all. And for once in his life, just once, he wouldn't be a joke of an old, fat man, stealing money from widows. He'd be an honest-to-goodness oilman who'd brought in a well!

Dad wasn't the only one bit by the fever of high hopes. The Dials owned the general store in town, and they'd promised to tear up the credit slips of all their customers when the oil came in. So there wasn't a rancher or farmer for miles around who didn't show up and pitch in, hoping the Dials would strike it rich, their debts would be wiped out, and new jobs would spring up to where a hardworking man could get an honest day's pay for an honest day's work, feed his family, put a roof over his kids' heads, and maybe buy 'em new shoes at Christmas.

Such were the modest dreams of the humble folk who showed up to help, to be directed by the old, fat man who held each part of their two-bit rig so lovingly with such practiced hands that moved with the skills of a surgeon.

They weren't just white folks either. There was a sizeable Black population in Cornville, and what folks didn't know was that back in the Great War, or what some still called the 14–18 war—when America suddenly needed oil more than ever to fuel the killing machines in Europe that were supposed to make the world safe for democracy, in what was supposed to be the war to end all wars—back then when oil was discovered in Oklahoma, it was the Black folk who were the wildcatters, who drilled the wells, and some of them struck it rich too.

Dad had worked the oil fields with those wildcatters and reckoned they were some of the best folks he'd ever known. When you worked with another man on a rig, you literally put your life in his hands, and whether those hands were white or black didn't make a bit of difference. The only thing that mattered was the man's skill and character because a lack of either could cripple or kill you as easy as pie.

When the Great War ended, so did the Black man's reign in the oil business. White folk came back, and if a boss had a choice between hiring a white or a Black man, the white man got it every time.

Still, there were as many Black folks living on credit at the Dial's general store as there were white folks. Junipera Sue and Thurman sold to everyone alike. It cost them with some people, but that didn't bother them either.

So when Dad and Doc put out the word that they needed help to spud in the Junipera Sue Number One, as many Black folks showed up to help as white, and a few of them knew the trade from the old days up in Oklahoma. Dad even remembered a couple of 'em. Real cable-and-tool men.

One of the Black men who showed up was Tanner Irving Sr. Oil wells worked on steam engines, and steam engines had boilers, and those boilers needed plenty of wood to burn. Tanner Irving Sr. was a wood carter. He approached Doc and Dad with what he said was a business proposition. The two con men asked him what it was.

Tanner Sr. said, "Well, sir, why don't you come over to my place? My missus is a mighty fine cook, and we can talk it over then. As long as you don't have nothin' against doin' business with a Black man."

Well, Doc Boyd and Dad Everett knew how to stretch a dollar, and they figured if Tanner could give them wood cheaper, they'd buy from him, no two ways about it.

"Mr. Irving," Dad said, "when that gusher comes through and sprays each and every one of us, we'll all be black and grateful for it."

That night, Doc and Dad drew quite a few looks in their magnificent black, chrome-wheeled automobile as they drove the dusty streets of Cornville to the side of town where the Black folk lived. At the very edge of the Black neighborhood, there was as pretty a log cabin as any man had ever seen. You could tell each and every log had been handpicked and expertly hewn. It was the kind of place a man could rightly be proud of. As they parked the Ford convertible next to the cabin, the smell of Della May Irving's pig's trotters and fried chicken greeted them both like an old friend, enveloping them in childhood memories.

In addition to the aforementioned pig's feet and buttermilk-crusted fried chicken, the meal included molasses and bacon baked beans, turnip greens, sweet potatoes, and poke salad. Della May must have been cooking since the day before since poke salad was not, as a city slicker or person of means might surmise, a simple bowl of tossed, chopped greens. It entailed a laborious process involving multiple rinsings and boilings of a noxious weed. Through sheer force of need and will, Della May, like so many others before and since, had transformed a plant that could cause violent illness or even death into a dish fit for a king. To top it all off, there was cornbread and, for dessert, cheddar cheese–crusted apple pie. And when it was all done, there wasn't a speck left on either man's plate.

"Mighty fine cooking, Mrs. Irving. Mighty fine," said Dad.

Della May was a tall, impressive-looking woman. There was something regal and statuesque about her, and when she moved, she seemed to float more than actually walk. Her husband, Tanner Irving Sr., was probably three or four inches shorter and of a wiry build, though pound for pound, folks from every part of the county would testify that he was one of the strongest men they had ever seen. And despite his limited stature, he bore himself as if he were as tall as Big Thurman.

Della May thanked Dad for the compliment and asked if he'd care for a bit more.

"No, ma'am," Dad said, patting his ample belly. "I've reached my limit."

"There are quite a few people in this town who wouldn't look kindly on you having dinner with us," Tanner said.

"That's the gospel truth!" Della May added.

"Well, that's their problem, not ours," Doc replied.

Dad wiped his lips, delicately for a fat man, then burped discreetly into his napkin. "And I have never been known to turn down a free meal. Especially glad I didn't start with this one. Can't recall ever having ate better."

Doc turned to Tanner and said, "Mr. Irving, you said you had some kind of business arrangement you wanted to discuss with us."

Tanner Irving took a deep breath, looked Doc straight in the eye and asked, "Are you a real geologist, Doc? Or is this some kind of flimflam you're pulling on folks? I don't mean no offense. I just got to know."

"You got to know?" Doc laughed. "Why is that? Did somebody appoint you sheriff while I wasn't looking?"

Tanner leaned in a bit farther, his jaw jutting out, as if to confirm his intent.

"I got to know, Doc, because I'm thinking of investing."

Doc and Dad looked at each other. "Well," said Doc, "that's another story."

"Very prudent of you, Mr. Irving, to do your due diligence," Dad continued. Doc reached into his well-worn carpetbag and produced a finely wrought diploma.

"Here you are, sir," Doc said grandly. "PhD in geology and petroleum engineering. Granted by the University of Heidelberg."

Tanner and Della May leaned over the document festooned with ribbons, wax seals of every description, solemn mottos in Latin, and the florid signature of the august institute of higher learning's dean, the honorable Herr Professor Manheim T. Muenschausen, PhD. The diploma itself, one had to admit, was a handsome one, though it had been printed up on the backside of a poster advertising a seven-reeler talkie starring a curvaceous Clara Bow. The drawn rendering of Miss Bow had been covered over, with a level of artistry that any doctoral candidate might well envy, by a blank sheet of parchment to conceal its origins.

There was one tiny flaw. The hand-drawn portrait of the "It Girl" had bled through from the poster onto the diploma. Miss Bow's bare-armed figure was enhanced by a flowing white gown while her chestnut curls framed the impish face of America's "red-hot mama." She looked out of the diploma with an unmistakable "come hither" smile, which Della May, as only a Christian woman with a discerning eye could, noticed right away.

"And what's this lady up here in the corner?" she asked, with no small amount of suspicion and distaste.

"That?" asked Doc Boyd.

"That!" she answered emphatically.

Doc was neither intimidated nor even flustered about the query. Without missing a single beat, he said, smiling proudly, "That, madam, is the Greek goddess Petrolia."

"Goddess of, uh, all matters petroliferous," Dad added, by way of explanation. Tanner Sr. looked at his wife with no small degree of skepticism himself. But still, the opportunity to own a share in an oil well, which could ensure his family's future, was too much to resist—lady or no lady.

He pondered the document a bit longer. The Latin motto at the bottom of the diploma read "*Verum in oculis aspicientis.*" Tanner read out the words and asked, "What's that mean?"

Doc, with the solemnity and respect due the motto of his alma mater, replied, "That, Mr. Irving, is the motto of the University of Heidelberg, the solemn oath by which it and all its students live. It means 'Truth…', that's the word *verum*, 'is what the eye…', that's the word *oculis*, 'must always behold.'"

"Truth is what the eye must always behold," Tanner Sr. repeated, swirling the words in his mouth like Kentucky sipping whiskey before swallowing them. "Well, seeing as how you got an official diploma and all, with a Greek goddess on it, I'll take a chance on you."

He proffered his hand, and Doc shook it enthusiastically. "Well, that's just fine, Mr. Irving. Now for only five hundred dollars—"

"I don't have five hundred dollars," Tanner quickly corrected him. "But I can supply you with firewood, and you can pay me with stock certificates," he said, his eyes still staring straight into Doc's, searching for the hint of flimflam about the man.

But yet again, Doc assumed a noble bearing and said, "Mr. Irving, you've done made yourself a deal!"

They shook on the terms of their new agreement once again. Tanner felt obliged to advise Doc, who was a newcomer to these parts, about the social realities of Cornville, Texas, and certain of its citizens. "There's gonna be quite a few white folks who aren't gonna be too happy with you having a Black partner."

"Mr. Irving," Doc said, with what he hoped would pass for nobility of spirit rather than greed, "I can honestly say that when I look at money, I don't see black, and I don't see white. I see green. It's the only color that concerns me."

"Well," said Dad Everett with a hearty smile, "a happy conclusion to a festive evening. And now, if you will excuse me, I have a condolence call to pay on the Widow Tyler." This last was uttered with fitting respect for the grieving widow to whom he was about to pay his respects. He took his leave of Mr. and Mrs. Irving, graciously thanking Della May once again for her fine cuisine, put on his beaten fedora with what could only be called a remarkable je ne sais quoi for an ancient fat man, and departed.

Doc Boyd waited until Dad was out of earshot and then looked at Mr. and Mrs. Irving and, referencing Dad's earnest desire to comfort a bereaved widow, said, "The man is a saint."

Chapter 10

In retrospect, Dad Everett would have found it difficult to say what had transpired on the ride from Tanner Irving Sr.'s well-crafted log cabin to the Widow Martha Jean Tyler's slat-boarded, tidy home, perched at the other side of town upon the slightest rise on the endless flat horizon.

Dad was certainly not an inarticulate man, especially when it came to the widows. But that presupposed he was quoting from the Scriptures or the sonnets of the immortal bard. Left to his own devices, he was all but mute in the expression of the meditations of his heart. Indeed, the very notion of meditations of the heart was foreign to him.

His life, he reflected, discounting the swindling of the widows, was almost monk-like. He arose before dawn, splashed water on his face, performed his daily needs, took a hearty enough breakfast to last him through the day, and set out to perform whatever labors lay before him. He bathed three times weekly and had three sets of clothing: work clothes, after-work clothes, and widow clothes. He was happiest, of course, when his hands spoke for him. They bore the scars of every well he had ever drilled: rope and cable burns, oil fires, the harsh bite of iron into his palms, the tip of a finger cut away, spots burned into him by a lifetime spent laboring beneath the sun. They were good hands, skilled in his profession to the point of mastery and worn not only with scars of misfortune but also with the passing of time itself. As it said in the Ninetieth Psalm, verse ten: "The years of our life are seventy, or even by reason of strength eighty; yet their span is but toil and trouble; they are soon gone, and we fly away."

By that reckoning, he realized, it was almost time to sprout his wings.

And yet, though of advanced years—but two years shy of the promised four score—by reason of strength, his well-worn hands were still powerful enough to wrench in any section of pipe, stronger than the younger men whom he guided on the rig and who marveled at the old, fat man's stamina.

Yet when it came to matters of the heart, that was a light extinguished and grown cold in a Shreveport boardinghouse decades before. He woke and ate and worked and ate and slept and occasionally bathed. He awoke more frequently in the night, as was the wont of men of his advanced years, but aside from fulfilling the most basic of bodily needs and work, his days were occupied with nothing else. He did not fish or play cards. Gambling held no charm for him. He would imbibe a dram of whiskey to ward off the cold or for what he deemed medicinal purposes. But, outside of that, there was nothing in his life. There were neither children nor nieces nor nephews. There was a distant cousin who had long since been a stranger to him.

As for Doc Boyd, the two men were business partners. They shared the rigors and risks of their profession. They could finish each other's sentences. But could it be said that they were truly friends? If he died tomorrow, would Doc mourn him? He'd raise a glass to his memory, there was no denying that, but that was a low bar indeed. Doc Boyd would simply find another partner with whom to continue his nefarious labors.

Love had come relatively late in life to D. H. Everett and departed all too soon. He had few childhood memories, owing to the fact that his own childhood had been so short-lived. He was a field hand with his sharecropper parents, by his reckoning, at the age of five or six at the most. Not long thereafter, his mother died in childbirth, and the baby brother she bore him followed her into the grave within a fortnight. His father was a harsh man with no particular fondness for children. When the war erupted between the states, or as they referred to it in Dixie, the War of Northern Aggression, his father had donned a uniform and was killed, so he was told at the foundling home, at the Battle of Chickamauga.

His entire life had been one of work, bereft of the tender mercies a child remembers from a loving mother. Lou Della Havermeyer had been the single brightest light, the moment of softness, the warm comforter in a harsh life. She was gone in the wink of an eye, and all those things that rekindled her memory within him became his enemies. They could destroy him, drive him to drink or rack and ruin, and so he burned them one lonely, drunken night. They were like a drowning man clinging to him in a shipwrecking sea, and in order to survive, he had to cast them off and let them sink to the bottom.

Thus he lived like the lone member of some odd religious order, performing the same rituals each day as if adhering to vows. And yet he had made no vows, sworn no oaths, entered no monastery out of a desire to be closer to his Creator. What he did was done out of habit, not conscious decision. And there was this as well: he had fashioned an armor out of those labors and rituals in order to protect a lonely and wounded heart.

Chapter 10

But as poignant as these observations were, had D. H. ever allowed himself to observe them, they were not the cause of the transformation he later realized had occurred on the short drive between Tanner Irving's log cabin and the Widow Tyler's snug little home on the other end of town.

It was, Dad would later recall, somewhat to his own amazement, the sunset—and the certain knowledge that the last days of that summer of 1930 were fast approaching and too soon gone. There was just the slightest hint of chill in the air, and for the first time in his life, he became cognizant that, in all likelihood, he had very few summers still before him—even should he live well past the biblical four score, attained only through strength and force of will—fewer summers than there were fingers on his hands. And considering that one finger was partially chopped off, that further increased what was not a sense of melancholy but the simple realization that his days upon the earth were drawing to a close.

That the number of summers left before him was literally little more than a handful oddly enough came as a surprise to someone to whom the fact should never have come as a shock. But the simple truth was he had been too busy working to notice he had grown old, full of years, and, in the words of the Old Testament, was nearing the time when he would sleep with his fathers.

It was the sunset that did it.

He noticed, as if for the first time, its delicate hues changing from red to violet to an orange tinge beneath the clouds and back to a kind of bruise-like purple. It was both so beautiful and so altogether fleeting. And he had never noticed it before.

And now there was one fewer sunset that he would behold in his days upon the planet, and it could not be replaced, not for all the gold or oil beneath the surface of the earth. No king's treasure could ransom back one single sunset, and he had taken them all for granted, as if there were an infinite supply. But the truth he now realized was equally as biblical as it was inescapable. The sun would also rise without him and set, long after he was food for worms.

His days, he now knew, were indeed numbered. And with the setting sun were fewer than they had been only that morning.

Quite unexpectedly his eyes began to well with tears as he watched a boy chase a hoop down the dusty road that ran through the center of town just as he had done three score and almost eighteen years before. He longed to stop the car, chase after the child, and beg him to give him just one swat to the hoop with his stick, to reenter, if only for a moment, that magical world of a childhood largely denied him.

But the boy disappeared and with him the last rosy fingers of light beneath the clouds as Cornville plunged itself into a darkness broken only by occasional splashes of yellow streetlights on this moonless night.

Thus by the time he arrived at the Widow Tyler's, he was a changed man from the one who had left Tanner Irving fewer than fifteen minutes before. The armor he had labored so long and hard to build around his heart was cracked and, he now believed, irreparable. His life was slipping away between his workman's fingers like grains of sand, and precious few were left in his palm. He was an old man who shared a series of rented rooms with a ne'er-do-well swindler. There was truly no one he could call a friend, let alone a soul's companion. His life would end in the not-too-distant future, and he would leave this world unnoticed and alone. When he breathed in his last, in all likelihood, it would put not a dent in anyone's day. He drilled holes into the earth, and there was no shortage of men who could do the same.

He swindled widows and swore to them false fealty and escaped into the night, always, before they could find him out. And for what? What was the purpose behind all his labors under the sun?

"Vanity of vanities," said King Solomon, and yet his manners met not even that lowest of standards.

There was no self-aggrandizement in his work. The only difference between Dad Everett and an Aboriginal hunter-gatherer was that instead of roots and berries, Dad plucked the meager savings of lonely, old women. It was mediocre larceny. It did not make him rich, so it could hardly be called greed. It was mere subsistence at the expense of others. He had come so very close so many times to striking it rich only to finish a day late and a dollar short. He imagined at times that had his luck been different, had his Maker smiled down upon his efforts instead of frowned, there might have been some good works left behind by which others would remember him, some meaning to a life that he now realized, in the setting sun and twilight of his days, was without meaning. He labored with worn-out tools and worn-out shoes for worn-out dreams. The sudden weight of the realization was as heavy upon his heart as the fleeting elation of the beauty of the sunset.

With equal pain, he realized that the absence of good works by which others could remember him was not due to the fact he had never struck it rich but due simply to the fact that Dad Everett had never performed any good works. There were poor men whose deeds were remembered long after their demise. The same would not be true of Dry Hole Everett. The best that some might say in remembering him was that he had been a skilled tool-and-cable man. His could hardly be called a life well lived, and he saw that clearly now, for the first time, in the setting sun and growing darkness of the day and of his years.

He parked the Ford automobile beside the Widow Tyler's comfortable-looking cottage. He had already introduced himself to her and told her, as he had told seemingly countless widows before, that he had been acquainted with her late husband and had a business matter of some importance to discuss. She had asked him to return at a later date as she was overwhelmed by the number of business affairs to which the newly departed Mr. Tyler had evidently neglected to attend. She begged his indulgence. There were tax matters, matters of probate, and unpaid bills from the dry goods store he had owned and operated for over twenty years—bills of which she was completely unaware, which he had neglected to pay, and which were now her responsibility.

D. H. had told her to take as much time as was needed. He would not add to her burdens. For that she was truly grateful. He quoted Psalm 103 to her: "We are dust. As for man, his days are like grass; he flourishes like a flower of the field; for the wind passes over it, and it is gone, and its place knows it no more. But the steadfast love of the Lord is from everlasting to everlasting on those who fear him, and his righteousness to children's children."

The Widow Tyler's eyes had brimmed over with tears as she said, "We were not blessed with children, Mr. Everett. They would have been a comfort."

"We are all God's children, dear lady," D. H. replied. "And his love and righteousness, I promise, are with you."

Her eyes had brimmed over again, and she remarked favorably on how beautifully he quoted the Scriptures. Thus they had agreed on a day and time for him to visit, perhaps over dinner. D. H. allowed that it had been some time since he had enjoyed a home-cooked meal. And so they had assigned the date and time.

But now standing on her doorstep again, the words of the psalmist came back to him, "We are dust. As for man, his days are like grass; he flourishes like a flower of the field; for the wind passes over it, and it is gone, and its place knows it no more." And now there was one fewer sunset left to see, and soon one fewer summer whose sun would warm him.

What he was not prepared for when he knocked upon her door was the way the light framed her face or the way the soft blond hair streaked with gray softened the look of her, made her look more youthful than she had upon their first meeting. And then he smelled the fragrance of powder and the hint of perfume as well as the smell of home cooking, prepared not in anticipation of a business deal with him and Doc but for him, regardless of any business that might have existed between D. H. and the late Mr. Tyler.

It was not, by far, the first time a widow had gone out of her way to cook for him, but there was a softness in her voice, a warmth in the touch of her hand, and a simple joy in her look as she bade him "Come in," which quite disarmed him.

He stepped into the warm light of her parlor, decorated lovingly with what his discerning eye could tell were family treasures, heirlooms, newly made curtains framed with a delicate lace, and fresh-cut flowers that added, like a master painter's brushstroke, a splash of color and gaiety into the home she had made for the late Mr. Tyler.

The smell of home cooking enticed him, as did the sweet melody of her voice when she said, "Here. Let me take your coat." He felt her hands brush his shoulder as she helped him remove the once-elegant, now-worn blazer. She hung it upon the empty hat rack, which he imagined had once held her husband's topcoat when it was winter, his umbrella when it rained, and his duster in the summer months. A small stand nestled beside the hat rack, and when Mr. Tyler had returned from provisioning his store, that rack must have held the slippers she, Dad imagined, would have laid out for him.

"My goodness, ma'am," he said. "Your cooking smells…" He was about to say, "mighty fine," as was his wont, but, for whatever reason, he said, "Your cooking smells like home."

The Widow Tyler blushed, put her hand reflexively to her bosom, and thanked him.

As a practiced swindler, D. H. knew it was never good salesmanship to simply cut to the matter at hand. One always had to notice what he referred to as "the baby pictures or the fish on the wall." Were he conning the male of the species, he would look for the latter. He'd say, "By golly! Did you catch that?" thus encouraging the mark to talk about what was obviously his pride and joy. After all, he had not only caught the fish but undertaken some expense at having it mounted. Dad's appreciation of the man's prowess as a fisherman or hunter, if there were a dead beast's head or a piece of antlers on a wall, immediately created common ground. It put the mark at ease. The mounted fish or buck's head or set of antlers was the pro forma baiting of the trap.

D. H. was a man who appreciated that which the mark held dear. If there were tintypes of offspring, in the case of a widow, even if the children were as ugly as monkeys and his first inclination was to offer each of them a banana, he would gush forth in exclamations of how precious the little tykes appeared to be.

"I have grandnieces and grandnephews myself!" He would say. "But though I love them dearly, I can say without hesitation that those"—pointing to the pictures—"are some of the most beautiful children I have ever seen! Little wonder they are the apple of your eye. And this one, over here, bears your likeness, as if I were gazing at your reflection in a mirror."

But in this sweet cottage, there were no pictures of progeny nor decapitated heads of dead beasts along the walls. Rather, there was an heirloom hutch containing porcelain figurines—a maiden with a pitcher perched delicately upon her shoulder and supported by the maiden's shapely arm. There were bone china teacups lovingly displayed. Being the practiced flimflam man he was, Dad remarked upon them as if he had suddenly stumbled on the holy grail.

"They belonged to my mother," the Widow Tyler said, "and her mother before her and her mother before her."

There was something in her voice, almost as if she were humming to herself some dainty, long-forgotten melody. Widows tended to prattle, and it became increasingly difficult for Dad to mask his discomfort. But the Widow Tyler did not prattle. She spoke with a kind of joy in sharing tender memories. It was as if she were opening a box of treasures and wanted to make sure that he received as much pleasure from them as she did.

In the normal flow of events, when swindling a widow, Everett knew it was best to keep conversation to a bare minimum. The point was simply to form a common bond. From thence, one complimented the home cooking and—even if it was burnt through and through, as dry as dust, or tough as a brick—to smack one's lips and remark favorably on the quality of the victuals. One then sprinkled that with a coat of Scripture and a dash of the sonnets and then got on to the business at hand. Otherwise, the widows, irritatingly and seemingly without end, could prattle on about nothing.

But such was not the case with the Widow Tyler. D. H. delighted in her memories of childhood gaieties. Her laughter quite bewitched him. And then she asked, as if discerning his innermost thoughts, if he had noticed the particular beauty of the evening's sunset, the delicacy of the gathering hues of twilight. She made it a habit, she said, never to miss a one, especially as she neared the twilight of her own years.

"Twilight is not a term I would associate with you, Mrs. Tyler. There is about you a girlish delight, whose joy is contagious."

Once again, the Widow Tyler blushed, indeed like a young girl, and once again, D. H. could not help but notice how becoming such modesty was on her. As for her home cooking, even though he had already finished a full meal excellently prepared by the very capable Della May Irving, he ate every morsel the Widow Tyler placed before him. Indeed, he could not recall in all his days ever having eaten a juicier chicken fricassee nor tastier biscuits and gravy. As for her peach cobbler, he was willing to swear that its equal was not to be found anywhere on the continent.

"Won't you take another serving of cobbler, Mr. Everett?"

"I have to confess, Mrs. Tyler, I already ate before I came here."

"Please. You can call me Martha Jean."

With that, Dad entirely forgot to get to the business at hand: the supposed contract that the Widow Tyler's dear departed husband had signed regarding his investment in D. H.'s oil venture. Before he could recall his well-rehearsed speech, Martha Jean said, "You know, I have a confession as well."

"What is that, Martha Jean?" Dad asked, noticing for the first time how beautiful her blue-green eyes appeared in the candlelight.

"I'm not quite sure how to…you see…Woodrow and I did not have…Well, there was a certain passion, a flame, you might say, that went out many years ago."

"I find that hard to believe," said Dad, once again forgetting entirely about the supposed business venture that was the purpose for their meeting.

"It's been a good long time since I've had a man in my parlor," said Martha Jean, "with whom I've exchanged more than a few sentences. 'Pass the greens' or 'More chicken' was about all the conversation we ever had."

"Well, if that was the case, dear lady, your husband deprived himself of the most charming of companions." There was an embarrassed silence between them, an unexpected intimacy that took them both by surprise. "I apologize for that," Dad said. "You must think me forward, for I must be a good twenty years older than you."

There was a sadness suddenly thrust upon him. He was no longer sticking to the script of his con but speaking, to his amazement, from his heart. "No matter what my intentions, ma'am, I don't believe there could be a happy ending in store for us. But please believe me when I say I have developed the greatest fondness for you. It was the last thing I would have expected."

"Mr. Everett, you appear to be crying. Are you all right?"

"Tears of joy, my dear, simply at being able to confess my affections openly and without guile for the fairest creature I believe I have ever met."

Dad could not tell, as he dabbed away a tear, whether he was falling for his own con or if his feelings were genuine. Either way, they had the same effect. Martha Jean reached out and covered his weathered and scarred hand with her own.

"Oh Mr. Everett!" she exclaimed.

"Please," Dad said. "Call me D. H."

"You…you are a wonderful man, D. H."

They retired to the parlor for coffee, and despite his feelings, D. H., like a monk remembering his vows, said, "Martha Jean, though I have every legal right to hold you to the contract that your dear departed husband, Woodrow, signed, I will not add to the burden of your grief."

"Why," said Martha Jean, "what contract is that?"

And, condemning himself as a fool, D. H. told her.

Chapter 11

In later years, Doc would ruminate over the fact that perhaps there was something in the air of East Texas at the time. For while Dad Everett was being smitten by his first sunset, his armor cracked open by the sense of his own mortality, and his heart vibrated in sympathy with the melodious voice of the Widow Tyler, Doc found himself drifting back, despite his best efforts, to sunlit days in Lathrope, Oklahoma, and late-afternoon, meadowed picnics with the comely Flora May Simms.

He allowed as how those were perhaps the happiest days he had ever known, lying back on a picnic blanket with Flora May, eating watermelon, sipping homemade lemonade, and watching clouds roll themselves up into cotton candy animals, floating in the skies above them, as Flora May rested her head upon his shoulder and his hand brushed back and forth against the incredible softness of her skin. He remembered that faint scent of lilac upon her cheek, and try as he might, he could not free himself from the spell she seemed to have cast upon him, when every lie he ever told became his profoundest truth.

He knew that no good could come from such ruminations. He knew, like Dad, there were no happy endings to this story. He was a swindler and a flimflam man and not much of one at that. Not that he lacked in technique; it was simply that he was in such a low-stakes game. Like Dad, among swindlers, he was little more than a hunter-gatherer.

More than likely, the Widow Simms had already found him out. Perhaps she had filed a complaint against him with the local constabulary, though he doubted it. More likely than not, had she discovered his deception, she would have kept to herself the shame of having been deceived by him, and all the sweet affections—the tender endearments spoken between them—would have turned to bile.

Yet, she still haunted both his waking and sleeping hours. He daydreamed of her as they spudded in the well. At night, when fatigue had pushed him past the boundaries of Dad Everett's epic snores, he drifted back in dreams to sunlit meadows, to Flora May brushing a lock of his hair away from his forehead as if he were but a lad once again.

Trying to live up to the self-made image of a man of science in possession of a diploma from one of Europe's most esteemed institutes of higher learning, Doc labored to analyze the attraction he felt for the Widow Simms. It was unlike any that had ever come before, and he suspected none would ever be its equal, no matter how many days upon the earth the Almighty would grant him.

Certainly he had known many a young maid and had stolen his share of kisses on the village green on summer nights made heavy with the perfume of jasmine and honeysuckle. He was no stranger to the many charms of the female of the species. But he had never succumbed. The urge to do what others referred to as "settling down" was anathema to him. He had once been all but offered the hand of a wealthy merchant's daughter in marriage. The merchant in question, whose wife had borne him but one child and no sons, yearned for a male heir to whom he could pass down all that he had accumulated and who would propagate his memory for generations to come. The merchant was that peculiar type of southerner who branded with his name everything within reach. Big Daddy Polk claimed to be a descendant of the eleventh president of the United States, James Knox Polk, who not only had been a protégé of Andrew Jackson but also had been responsible for the realization of America's manifest destiny in its westward expansion by annexing to the United States of America the Republic of Texas, the Oregon Territory, and all that was lost by the country south of the border.

Big Daddy Jackson Polk, who had been named after his ancestor's mentor, owned not only the Polk General Store, the Polk Emporium, and the Polk Livery and Stables but the town of Polk Corners, Louisiana, itself, to which Big Daddy had migrated from the Polks' ancestral home of Pineville, North Carolina, by way of Duck River, Tennessee.

Big Daddy Polk had only one legitimate child of which he knew: a schoolmarm, spinster daughter, Sarah Childress Polk. She was, Big Daddy reckoned, simply too particular in her choice of male companionship. No one was ever refined enough or well-mannered enough to suit her fancy. That is, up until the time that she met Henry Clay Jefferson, which was one of Doc Boyd's earliest incarnations, at a time when he was considering reading for the law. Having passed through Polk Corners and sizing up Big Daddy Polk upon their first meeting, he alleged to be a product of the families of both Thomas Jefferson and Senator Henry Clay, for whom he claimed to have been named.

Both Big Daddy and Sarah Childress were mightily impressed with the budding young, tall, and handsome attorney who knew, even then, all of Shakespeare's sonnets by heart. Young "Henry" had just passed his nineteenth birthday, and Sarah Childress was an old maid of twenty-seven. Big Daddy sought to act quickly and decisively.

For three days and nights, he and young Henry engaged in arduous negotiations over exactly what properties would pass into Henry's hands and when. When they reached an impasse, Big Daddy suggested a novel solution. He wanted heirs, male heirs. It was not enough to see his name on every storefront; he wanted at the holidays to behold a grand table of male Polk offspring, bearing his likeness, gathering for family festivities and, most importantly, for the anniversaries of his birth. Thus, he created a kind of bonus system. For each male offspring that issued forth from the union of Henry Clay Jefferson and Sarah Childress Polk, there would come another trust deed to land that would pass into Henry's possession upon Big Daddy's demise. There were prodigious amounts of sipping whiskey imbibed and fine cigars smoked as the two men drew up the dowry in infinite detail.

As for Sarah Childress herself, young Henry felt more than a passing affection for the older woman. She was blond, shapely, and fair and shared his love of poetry and the finer things in life, which her father's fortune could afford. It was as close as Heinrich Bumstetter had ever come to marriage, excluding, of course, the childhood sweetheart from whom he had stolen his first kiss and from whom he had fled at the thought of a life of labor and responsibilities.

The marriage to Sarah Childress Polk contained no such impediments. Indeed, it held benchmarked enticements. But, as was always the case with Doc, the game afoot was worth more than the prize. The deal having been negotiated and young Henry feeling he had bested Jackson Polk, the thought of quite literally being put out to stud, having to pay ongoing obeisance to the Polk patriarch, showing up at ever-noisier family gatherings, and being forced to act the gentleman when, at heart, he knew he was and always would be a rogue was simply too much for him.

The night before what was to be the grandest wedding in the history of Polk Corners, Louisiana, he packed into his carpetbag the same belongings with which he had come to that part of the country and fled like a thief in the night, leaving behind a humiliated spinster, stood up on the way to the altar, and an irate almost father-in-law, who swore by all that was holy and profane to have the scalawag tarred and feathered should he ever catch sight of him again.

Thus, to cover his tracks, Henry Clay Jefferson left the practice of the law and his prestigious, ancestral name and entered medicine, eventually to metamorphose into Dr. Enrique Alonzo, an identity he maintained, on and off, for well over twenty years.

What was it, then, about the Widow Flora May Simms that had laid hold, it seemed, to his very soul? Fair, she was, but no blushing maiden, having been married for over thirty years to the late Mr. Simms. Try as he might, Doc simply could not explain it.

He did not, for a moment, entertain the notion that it could be love, since he placed no stock whatsoever in even the idea of it. Love was for suckers, rubes, chumps, and marks, not for Horatio Daedalus Boyd. Or Heinrich Bumstetter, for that matter. Yet, whatever hold she possessed upon him tempted him into a kind of foolishness in which, heretofore, he had not dared to engage.

He began to write her letters. He was careful, of course, to send them to other acquaintances in other states and have them forward the epistles on to the Widow Simms so that, if she bore him ill will, his tracks would at least be covered. But write her he did.

He still maintained, of course, the fiction that he was a fugitive on the run, never allowing himself rest or respite in order to protect her from the imaginary creditors who would see to his incarceration. The letters contained no clue of what he was up to since what he was up to was swindling other widows as he had swindled her before. Instead, he confined himself to reminiscences of the tender moments that had passed between them.

He wondered at himself for engaging in the correspondence since he could give her no address to which she could reply. But without knowing why, he simply felt the need to tell her of his affections, and many a night, as he lay awake listening to his partner's sawmill-like, nocturnal rumblings, he allowed himself to wonder if she had received his letters and whether she shared those affections he had expressed—or if they had turned to ash.

Eventually, he would fall asleep, and more often than not of late, his dreams were of Flora May Simms. Usually they were variations on the themes of their picnics, their sweet walks, lying side by side with the clouds by day and stars by night, their own private kaleidoscope, sharing dreams of things that never would be but for which now, contrary to all his experience, he found himself longing.

At times, however, there were nightmares as well, in which he was hauled before a heavenly tribunal to answer for his sins, and Flora May Simms was there to testify against him. The next morning, upon awakening from just such a dream and trying to shake off its ill effects with a strong cup of black coffee, he drove out to the Dial Ranch in order to maintain the pretext that they were on the cusp of finding a treasure beneath their feet that all the kings of the earth might envy. He stopped near the lone cottonwood tree on the little rise above the ranch, where Thurman Dial was dutifully feeding into the steam boiler the wood that Tanner Irving Sr. had dropped off that morning.

"How's she runnin', Thurman?" Doc asked, trying to add a cheerful lilt to his greeting to shake off the strange sense of foreboding that still clung to him from the dream of the night before.

"Runnin' good, Doc," said the giant of a man in his laconic, rumbling basso profundo. Thurman took off his hat, wiped the sweat from his brow, and then continued. "You know, every day I remember a little bit more and more, but I swear I can't remember a thing about you or Dad or any fortune teller. You'd think a man would remember something as important as that."

There was no accusation in his tone, merely a sense of wonderment that he could not retrieve from the bank vault of his memory something as portentous as a prophesied oil well.

"Well," said Doc, "mustn't be impatient, Thurman. The good Lord works in his own sweet time. I'm just gonna have a little look-see at the cuttings bucket. It won't be long before we're gonna bring it up and find the old Woodbine sand."

Doc walked eagerly toward the back of the rig. It was all part of the show, all part of the P. T. Barnum circus act. He knew there would be nothing in the cuttings bucket but dry, pulverized rock. But he had to maintain the illusion until he and Dad had reaped the full harvest afforded by the widows of Cornville.

For Thurman, however, this was no illusion. It was the single ray of light breaking through the clouds of gloom in which, it seemed, the entire country had become engulfed.

"I hope so, Doc," Thurman said. "Lot of good folks around here countin' on it. They all live on credit over at our general store, and I don't know how much longer any of us can hold out." He stretched his massive frame over to the woodpile and tossed another log into the boiler. Thus occupied, he did not see Doc as he went about the charade of examining the cuttings bucket. But what Doc saw jolted such a shock through his system that it blocked out all that Thurman had said.

"Anything good in the cuttings bucket?" Thurman asked, like an eager child inquiring about the tooth fairy.

"Not yet," Doc said, giving Thurman a hopeful-looking grin. "But only a matter of time, I expect. Only a matter of time."

As he spoke, he hid the cuttings bucket behind his body and secreted it on the floorboard of the Model A, then raced toward town.

Doc Boyd could hear Dad Everett's snores on the stairs through the flimsy wooden door of the room they shared above the Dials' general store. Upon entering the room, he loudly dropped the cuttings bucket next to Dad's bed. "Wake up, you old fool!" he demanded.

Dad snorted, harrumphed, then opened one eye, looking like a beached Moby Dick. "What time is it?" he asked.

"Past nine."

"Oh Lordy, let me sleep. The Widow Tyler prepared a meal big enough to feed two armies. Amazing appetite for a woman of her age. Wake me up at noon."

"I'll wake you up right now! Dad, what in tarnation were you thinking last night?"

Chapter 11

"I wasn't thinking, Doc!" Dad said plaintively. "I was putty in her hands. She's like a force of nature. Unstoppable."

"I'm not talkin' about the Widow Tyler," Dad snapped. "I'm talkin' about the cuttings bucket. I'm talking about the way we do things around here!"

"The way we do things?" Dad was confused. "We do things the way we do things. That's the way we do things. What are you talking about?"

"We've still got money to git from more widows before we salt that well, right?" Doc demanded.

"Right?" Dad said, as if asking a question.

"Right!" Doc said, as if answering.

"I'm still not following. I pulled five hundred from the Widow Tyler last night. Here's the check." Dad's grubby fingers fumbled around until he pulled the piece of paper from the sweatband of his fedora, which he then handed over to Doc, who quickly pocketed it.

"That's all good and fine," Doc said, "but what are you doing pouring Quaker State down the well shaft this early?"

"I didn't pour any Quaker State down that well. I was locked in the ample bosom of the Widow Tyler. I couldn't have escaped even if I'd wanted to!"

"You didn't pour oil down into the core samples?"

Dad sat up in the bed now, sniffing out the pungent scent of something amiss. "There's oil mixed into the sand in the cuttings bucket?" he asked, incredulously.

"Look for yourself!"

In the cuttings bucket, Dad saw sand mixed with black, gooey tar. He took a handful and sniffed at it, then looked up to Doc as if the worst had happened.

"Somebody's on to us," he said. "Somebody's tryin' to hustle a hustler here."

"You think somebody else salted it?"

"Of course somebody else salted it!" Dad declared. "They wanna get the rumor started that there's really oil out here. They're probably buying up leases on worthless mineral rights that they're gonna syndicate and sell. That'll make what we're getting look like chicken feed."

Doc's breast swelled with righteous indignation. "I'll bet it's that Thurman!" he fumed. "He's not as dumb as he looks. The *gall* of that man. To try and cheat us!"

Doc paced back and forth, trying to come up with a suitable counterstrategy to defeat the surprisingly wily giant, when his ruminations were interrupted by Dad, speaking ever so softly. "There is one other possible explanation," the old man said, with just the tiniest hint of a smile.

"What?" asked Doc.

And then it began to sink in.

The sheer impossibility made the thought absurd. But, as a man of science, it was a possibility that had to be taken into account nonetheless.

"No," said Doc. "Really?"

Dad simply nodded his head with that hint of a smile growing ever so slightly larger, like the proverbial boy in a room full of horse manure who holds out the hope that there must be a pony in there somewhere.

"How long would we have to wait till we can take a real core sample?" Doc asked.

"Twelve, fifteen hours at least, till it clears up," Doc replied.

Looking back, they would be the longest hours of their lives.

Chapter 12

Twelve to fifteen hours. Plenty of time for a man to think. And contrary to what one might have thought, Doc hated to think—unless the thinking led to a plan.

But there was no plan here. There was only waiting. And again, despite his will and everything he knew to be prudent, Doc's thoughts drifted back to the Widow Simms. To Flora May with the chestnut hair and the scent of lilac and the loving gesture of brushing away a lock of his hair from his forehead as if he were her own sweet child.

What hold did she have upon him? What secret spell? Was there a wax likeness of him stuck with pins and voodoo incantations chanted before a candle encased in glass with the likeness of some pagan saint imprinted upon it?

She is fair, 'tis true, he thought, recalling the bard, *'tis true, and pity 'tis, 'tis true.* Why could he not stop thinking of her? There were so many people in his life he had forgotten so completely without any effort whatsoever—couldn't remember their names, their likenesses, not a thing they'd said or done, as if they had vanished completely. Even more than that, vanished as if they had never existed at all!

And yet, Flora May's every gesture, the tone of her voice, the tilt of her head, the way she brushed her chestnut hair away from her forehead, the sweet, soft lines made by the thousands of smiles she had smiled…all of it indelible, almost every word, almost every gesture, and the electric sensation of simply lying on a picnic blanket next to her.

Doc was no rube, no callow youth, no mere schoolboy impressionable and gullible. He was a worldly man, a man of some culture. A diplomaed man—even though he'd printed up the diploma himself. Still and all, *he* was the one who had come up with the fake motto. And a fitting one it was.

Verum in oculis aspicientis. He had told the rubes and the marks that it meant "Truth is what the eye must always behold." But the fact was that *Verum in oculis aspicientis* meant exactly the opposite. "Truth is in the eye of the beholder." Now those are words to live by if you are a con man.

It was no mere relativism; it meant "Truth is whatever I could make you believe." And in his life, that had been the secret to Doc's success. *Well,* he thought, *perhaps* success *is too grand a word. You couldn't call swindling widows and sharing a foul-smelling room over a general store with a snoring, fat man much of a success.* But, as many an itinerant rodeo cowboy was wont to say, it beat wages. And there was enough success in that. And the secret of that success was Doc's chameleonlike ability to become whatever his mark wished to see.

Big Daddy Jackson Polk wanted to see a well-bred stud service for his spinster daughter, someone with as illustrious an ancestral name as his own. Big Daddy was of that breed of Americans who, though they proclaimed their love of democracy, worshiped—nay, longed for—fairy-tale royalty. And, lacking in any inheritable titles, they found it in connections to presidents past, to frontier heroes, to local baseball teams on which they never played an inning but wore the team's colors.

Thus, in the case of Big Daddy, Heinrich Bumstetter became Henry Clay Jefferson, the descendant not just of one of the country's founders but one of the nation's greatest orators as well. He outclassed Big Daddy and beat him at his own game, negotiating land and mercantile swaps in exchange for the issuance of his loins.

To the lonely wives of traveling salesmen, he was Dr. Enrique Alonzo, purveyor of a magical Elixir of Life. And it was no mere flimflam, for when he sweet-talked them, they felt as if they were blushing young girls once again. The magic was there, but it was not in the bottle that the good "doctor" purveyed; it was in the pitch, the tale he told, woven from a fabric of lies they wanted so desperately to believe, that, as if by alchemy, day turned to night and night became the stuff that dreams were made of.

He was no patent medicine salesman. He was their own personal Queen Mab of the frontier. To the ranchers whose dreams of eking a living out of the land that had turned, as if in a biblical plague, to dust, he created bubbling oil fields, sleeping black giants just beneath their feet, pooling up between the Sabine Uplift and the Rusk Depression. And they believed it, as fervently as medieval suckers who had bought splinters of the cross of their Lord and Savior, which had the magical, curative powers to ease the burdens of their plague-ridden lives. They believed it.

Under his spell, the widows cast off their widows' weeds to wear the blush of maidenhood once again. And even when the promised, bubbling oil failed to flow, and the earth, instead of bursting like a geyser of liquid gold, yielded up nothing more than a dry hole, they saw not a villain who had swindled them out of their meager savings but a modern-day Quixote, a knight-errant, a Flying Dutchman willing to roam the earth forever, knowing neither respite nor rest, in order to protect them.

With no trace of cynicism but an honest appraisal of goods received for goods paid for, Doc fervently believed he had given them their money's worth and left them with that which they would remember smilingly at their last. For no one counts their money when shuffling off this earthly coil. If they're lucky, they remember love. And if they are only slightly less lucky, they smile at the remembrance of the illusion of love—if the illusionist knew his stuff, which Doc knew he most certainly did.

These feelings—that he was not a flimflam man but a purveyor of life's greatest treasure—alternated with feelings of utter and total revulsion and self-loathing for the liar, cheat, and swindler he knew he truly was. He should be tarred and feathered. Run out of any town he had ever entered on a rail. He was not fit for human companionship. He should be an object of derision and scorn.

If his body reflected the makeup of the soul within, he should be leprous: something so hideous that small children would turn away with cries of terror, so hideous that no mother's love could erase the memory of what they had beheld, which would haunt them in nightmares all the days of their lives, a walking pustule of rotting flesh, oozing putrescence from a never-closing, gangrenous sore.

That's what twelve to fifteen hours of aimless thinking can do for a guy. A ping-pong match with himself, which he was destined to play forever, simultaneously winning and losing at every point.

Chapter 12

And then, it suddenly hit him like the lightning bolt that struck not a thousand yards away from the oil rig where he and Doc huddled in the middle of that night, soaked in the unexpected rain.

That was the secret of Flora May Simms.

With her, he didn't *have* to be anyone else other than who he really was, even though he didn't really know who that person might have been. As long as he could remember, from his earliest childhood with his German sodbuster father, he had lied and self-aggrandized at every opportunity. And it was not merely to escape the drudgery of being little more than an extra farmhand to a father who showed no emotion other than anger at any task imprecisely performed, no matter how small the imperfection. He lied for the sheer joy of lying! He lied because he was good at it. Even if it ended with the flesh-eating bite of his father's belt, he would lie and lie again and in those lies create something other than the life he seemed doomed to live.

But he didn't have to sell Flora May Simms on anything. The truth was that she was never really interested in the oil well. She hadn't cared nor missed a beat when he forgot her husband's real name. He didn't have to be Horatio Daedalus Boyd, PhD, petroleum engineer, geologist, and master of all things petroliferous. He could even have been Heinrich Bumstetter with her, and she, because of *her* goodness, not his, still saw in him a spark of the divine as well as the smile of the rogue.

He didn't have to con her, and she wasn't buying any snake oil. Whoever he was at his truest self, she saw him and didn't turn away in horror or run toward an illusion. She simply let him rest his head upon her shoulder, and there, tucked beneath her protective wing, he found peace.

Just then, the lightning and thunder struck once again.

"What a great idea!" Dad Everett said. "Go out to an oil derrick on a barren rise in the middle of a lightning storm." The heavens had opened, and the rain soaked them to the bone. "I should be over at the Widow Tyler's, eatin' pecan pie."

"I would have thought you'd had enough of her pecan pie for a while," Doc snapped, having been pulled away from his reverie of the secrets of Flora May Simms. "Just pull up the core sample."

The two men pulled the core up and dumped its contents into the cuttings bucket. Doc cranked up the Ford and turned on the headlights while Dad pulled over a lantern to view the contents. It was thick, black, oily, tar-like sand.

"Oh my Lord!" Doc exclaimed, like one of the twelve tribes of Israel standing at the foot of Mount Sinai with the tablets of the Ten Commandments revealed. "Oh my Lord, it's the Woodbine! We hit the Woodbine sand, D. H.! We hit the Woodbine sand!"

"Oh my Lord!" Dad cried out fervently. "Oh my Lord and Savior, Jesus Christ!"

And there, illuminated by the light of the Ford's head-lamps and flashes of lightning that streaked across the skies, Dad and Doc danced the most spectacular jig you or anyone else ever beheld. They danced, singing "Happy Days Are Here Again." When they had worn that out, they linked arms and do-si-doed to "Yankee Doodle."

"We done it! We done it, Doc!" Dad shouted.

"We're rich!" Doc cried and began climbing up the oil derrick. "We're richer than the Queen of Sheba! Richer than Pharaoh himself!"

Then suddenly, the rain ended, the clouds parted, and the two men danced their jigs silhouetted against the light of the moon. Without warning, there was another flash of lightning and a crack of thunder, as if a heavenly gavel had been brought down in judgment, and Doc's expression changed from jubilation to grief-stricken.

"What's wrong, you fool?" Dad asked, still dancing his jig. "Dance! Make a joyful noise before the Lord! How many times in your life do you become a millionaire?"

"Dad," Doc said softly.

"What?"

Doc descended the derrick and crossed over to the dancing, fat man and took him by the shoulders. "We can't bring it in."

"What are you talking about?"

"This well. We can't bring it in."

"Sure we can! We'll need to use the money we've got from the widders to buy a real rig. A new rig. Not this broken-down piece of junk."

"Dad," said Doc, "we've already sold close to five hundred percent."

Dad didn't see any problem with that. "Well, we'll just sell a little bit more. Whatever it takes. What's wrong with you? We can't quit now when we've got a gusher to bring in!"

"You're not listening! I said we sold 500 percent. You can only have a hundred percent of anything. We're crooks! We've conned all those old ladies."

Dad threw his arms up in frustration. "Of course we did! We've always conned old ladies. That's what we do. But this time, we told 'em the truth! Don't you see the hand of God in that?"

"If we bring this oil well in," Doc said, "and it's a gusher, everybody who has a stock certificate is gonna show up and say, 'Where's my piece of that pecan pie?' And we don't got enough pie to go around, Dad."

Suddenly, he could see the penny drop. It hit Dad like a ton of bricks.

"Wouldn't take more than a week, and you and me both would be sitting in the hoosegow," Doc continued. "Unless they up and tar and feather us first—or worse."

"Well, that's not fair!" Dad shouted, throwing his fedora to the ground. "We struck oil! You know how many men walkin' around on the face of the earth can say that for real? Not more than a handful. We struck oil! Great Caesar's ghost, I did it! For the first time in my life, I'm not Dry Hole Everett! I'm an oil-man! And you're saying we got to walk away from it?"

Doc crossed toward the older man. Along the way he picked up the fedora and wiped away some of the mud before handing it back. "There's nothin' else *to* do," he said. "We cap it up and tell the widows and old Thurman and Junipera Sue it's nothin' but a dry hole. Take what we got and get as far away from Texas as we can get, as fast as we can go. If we know what's good for us."

The two men were silent, both lost in the hells of their own private despairs.

But Doc was a thinker, especially when he had a problem that needed solving. And suddenly, he had the solution. "California!" he shouted. "They're bringin' in plenty of oil in California. It's the promised land, Dad!"

Dad just stared at him. The joy went out of Doc's voice completely. There wasn't any promised land; there was just a getaway.

"What are you looking at me for? Get that cuttings bucket and let's get outta here before somebody finds out the awful truth."

Chapter 12

And with that, the two men put the cuttings bucket on the floor of the Ford and drove off into the nighttime, the endless flat prairie, slicing across the moon up behind them.

Chapter 13

They drove off in the Model A, discovering how badly the convertible top had leaked in the pouring rain, which seemed only fitting. Neither man wanted to go back to the gloom of the garret above the general store, so they parked on what passed for a hill in East Texas, little more than a prairie dog mound, midway between the Dial Ranch and Cornville.

Dad always kept a bottle in the rumble seat, for medicinal purposes, and they were both in need of a cure that evening. The rain had let up into a light drizzle, and they gathered together the few sticks they could find and some tumbleweed and used the Woodbine sand as fuel. It made a mighty blaze.

"Might as well get some use out of it," Dad said.

They passed the bottle back and forth, each man lost in his own thoughts.

For Dad, it was a nightmare revisited, only worse. This was worse than Burkburnett, worse than Spindletop. This wasn't running out of money and having someone come in behind you, drill down another thousand feet, and strike it rich. This wasn't the same as breaking a drill bit and not having the wherewithal to fish it out.

Chapter 13

This was actually having *found* it. It wasn't coming in second. It wasn't almost-but-not-enough.

They had found it! Dad had drilled it. With a two-bit piece of junk held together with baling wire and spit, Dad had brought it in! There weren't ten men in the country who could match his knowledge.

He had been there when they had invented the fishtail bit at Spindletop. He had drawn up the plans for the two-cone bit with that idiot, Humason, while his sweetheart's rib cage ached with every racking cough and she spit up blood as he held her in his arms, saying, *God wouldn't let this happen to us.* While he heard her last gasp and then saw that briefest smile on her face, maybe because she got a glimpse of heaven or maybe because she was just glad to be out of the pain. That beautiful smile. And then, the low wheeze, and he could actually feel her soul depart her body, which instantly went limp and colder in his embrace.

While his heart was being ripped out, that idiot Humason got liquored up and sold the future of oil drilling in America to Howard Hughes for a measly hundred and fifty bucks, fifty of which he drank up in the saloon before he had the courage to face Dad the next day.

And somehow, this was worse. It was like losing the love of his life all over again, like that terrible night, and then having the last shred of dignity torn out of his hands.

Dry Hole Everett. He hated that name worse than death. Dry Hole. It was worse than failure; it was a joke. And he knew that this had been his last chance, and now it was gone. The more he thought about it, the more it seemed like it was almost worth going to jail just to ditch that moniker. Dry Hole. What was worse, bein' a somebody in jail or a nobody on the outside?

He had been a craftsman, a master driller, and he'd let a low-life flimflam man lead him down into depredation, and now, here they were, huddled on a muddy rise, burning up the signs of the fortune that was theirs for the taking.

And that's when the realization hit him. He wasn't gonna do it! Not this time. He wasn't gonna let them take it away from him. He wasn't gonna die a joke. No, sir! The drunker he got, the clearer he saw it. He wasn't gonna let 'em do it.

As for Doc, his thoughts ran in a totally different direction. He wasn't thinking about redemption. He wasn't thinking about a thing except not letting the Texas Rangers arrest him. This put an end to the dialog he had allowed to run through his brain during the long wait for the core sample. The ping-pong match was over, and the self-revulsion side won, twenty-one to zip.

He was the lowest-life con man there was. He made a living swindling little old ladies, and he didn't even get rich by it; he just got by. But that beat the heck out of whatever they were serving in the state pen.

As he received the bottle Dad was passing, he could tell everything that was going through the old man's mind. He knew the old fool was about to become his deadliest enemy, worse than a rattlesnake, because Dad still cared. That was his mistake. That was his weakness. That was the chink in his armor.

But Doc had already crossed that bridge, and the difference between him and the old, fat man wasn't just age and poundage. Doc didn't care. He was a low-life swindler, and it was the only skill he possessed, and though he was as skilled in that craft, if you wanted to call it that, as Dad was with cable and tools, he took no pride in it. He took no pride in himself. And he didn't care. He didn't care about money. He didn't care about daydreams or night dreams or memories of picnics and cotton candy animals floating by in the sky above Flora May Simms and him back in Lathrope, Oklahoma. He didn't care.

The only thing he cared about was his hide and not seeing it spend the rest of its life behind bars. He didn't care about not letting anyone take any supposed fortune away from him; he just cared about getting away—as far and as fast as he could. Tonight. This evening. Before sunup. It wasn't even worth going back to the room above the general store to get his carpetbag, shaving kit, or his clothes. Because if he stuck around, he'd get a new set of clothes, and they'd have stripes on 'em. He took a long swig and passed the bottle back to Dad.

It was different for old D. H., he knew. He didn't have that many years left anyway, so why not spend 'em in prison, bragging about the well he'd brought in? But if Doc wasn't a young man, at least he was a younger one. He had a good twenty years left ahead of him. And some of the widows weren't half bad looking!

The minute he let that thought creep in, he blocked it off because he knew it was a one-way road back to Flora May Simms. And one way or the other, that'd lead to the Oklahoma state pen instead of the one in Texas. She was a straitlaced, churchgoing woman. She might not be a foot-stomping Christian, beating on a tambourine and speaking in tongues and letting the Holy Spirit take hold of her, but she was a Christian, nonetheless, the kind that believed in right and wrong. The kind that wouldn't take kindly to knowing she'd been swindled. And he doubted she'd have much of a Christian air of forgiveness about her if she ever did figure out the extent of his depredations. She'd probably stand in line to be the first witness against him. It wasn't the money; it was that he'd told her he loved her.

And the minute he let that thought sneak in, there was that voice that said, *But maybe you do.* So he banished that one as soon as it lit, like a fly, on his mind.

There was only one thing that he could afford to think about now, and that was how to get away. Get out of Texas. Now. Tonight. As soon as they finished this bottle. And he couldn't afford to leave the old, fat man behind him because he knew, as sure as shootin', that, if left to his own devices, the old man was gonna bring in that well.

Thus, the two sat together, in totally separate worlds, watching the fire fueled by Woodbine sand, each of them making their own separate plans.

Dad took a twig, dipped it in the cuttings bucket so it came up coated with the thick, black tar, then just waved it over the campfire, and it burst into flame.

"Look at that," he said. "Look at the way it burns. That's oil, son. Pure and simple."

He took a long swig out of what was left of the bottle, passed it to Doc, then said, "What do you think it would take to bring this well in, Doc?"

"I'm not gonna play this game, Dad."

"I'd have to change my name if we did," Dad said, luxuriously. "Couldn't be Dry Hole anymore. I'd be old Gusher Everett."

"Gusher Everett," Doc said, with no small amount of bile. He'd known this was exactly where the old man was headed.

Dad was fully in his cups now. "You know, I was this close"—he held up his thumb and forefinger less than an inch apart—"to strikin' it rich at Spindletop. A fella named Lucas come in behind me and drilled not more than a hundred yards away. Hit the Woodbine at eight hundred feet and at eleven hundred—*pshoom!*" Dad spit as he made the sound of a gusher and shot his stubby arms out like a fat, old Isadora Duncan doing a modern interpretive dance on the glories of the petroleum industry. "Thing blew a hundred and fifty feet in the air," Dad continued, wiping the spittle off his lips.

"I know," said Doc. "Anointed you all in black gold, the way you anointed me in whiskey spit just now."

"Sorry about that," Dad mumbled, then he got to his feet. "Doc, I can't do it. I can't walk away from it." Dad walked, none too steadily, to the top of the rise. And there, in the distance, silhouetted against the moon, was the derrick of the Junipera Sue Number One.

Doc knew this was coming and knew he had to end it now.

"Walk away? Heck, we're gonna run away! We done it a hundred times before, and we can do it again. And if we do, we'll get away clean."

Dad turned to face the taller, younger man, and he put all his considerable weight behind every word he said. "I cannot walk away from a real honest-to-goodness oil well, and neither can you. Doc, that oil well is the vindication of my life's work!"

"I'm a two-bit flimflam man, Dad. And the only thing worse than that is being a two-bit flimflam man sittin' in the state pen for the rest of his born days."

Dad poked a stubby finger into Doc's chest. "You said we'd hit the Woodbine sand at thirty-five hundred feet. You know what the depth was of that core sample? Thirty-five hundred feet, on the button. That's a hand-o'-God miracle! And he chose you just like he chose Moses in the desert! *You* did it, Doc! *You* parted the Red Sea! That's what you done. Hand-o'-God miracle, that's what it is." For emphasis, Dad raised his arms, lifted his face to the sky, and, exultant as a new-baptized Christian, shouted, "Hallelujah!"

There was nothing left in the bottle, so Doc tossed it. "I ain't Moses. I ain't parted no Red Sea. I've been eatin' a lot of pecan pies made by little old ladies and stealing their money. I can face it. I don't know why you can't."

Dad turned his back on Doc and spoke more honestly than he had in years. "You know what? You live so long without self-respect, and you forget what it feels like. Well, we got a chance for it now, see, and I want it." He turned back and pointed at Doc. "And you're not gonna take it away from me. And you're not gonna take it away from them widders neither."

"The widows?" Doc cried out to the heavens.

"That's right!" Dad said, pleading now not just for his own dignity but for the saintly widows whom they had both been swindling for years. "Those sweet little old, well, not all of 'em little—an' some of 'em ain't so sweet neither. Downright rattlesnakes, some of 'em. But they're widders all the same. And yer not gonna take their fortune!"

"Dad, this is delirium incarnate. We have sold five hundred percent of nothing!"

"This time it's not nothin'!" Dad said emphatically. "It's an honest-to-goodness oil well! And yer not gonna take it from them, and yer not gonna take it from me neither. Jesus will not stand for it."

"Jesus?" Doc shouted incredulously.

"Yes, Jesus! Your Lord and Savior, before whom you will have to stand in judgment. And on that mighty day, when you stand before the Father, the Son, and the Holy Spirit, the only thing between you and eternal punishment might just be that you did right by them widders."

Chapter 13

"I'll take my chances," Doc said. "Right now, I'm more concerned with the Texas Rangers than the Holy Spirit. Not to mention the possible revenge of widows once they realize what we've done."

"No one's gonna kill us for bringin' in the black gold that'll be their salvation. No matter what the law does, they'll immortalize us. They'll build statues of us in public parks where little children play long after we're gone."

"And the pigeons will relieve themselves on our likenesses. Dad, you're drunk."

"Drunk as a skunk!" Dad said, leaning up against the Ford. "But I can't walk away from it, Doc. I can't do it. And neither can you. We cannot walk away from this."

Suddenly, Doc found himself kicking the rear tires of the Model A, bellowing at it as though everything were the Ford's fault. "Well, you lousy, two-bit sack of manure!" he screamed into the prairie night. "Aahhh!" He looked up at the heavens, toe to toe with the Almighty himself. "Why couldn't you've done this thirty years ago? Twenty years ago, when I was still an honest man! Before I became a tinhorn huckster! A defiler of widowhood! Why couldn't you have done this in Oklahoma when, for the first time, I believed every lie I ever told? Why'd you have to let me sink so low, Lord? And then dangle it right in front of my face! Let me be one or the other. A crook or a righteous doctor of geology in all matters petroliferous who struck it rich."

Doc was quiet, breathing hard, leaning against the Ford. Finally, he sank down onto the running board in defeat.

"You get it all out of your system?" Dad asked, sinking down next to him.

"Not all," Doc said.

"You know we're gonna bring this well in, don't ya?" The old man had the grace not to let his excitement show too much.

"You bet," Doc muttered.

"We're gonna be rich," Dad offered.

"Till they tar and feather us."

Dad, magnanimous in victory, was all silver linings now. "Well, if they do, it'll be with the oil we found."

"The good Lord surely does have a twisted sense of humor."

Off in the distance, a coyote howled, long and echoing toward them through the night air across the flat land, as long and loud as Doc had howled before him.

"When a coyote howls like that, you think it's rejoicing or a lamentation?" Dad asked.

"Hard to tell," Doc answered.

Then all was still in the night.

Chapter 14

Dad had to admit it was the craziest thing he'd ever seen in his life. When word got out that they had hit the Woodbine sand, farmers came in from all around to offer to help them bring in the well. No job was too big or too small. Seemed like each one of 'em was staking their fate, their future, and their families' futures on bringing that well in.

And it wasn't just white folks. There were as many Black folks who showed up as there were white folks. Dad reckoned word must've got out through Tanner Irving Sr. The Black folks in town had a pretty little church just outside of Cornville, near their end of town. It was called the Beth El Baptist Church, and Dad reckoned half the church's members were there, pitching in.

A good many of 'em lived on what they could get in credit from the Dials' general store, so the minute they heard that Thurman and Junipera Sue were going to tear up all the credit slips if they struck a gusher, they showed up to do what they could to make sure it happened.

But there were just as many folks, white and Black, who didn't owe the Dials a dime. They just heard there was a chance for an oil strike, and that meant jobs—and good ones too. Ones that paid a heck of a lot more than sharecropping during a drought. And it didn't seem to matter much whether they got the jobs or somebody else did. Jobs meant people would have money. And if they had it, they'd have some to spend. So there were even a few shop owners from town who showed up to do what they could.

They weren't much use with a drill string. None of 'em were cable-and-tool men. They didn't know their way around pipes, collars, or bits, let alone the mud pumps. But each of 'em did what he could, whether that was hauling over sections of pipe or feeding logs into the boiler. It just seemed like everyone wanted to lend a hand.

After a while, there were womenfolk too. Some of it made Dad and Doc downright nervous because not a few of them were some of the widows who had invested in the well, and all they needed to do was start yakking to one another about how one of them owned ten or twenty percent, and the two old swindlers would wind up in the hoosegow.

But still, the womenfolk came with pitchers of lemonade, baskets of chicken, corn on the cob, sandwiches, pies, and cakes. An onlooker might have thought it was a church picnic or covered-dish dinner. There were baked hams, slow-cooked chili, cornbread and beans, and pretty near anything that could be stuffed into a casserole.

After a while, it was almost like a picnic. Folks who hadn't talked in years were hauling wood together, laughing, telling jokes, and eating everything in sight.

"Well, if that don't beat all," Dad said to Doc.

"What?" Doc answered, wiping the sweat off his previously unstained white derby hat.

Chapter 14

"Black folk and white folk all working together, like there wasn't hardly any difference between them at all. Never seen the like of it!"

Doc turned and looked at the scene, which he wouldn't have believed either if someone had told him about it the week before. Heck, there were even some men drinking out of the same cup whether they were Black or white.

"It's because they believe in us," Dad said. And when he said it, he had to fight back tears welling up.

"What's wrong with you, you old fool?"

"Nothin'," Dad said, wiping his eyes on his sleeve and looking away so Doc couldn't see just how much emotion he felt. "Must've been a cinder or somethin'."

"Yeah, more than likely," Doc said. But he patted the older man on the shoulder and gave it a squeeze.

"They really do believe in us," Dad said, clearing his throat. "And not 'cause we conned 'em either. We earned it this time. We deserve it."

"You better hope deserve has got nothin' to do with it, Dad. 'Cause if we ever get our just desserts, it won't be pecan pie; it'll be a one-way ticket to the state pen."

Doc turned away from the old man and went back to work. In a sense, he had amazed himself. He actually *did* know a thing or two about how to bring a well in. He had pretended to do it so many times, he figured something must have rubbed off. And these folks looked at him just as if he were General Lee himself, sittin' astride ol' Traveller with a spyglass on a battlefield. He had to admit, it was quite a thing.

For the first time in as long as he could remember, he wasn't working a con. He was spudding in a real-live, honest-to-goodness oil well. And it wasn't a question of *if* they'd hit a gusher. He knew that much about petroleum engineering, even if his fake diploma was printed up on the backside of an advertisement for a Clara Bow seven-reeler. No, sir! For once in his life, he felt like the figure of his own creation: Horatio Daedalus Boyd, PhD, petroleum engineer, geologist, and master of all things petroliferous.

And it felt…well…for a while there, it felt good. And then he realized it. Hit him like a ton of bricks. Like a sucker punch to the gut in a barroom brawl. He was falling for his own con. And there was absolutely nothing good that could come from that.

They worked till sundown, and all the men alike tipped their caps to him, called him "Dr. Boyd," and said they'd see him tomorrow—said they felt like they'd put in a good day's work and asked, hopefully, "It won't be long, now, will it Doc?"

"No, sir," Doc said to one and all. "I don't believe it will."

For them, just his word was good enough to hang their hopes on. There was a kind of rejoicing. Doc Boyd said it won't be long!

For Doc, however, it had exactly the opposite effect. He knew that it would not be long, indeed, until they struck oil and that it would not be long after that till they were on the run from the law. Probably not more than a day or two after they brought the well in, the Texas Rangers would be after them.

With a little luck, they'd get away clean, maybe make it to California after all, and start all over again. But even as he tried to convince himself of that, he knew it was just a con. And he also knew that he was too smart to fall for it. They wouldn't make it to California. Maybe, if they were lucky, they could sneak out across the border into Mexico, but that was a pretty good stretch too.

Chapter 14

And what would they do once they got there? Neither one of them spoke the local lingo, so they weren't likely to pull off any kind of scam once they crossed the border. They'd be reduced to working for a living. Either that or become bank robbers, and there certainly was no future in that.

After they knocked off work, he and Dad headed over to what they had rechristened the New Dugan's, both for a meal and a bit of liquid refreshment, to which both men felt they were entitled. After imbibing two stiff shots of New Dugan's finest hooch, which were served up in porcelain coffee cups like at the cigar store, Doc's thoughts drifted back to Oklahoma, and he knew that was even more dangerous than falling for his own con. No good could come from thinking about the comely Widow Flora May Simms. He knew that. There was no question of it. He knew it was the last thing on earth he should be doing.

He ordered another coffee cup of liquid courage, finished the last bite of New Dugan's famous stew, which, he suspected, contained parts of an old boot for meat, and then abruptly announced to Dad that he was taking off for a few days.

"Takin' off? What do you mean, takin' off?" Dad demanded.

"I mean takin' off," Doc said. "I got a prospect, maybe a hot one."

"We done hit all the widders in the local papers. And we agreed, now we hit the Woodbine, we're gonna hit 'em up a second time."

"We did, and that's exactly what we're doin'. I'm just castin' my net a little wider, that's all."

"What's that supposed to mean?"

"Well, this one isn't in the local papers, okay?" said Doc. "She's somebody I knew."

"From where?" Dad asked, wiping the greasy stew off his mouth with what passed for a napkin but might have been used to wipe down surfaces that were better left unknown.

"From someplace else, all right? Did it ever occur to you that I might know people from someplace else?"

"Someplace like where? I been every place you've been, and I don't recall any widders that we haven't already bamboozled."

"Well, maybe I got a better memory than you. I don't recall as how we ever had an agreement that I had to ask your permission to check out a prospect."

"That's what you're doing? Checking out a prospect?"

"That's just what I said, isn't it?"

"Why don't I believe you?"

"You want to know the truth?" said Doc.

"If that was a commodity I was in search of," said Dad, "you would not be my first stop. But go ahead. Give it your best shot. Here we are, about to bring in an honest-to-goodness oil well, and you want to take off because, supposedly, you got a prospect."

Doc just looked at the older man. "Number one," he said, holding up a finger to amplify the order of things, "we are in the process of drilling. Number two, you are the driller in this operation. Number three, I thus feel I am leaving the Junipera Sue Number One in the ablest of all hands. And number four, I do not rightly care about what you do or do not believe, Dad. I'm takin' off."

"For how long?" Dad called out to him, as Doc had risen and was headed through the door.

"Till you see me come back," Doc answered. Then, he pushed through the swinging doors that marked New Dugan's

Chapter 14

as the saloon it used to be, got into the Model A, cranked up the engine, and set off for what he knew would be quite a drive. It was a long way to Lathrope, Oklahoma.

Chapter 15

The problem with making a getaway from a town like Cornville, or even the larger metropolis of Mule Chute, was, first off, the road.

It was a dirt, pitted, dusty in the summer, up-to-the-hubs mud in winter country lane, rutted deep by wagon wheels, which had had fifty years more than the automobile to make their impression upon the earth.

There were livestock of every species that could dart suddenly across the road in the dark and were as much a hazard as a minefield in Belleau Wood was to an infantryman in the 14–18 war. It wasn't just armadillos, mule deer, and whitetails; bobcats, the occasional mountain lion, and, just as easy, a stray herd of cattle could all put a meaningful dent in a Model A and an unexpected end to one's journey, not to mention one's getaway if not one's very life.

"Getaway" had not been Doc's original intent. His original intent had been to travel west on Route 67 into Dallas, then head north on Route 75, cross the state border into Oklahoma, then head up to Lathrope, which was just midway between McAlester and Muskogee.

Chapter 15

He figured it would take him a good eight hours, as the journey between Dallas and Lathrope, according to the American Automobile Association road map, was almost 350 miles. That would put him in the vicinity of the Widow Simms, with any luck, somewhere between three and six in the morning. He did not expect she would appreciate a call at that hour, which would mean that he would have to put up at a motel. He didn't recall seeing one in Lathrope. There was a AAA-approved motor inn in McAlester: little cottages right next to a hamburger joint. He could lay up there, then pay his visit to the Widow Simms after catching some sleep and taking a shower, getting the road dust and smell off him.

That was the original plan. But once he got to Dallas, he gassed up at a Texaco station, and there in the light of the filling station, while the fella in the cap was washing his windscreen, he pulled out that old auto club map and saw Route 70.

Route 70 was up near Durant, just past the Oklahoma state border. And if one took a left on Route 70, one wasn't heading farther into Oklahoma. One would be headed, if one were so inclined, through Oklahoma, across the Texas panhandle, and into the badlands of New Mexico. One could stop in Clovis, which was just below Albuquerque, lay up for a good eight hours' sleep, fill 'er up, and head west to Flagstaff, Arizona. From Flagstaff, a fella could jump right onto Route 66 and take it all the way to the Golden State—Califor-ni-ay. They had orange groves and pretty girls in bathing suits who had come to Hollywood to become movie stars and ended up waitresses and carhops instead.

Route 66 ended at the Santa Monica Pier. He had seen pictures of it. They had corn dogs on sticks and one of the prettiest merry-go-rounds he had ever seen. They had a ballroom at the end of the pier called the La Monica. Five thousand people could dance there to some of the best bands in the country. And there was a place there called The Lobster. Movie stars went there and dined on the best seafood the Pacific Ocean had to offer.

It was a real paradise, especially for a flimflam man dealing in fake oil wells. They had the real deal up on Signal Hill, near a place called Long Beach, that supplied one-fifth of the nation's oil supply. And, Doc figured, with as much fast living as was reputed to go on in Los An-gull-ease (Doc did not pronounce the *g* like a *j*), it had to have more than its share of widows. Probably a good many of 'em came out there in the first place because they wanted to be movie stars. Probably the best-lookin' widows in the country were in Los An-gull-ease!

The more Doc thought about it, the more appeal the idea held for him. He didn't owe Dad Everett a thing. Didn't owe him beans! He had told Dad Everett that the smartest thing they could do would be to cap the well and hightail it out of town before the rangers could get ahold of 'em. And that old fool had talked him into the stupidest thing he'd ever done in his life—exposing himself to the law!

Well, if Dad wanted to bring that well in so much, let him do it. Let him take a hundred percent of the glory and a hundred percent of the cell they'd stick him in. Why should Doc stick his neck out for anybody? Especially a hard-luck, fat, old loser like D. H. Everett? The men weren't friends; they were business associates.

Friends were millstones. They were an albatross around the neck of any self-respecting con man. They were a luxury a con artist could scarcely afford. The only way to survive in this business, the only way Doc had survived all these years, was to not own anything he couldn't leave behind at a moment's notice. If it couldn't fit into his carpetbag, he didn't need it. And, the truth was, he didn't need the carpetbag either. More than once the only way he had prevented his backside from being peppered with double-aught buckshot was to drop everything but his pants and skedaddle. That was just what he should do now, and he knew it.

The only thing that was more of a fool notion than bringing in that well was just what he had set out to do only a few hours before: head north across the state line into Oklahoma to see the Widow Simms, confess his sins, and give her back her money.

What did he think she was gonna do? Fall into his arms? Say, "Oh Horatio! I've been waiting, all this time, for you to return. I don't care how you swindled me, how you abused my affections, how you've bamboozled me. You've come back into my life, and that's all I care about."

Flora May Simms may have been a lot of things, but a fool wasn't one of them. She was a straitlaced, sanctified woman and not the kind who would cotton to bein' lied to.

Course, that was the whole point. For once in his life, he *hadn't* lied to her. He had told her the truth. His affections for her were as real as they came. Otherwise he wouldn't be in this car right now doing something as stupid as driving all the way to Oklahoma to confess his crimes. It made it all the more galling to him that his affections for her were the fondest he had ever felt for any woman in his life. He hadn't lied about that a bit!

Course, there was the matter of the Classafay Vaudine Number One oil well. That was technically a lie. But then, so was the Junipera Sue Number One, and they were actually finding oil there! So, when you thought of it, he *could* have been tellin' her the truth about the Classafay Vaudine oil well. It wasn't *his* fault they didn't strike oil there. In fact, he had tried just as hard in Oklahoma as he had at the Junipera Sue. Moreover, he had used the exact same words, the exact same charts. He had cited the exact same Sabine Incline and Rusk Depression, the salt dome, the anticlines, the Yegua and Cook Mountain formations—in every single oil scam he had pulled off, the words were no different. And yet, in one instance, they turned out to be the absolute, a hundred percent, without a doubt, gospel truth!

He had, in fact, predicted that they would hit the Woodbine sand at thirty-five hundred feet, and as Dad Everett had so rightly pointed out—and say what you will about Dad Everett, but he was certainly no fool when it came to the oil business—they *had* hit the Woodbine, at *exactly* thirty-five hundred feet, precisely as he had foretold.

So what made anything that he had ever told anybody a lie? The only difference was the results. The predicated predictions were the same. However, the results were not in his hands but the Almighty's. Had the truth he had spoken to Junipera Sue Dial been a lie when he described the Classafay Vaudine simply because they had not struck the Woodbine at thirty-five hundred feet? It was not as if they hadn't drilled down to thirty-five hundred feet. They *had*! So what made one a lie and the other the truth?

It wasn't as if he had employed charlatans to carry out some nefarious scheme. While it was true that he had not completed the mandatory coursework demanded by the University of Heidelberg to obtain doctorate degrees in geology and petroleum engineering, he was not the man in actual charge of the drilling operation undertaken at each of the wells. *That* man was D. H. Everett, a highly respected, well-known professional driller of great esteem. Respected by all his peers. It was true that he was unlucky, but no one could claim that he was not skilled, that he was not, in fact, a master of his craft.

So where was the lie? Where was the con? Was it in the fact that they poured Quaker State down the drill shaft on a moonless night? They were prepared to do the same thing at the Junipera Sue Number One. Would that action have negated the finding of the Woodbine sand? It would not have. Indeed, on every oil lease he sold, there was an admonition that oil exploration was a highly risky venture and that past results were no indication of future ones. Caveat emptor! Buyer beware!

It wasn't Doc who had made that up; it was the ancient Romans. And it was as true now as it was then. The buyer bore a responsibility. Was it Doc's fault that they did not exercise it? Could he be held accountable for everyone who made a foolish investment in the continental United States? There was a warning, in black and white! Did he hide it from anyone? It might be true that the print of the warning was somewhat finer than some other details, but he did not recall a single widow who did not possess a pair of spectacles.

Many a man, and not a few women, put their chips down, hoping the ball would settle on red, and instead it came up black. Could the roulette table be charged with any crime for being true to its nature? And was there anyone who had ever known Doc Boyd who could ever claim that he was untrue to his? A roulette table was a roulette table, and Horatio Daedalus Boyd was…well, it didn't matter what he was. Let the buyer beware! Doc wasn't their babysitter; he was a purveyor of hope in a hopeless world. Of optimism in a land of despair. Of entrepreneurship against a surging tide of a slavish mentality.

It was the same thing with those newfangled stoplights. They would mean the end of civilization as mankind knew it. They would cripple any sense of initiative and turn the paragon of God's creation into mere zombies, forgoing common sense in exchange for mindless obedience to soulless, electrified signage.

A man didn't need an electric light to tell him when to stop. It was *his* job to look around and see if it was safe to proceed or not. Was there an armadillo on a highway or byway that gave two hoots about what a stop sign said or did not say? It was the *driver's* job to beware. Was it the armadillo's fault that he wanted to cross from one side of the road to the other at the same moment that some careless automobile driver failed in his obligation to exercise due caution and turned said armadillo into a four-legged landmine? Dr. Horatio Daedalus Boyd bore no more guilt, in his own eyes, than that innocent armadillo.

When you got right down to it, the only thing he figured he *had* lied about was the affections he had sworn to the *other* widows he was swindling at the same time he was sweet-talkin' the Widow Simms. So, if you wanted to get technical, it was *they* who had a real claim against him. He had lied to *them*. That was true. But he had *not* lied to Flora May Simms. He had not lied about the thrill he felt at the touch of her skin or the sound of her voice. He had not lied about what that scent of lilac did to him or the feel of her hair against his face when they embraced. He had not lied to her about a single thing!

As a matter of fact, he took umbrage at the mere hint of an allegation that he *had* lied to her! Here he was, a fella who had poured out his heart to her, had told her the truth in every way, no matter the fact that the words he used were the exact same ones he had used a hundred or so times before with the widows he *had* lied to and swindled.

But Flora May Simms wasn't one of 'em. How *dare* she accuse him of such a thing! After he had confessed, with an open heart, his true and unbounded feelings of affection for her? It just went to show you how ungrateful certain people could be—not to mention suspicious. And jealous. Unbelieving. Without reason. She was one coldhearted customer, and there were no two ways about it.

And here he was, risking skidding across a highway after he popped open an armadillo, risking life and limb—not to mention an almost brand-new automobile—to travel between two states in order to give her money back, and she didn't even have the common decency to show a single sign of appreciation?

Well, that did it. She'd had her chance. He had certainly made more than a gesture. He had set out on a *journey*, practically a quest, like a knight in a fairy tale, to make things right with his ladylove. And what did she do? Spit in his face for his troubles! Well, that settled it. As soon as he got to Durant, he was makin' a left-hand turn and saying, "California, here I come!"

***

By the time he got to Greenville, he had built up quite an appetite. *Arguing with Flora May Simms can do that to a fella,* he thought. He found a late-night diner that served passable chicken-fried steak with all the trimmings—mashed potatoes and cream gravy—and washed it all down with an RC Cola. At the filling station, he gassed up again and bought another RC and a couple Moon Pies.

In McKinney, for some reason, he mistook gas for hunger pains and had a chili dog, which proclaimed it was made with

Clyde's Firehouse Chili. And whoever Clyde was, he wasn't messin' around. He had home-fried potato chips along with the dog and another RC.

Gassed up again in more ways than one, he headed north across the state line toward Durant. And it was there that fate, chicken-fried steak, three RC Colas, two Moon Pies, and Clyde's Firehouse Chili intervened.

Doc made a dash for the outbuilding at the Esso station. Later he would recollect that he sat there for quite a spell. And when he had done what he came to do, he reckoned that he was plumb done in.

Happily for him, there was the U-Smile Motor Court Cabins and Tent Ground just across from the Esso station. It beckoned like a shimmering oasis in the sands of the Sahara.

Thus, instead of making the much-anticipated left-hand turn and heading west on Route 70 to Clovis, New Mexico, and continuing on to Flagstaff, Arizona, where he would take Route 66 all the way to the Santa Monica Pier and widows in bathing suits who had come to California to become movie stars and wound up as waitresses married to plumbers who died before their time, he drove across the street from the Esso station to the U-Smile Cabins and Tent Ground, like a seafarer to a light-house and the illuminated sign that said Vacancy.

He rapped loudly upon the door of the cabin that looked like all the others in the U-Smile Cabins and Tent Ground but which bore the sign Manager. He was greeted by a brown-toothed, bald-headed man in torn long johns, who had just pulled one suspender strap up over his shoulder in order to greet his late-night customer with the dignity befitting his position.

"Evenin'," Doc said.

Chapter 15

"More like the middle of the night," the manager said and let fly a stream of tobacco juice suitably far enough away from Doc's personage so as to cause no offense.

"You got a cabin to let?"

The manager looked at Doc as if he were the village idiot and let fly another stream of tobacco juice that struck a gecko stealthily making its way toward his door.

"Bingo!" said the manager, in a self-congratulatory tone. Then, he looked back up at Doc. "You see a No in front of that sign that says Vacancy?"

"Nope," said Doc.

"Because," said the manager, completely ignoring him, "we *do* have a little sign that says No, which we flip over when we ain't got no more cabins to let. You know why we ain't flipped that sign over yet?"

"Because you've got a vacancy," Doc said, growing wearier by the minute.

"Bingo!" said the manager and spat again at the spot where the gecko had just been and from which it had since retreated, doused in tobacco spit and shame. "Cabin without a mattress will cost you a dollar," he continued. "Mattress is twenty-five cents extra. Blankets, sheets, and pillows're 'nother fifty cents."

"Buck seventy-five, fully equipped."

"Bingo," answered the manager. He retreated within his abode and returned with two blankets, two sheets, one pillow, one pillowcase, and a key.

"Cabin number four," said the manager. "You'll find 'er twixt three an' five."

Doc peeled off two dollars, took the pillow, pillowcase, sheets, and blankets, and waited for the manager to make change. He got a dime, two nickels, and five pennies, then stumbled his way through the gravel-covered courtyard to the small cabin between numbers three and five, illuminated in a dirty pool of yellow light by a single dangling bare-lit bulb.

Doc opened the door, smelled the familiar smell of left-over canned goods and the odor of workingmen, then pulled his car into the space beside the cabin, went inside, shucked off his high-top boots and breeches, white shirt, and derby hat, and snuggled in between the sheets.

Had it not been for the dream, the next morning he would have gotten into the Model A and headed west in search of widowed bathing beauties frolicking in the sand beneath the Santa Monica Pier.

But dream that night he did—of the Widow Flora May Simms and the sunlit meadow through which they once had walked, whispering tender endearments, till they came down beside a rambling creek in a little grove of black walnut trees, where they spread their picnic blanket and Doc leaned back into Flora May's lap as she reclined against a walnut tree and brushed away his forelock, as was her wont.

There, beside the almost Japanese-looking creek running swiftly over dark river rocks rubbed smooth, as if they had been there since the first day of creation—which was what that day felt like—it seemed to Doc that the entire world was new and full of possibilities and all his sins could be washed away. He could be baptized in that creek that ran alongside the grove of black walnut trees where they made their picnic and talked of the future, when the well would finally come in, and of the time, and love, and money, theirs to spend.

There were no curtains in cabin number four of the U-Smile Cabins and Tent Ground, and thus the first rays of morning light peeked in through the single window and

Chapter 15

roused Doc from his nocturnal reveries. He lay there, feeling the warmth of those first rays of sunlight on his face, much as it had been in his dream, much as it had been on the day he and Flora May picnicked by the creek down from the meadow in the little grove of walnut trees.

He allowed as how that day was probably the happiest one he had ever known in the almost six decades he had walked so aimlessly upon the earth. He allowed as how he had never been happier. He figured he could make Lathrope just after she'd be finishing up breakfast.

Chapter 16

While Doc Boyd was heading north from Dallas toward the Oklahoma state line, about to gorge himself on chicken-fried steak, mashed potatoes with cream gravy, Moon Pies, RC Colas, and Clyde's Firehouse Chili, Dad Everett was preparing to take the evening meal with the Widow Martha Jean Tyler.

He was not looking forward to the occasion. It was not that Martha Jean was not an excellent cook. He had to admit that she was one of the finest cooks he had ever met. Her fried chicken had the crispiest crust and the juiciest thighs he could recall. Her biscuits and gravy knew no equal. She had a little vegetable garden outside her farmhouse, which, even in the harshest climate, flourished under her care. Dad Everett was partial to turnip greens, and the Widow Tyler's were the best he had ever eaten.

And as for pies, she made a buttermilk shoofly chess pie that was buttery, sweet, salty, savory, and custardy. All the earthly pleasures of pie were contained therein. To top it all off, she had a cousin in New Orleans who shipped her coffee with chicory from Café du Monde, which brought back to Dad Everett the savory smells of youthful adventures, when life was new and everything full of promise.

Chapter 16

Indeed, despite his advanced years, that's exactly how the Widow Martha Jean Tyler made him feel every time her hand touched his. As if life were new again and full of endless possibilities, not for oil wells or get-rich schemes but for the warm comfort of her companionship.

Dad Everett was not, nor had he ever been, what one might call a lusty man, except perhaps where food was concerned. He preferred the delicious comfort of hand-holding to the fleeting passions of canoodling.

For a man who had lived so long in canvas tent camps and bare-bones boardinghouses, his fervent prayer was for hearth and home. When he added to that the merry twinkle in the Widow Tyler's eyes every time they spoke, the unbridled joy she seemed to take in their company, he had to admit that, for the first time since the tragic demise of his beloved Lou Della Havermeyer, he believed he was positively smitten.

The Widow Tyler was petite where Lou Della had been large and rawboned. And though Texas prairie life had left its mark, there was a softness to the touch of her hand that moved him almost to tears. The last time they had supped together, there was a chill in the air as an early fall seemed to be approaching. Martha Jean had made a fire in the hearth, and they'd sat on her love seat, hand in hand, by its rosy glow.

For a man who had made his living all his life by the sweat of his brow and the work of his callused hands, Dad Everett had acquired a taste for poetry, which quite surprised even him. His introduction to the works of the great poets had been, of course, through Doc Boyd, who insisted that, when it came to swindling widows, poetry was as much a tool of the trade as cable, hemp, and sections of pipe were to the driller. Thus, Doc convinced Dad to memorize Shakespeare's sonnets. But in so doing, Dad had come across the works of Robert Browning, one of the foremost Victorian poets, whose life had mirrored Dad Everett's in its personal tragedy.

He knew that Browning had married an older woman, the poet Elizabeth Barrett, and that the two of them had gone to live in sunny Italy. He had seen pictures of Barrett and Browning, she six years his elder. Doc knew their love story, which began in correspondence and led, ever so gently, into the deepest of affections. Elizabeth's father disapproved of the marriage and disinherited his daughter, and it was Browning who paid for the second edition of his wife's poems and love sonnets.

The two went to Italy because of her failing health. They lived first in Pisa, and Dad had seen autochrome photos of the Leaning Tower. And then they moved to one of the fairest cities in the world: Florence, home of the statues of Michelangelo, of the artworks in the Uffizi, of all the great masters of the Renaissance. They took an apartment at Casa Guidi and had a child, whom they nicknamed "Panini." They were madly in love, and they expressed it perhaps more beautifully than any couple had done before them, until death took her from him.

Browning had written a poem, perhaps more prayer than poem, beseeching Elizabeth to live on when he knew the life was ebbing from her. Dad had committed those words to memory and recited them to Martha Jean Tyler that evening before the rosy, warm glow of the fire in her hearth.

"Grow old along with me," he intoned Browning's words, looking into her eyes, made even bluer by firelight. "The best is yet to be, the last of life, for which the first was made."

Martha Jean squeezed his hand, thinking what a beautiful voice he had, as he recited, "Our times are in his hand who saith, 'A whole I planned, youth shows but half; trust God: see all, nor be afraid.'"

Tears had welled up in both their eyes as he whispered, yet again, "Grow old with me."

She'd leaned her head upon his shoulder, and the warmth of her hand caressed his callused palm, and he'd known a contentment there that, in truth, he had never known before, not even in his youth, when thoughts of growing old were strange.

Why, then, one might have asked, having known such joy and contentment in the Widow Tyler's company, having smacked his lips in delight with the first bite of juicy fried chicken thighs and forkfuls of country biscuits cooked in a cast-iron skillet and soaked in gravy, would he be dreading the thought of seeing her that night instead of counting down the hours until their assignation?

The reason was painfully clear to him. He was going to her home and hearth not as the suitor he desired to be but as the low-down swindler he had become as a result of his association with that cad, Heinrich Bumstetter, a.k.a. Horatio Daedalus Boyd, whom he now feared had absconded with their automobile and was, more than likely, making for the sunny climes of California.

Dad Everett knew his fair-weather partner like the back of his own workingman's hand. He wasn't going to milk any new prospect in order to bring in the gusher of a well they had finally discovered; he was making a getaway and sticking Dad with the bill. Dad knew it in his bones. Could feel it, down to the marrow. "He that lieth down with dogs shall rise up with fleas," old Dr. Benjamin Franklin had said. And more to the point at hand, as George Bernard Shaw had put it, "Never wrestle with pigs. You both get dirty, and the pig likes it."

Well, Dad's association with Heinrich Bumstetter had left him feeling both like he was crawling with fleas and smelling like swine. Once he had been an honest workingman who could hold his head up as high as any other man any day of the week and twice on Sundays. His only fault had been in being unlucky and then being fool enough to wallow in the muck and the mire of Bumstetter's making.

He had allowed himself to become that which he had despised in his youth: A huckster. A matchstick man. All hat and no cattle.

And, finally, when they had found redemption, when his entire life's work was about to be validated by bringing in what he *knew* would be a gusher that would blow a hundred and fifty feet high, Bumstetter had deserted him and left him holding the bag. The well that was to be his redemption was now his downfall, for in order to bring it in, he was forced to further enmesh himself in the web of Bumstetter's design. He would have to go back to the Widow Tyler and pull another check for five hundred dollars.

There was, of course, always a chance that Bumstetter would return. He might be headed north to Oklahoma to further swindle that chestnut-haired widder who, he knew, had left her mark on Bumstetter just as surely as Martha Jean Tyler had already carved her initials into Dad Everett's own heart. But either way, tonight's assignation filled him with dread instead of the anticipated pleasure of the Widow Tyler's company.

For though the Woodbine sand he had examined from the cuttings bucket promised as rich an oil strike as any he had ever dared to imagine, he was nonetheless filled with self-loathing at what he had become, and no amount of self-congratulatory rationalization could alter the fact that he was about to compound his sin by swindling the Widow Tyler a second time.

The one thing Bumstetter had said that was the truth, which Dad had ignored when they discovered the Woodbine, was that you could only sell a hundred percent of anything, and they had already oversubscribed the syndication to the mineral rights of the Junipera Sue Number One fivefold.

It was Bumstetter who had led him down this path. Bumstetter was the quicksand in which he had allowed himself to sink, the moral morass in which he had allowed himself to flounder. Bumstetter. The man was Satan's slave, if not the devil himself. But even as those thoughts echoed in his brain, Dad knew that no one had held a gun to his head. Bumstetter had not slipped him a mickey. He had simply supplied the rope with which Dad had fashioned the noose of his own making.

"Vanity of vanities," said the author of Ecclesiastes. "All is vanity."

Dad had let the scorn and derision of others, the nickname "Dry Hole" Everett, eat away at his very soul and turn him from the simple pleasures of daily life that old King Solomon spoke of in the Good Book, of eating when hungry, drinking to slake one's thirst, taking enjoyment in the works of one's hands—all of which were gifts from the Almighty.

He had let coming up a day late and a dollar short beat him down, like an aged boxer felled by the blows of a younger and stronger man, struggling to get up only to be beaten down once again, lying there on the canvas, knowing he still possessed the strength to rise once more and yet dreading the blows that would greet him, and instead of fighting on, instead of being bloodied but unbowed, he feigned unconsciousness and, embracing defeat, kissed the canvas instead of rising in defiance of whatever life still had in store for him.

He was not the first man to be faced with life's adversities, nor would he be the last to succumb to them. But succumb he did and, at his lowest ebb, met Bumstetter, who had not caused his demise but simply opened the door through which Dad had all too willingly, he now knew, entered of his own volition. And all of that would lead him, tonight, to betray his beloved.

He couldn't claim that he'd forgotten the last lines of Ecclesiastes in the Good Book, but he'd merely ignored them: "The end of the matter; all has been heard. Fear God and keep his commandments, for this is the whole of man."

Those were the final thoughts that occurred to him as he knocked on the door of Martha Jean Tyler and she cheerfully bade him, "Come in," to the smells and warmth of home and hearth, which he so devoutly desired and was about to destroy.

Chapter 17

Doc had slept five hours, showered, shaved, put on a clean pair of flared riding breeches and a new white shirt, brushed the dust and smoke smudge off his white derby, cranked up the Model A, and headed north. He hit McAlester by 8:30 a.m. and availed himself of Polly Ann's Diner.

The Polly Ann in question was a hard-faced, heavyset country woman whose diner had been open since sunrise to catch those just finishing a night shift and those just beginning their day's labors. He ordered bacon and eggs, grits, and biscuits and gravy, for good measure, and washed it down with coffee that still had some of the grounds floating on top.

He was dawdling, and he knew it, trying to avoid the inevitable. But there was no backing out now. He gassed up the car and, within an hour, was pulling up the long gravel drive to the Widow Flora May Simms's handsome farmhouse.

The drive itself hit him with a wave of nostalgia that seemed to wash over his very being as he drove up the winding, narrow, gravel lane. Just the smell of the place as he stepped from the Model A flooded him with memories. Off to his right was the meadow that led down to the little grove of black walnut trees and the winding creek meandering this way and that, silver colored in the sun that splashed down beneath the leaves, green and backlit against the sky.

Then he caught sight of Flora May, carrying a basket of laundry out to the clothesline behind her home. She had neither seen nor heard him pull up, and so he simply watched her a while, tall and slim and graceful in her movements as she pinned bedsheets and towels to the two lines strung out behind the farmhouse. A slight breeze blew across the prairie and flapped the sheets lazily back and forth as if they were damask curtains in an alabaster palace. That same breeze blew her chestnut hair. And as she raised a hand to brush a lock of it aside, squinting in the direction of the morning sun, she saw the familiar silhouette of the tall man in high-top boots and riding breeches and a derby hat. The sun was behind him, and she could not make out his face, but there was no mistaking him for any other man but the one of whom she had dreamt, almost every night, since he broke the news to her of the dry hole, which ended all their dreams of marital bliss, and of the creditors who might seize upon her home to satisfy his debt.

He had taken on the life of a fugitive because of her. He had become a wanderer in order to protect her. He knew neither rest nor respite because of his affections for her. And now he had come back. She was filled with both elation at his return and fear for his safety from the law. He was, for her, an almost mythic figure: the outlaw cowboy who risked the mounted posse for one last embrace from his own true love.

Without care, she dropped the sheet she was in the process of hanging out to dry. Let it be blown to the four corners of the earth. Her Horatio had come back to her at last!

Doc just stood there as if his feet were nailed to the ground, so filled with shame was he at the sight of her smiling face and outstretched arms as she ran toward him, calling out the name of the character he had created and who, he now realized, had dashed to bits his last true hopes for happiness.

Not knowing what else to do, he held his own arms out wide, and she ran into them, throwing her slender arms up about his neck, holding him close, as if she'd found her precious child, her one true love, and would never let him go again. He felt the warmth of her cheek, soft against his own, wet with tears she wept unashamedly, saying, over and over again, "Oh Horatio! I knew you would come back!"

As if out of instinct, his brain scrambled to find a lie convincing enough to mask his betrayal of this sweet soul who offered her heart so openly and without fear. It was as if he thumbed through a catalog of falsehoods in his mind, searching for just the right one that would save him from the awful moment of truth that he had chosen to bring about.

"We—" he said, holding her close against him, feeling her heart race next to his, basking in what he knew would be their last embrace before she cursed him for the dog he was. "We should go inside."

"Is it not safe for you, my dearest?" she asked, furtively scanning the horizon, as if a posse of mounted lawmen would come galloping across the rise at any moment, like in a lonely country song. "Perhaps you should put your car in the barn, where no one else can see it?"

Her concern for him was so poignant, so genuine, so without guile. Here she was, this pious woman, so concerned for her outlaw love who had risked life and limb to see her once again.

He looked at her sweet face and saw his reflection in her eyes. He was, to her, a tragic hero, the sweet soul companion of her dreams, a doomed knight-errant, willing to die for one last embrace. And the self-loathing rose like bile in his throat.

"We should go inside, Flora May." He relished saying her name, knowing full well it would be the last time he could say it without hearing her reproach in return.

She took his hand as if he were a blind man and led him up the steps to the threshold of the home he had once dared to dream of sharing with her. The sweet familiarity of the place made his remorse all the greater.

She showed him into the parlor, offered him coffee, which he declined, sat with him on the love seat far too delicate for the Oklahoma prairie—an heirloom, perhaps, handed down from someone who'd lived a more genteel life. Before he could begin, she pulled a bundle of letters bound in a blue ribbon from the side table and said, "I kept every letter you wrote during your wanderings, Horatio. I've read each one, it feels like, a thousand times and imagined this day. Longed for it. Prayed for it! And never truly believed it would happen. How long can you stay?"

"Not long," Doc said.

"Are there men pursuing you?" she asked.

"They will be," he said, clearing his throat, hating the fact that the answer reinforced the image he had created for her of the tragic lover who had burdened himself to wander the earth forever in order to protect his ladylove.

"Lawmen?" she inquired, choking back the emotion that swelled in her breast.

"Yes," he said. "They'll be after me soon enough. And I deserve what they have in store for me."

"Don't say that!" protested the Widow Simms. "You acted to protect me! You may have broken the law in the eyes of some, but—"

Chapter 17

"Flora May," Doc stopped her. "I'm a swindler and a liar."

"What?" she said, as if he'd spoken in a foreign tongue beyond her comprehension. "I don't understand."

"Everything I told you," Doc said, still holding her hand, "except my expressions of affection for you, my love for you, my hopes for a life with you—everything but those words was a lie. Not even my name was true."

"What are you saying?" she asked plaintively, as if the world was crumbling around her.

"It was all a lie," Heinrich Bumstetter said.

"But the oil well?" she asked. She had seen it. It was real! She had talked to Classafay Vaudine, on whose land the well was drilled. That woman was the salt of the earth. Nothing false about her.

"The oil well," he said, "was worthless. Not only that, the shares you owned were worth even less. The money you paid me as an investment was money I stole from you."

Flora May withdrew her hands from his, as if slowly comprehending something more horrible than anything she could have imagined. "But why?" she said. "Why would you steal from me?"

"Because I am a swindler. A con man. A snake oil salesman. But I swear to you, Flora May, for the first time in my life, every lie I thought I was telling you was true when it came to my affections for you. And I've come to make amends."

"Make amends?" she said, again uncomprehending.

Bumstetter felt his own heart break within him at the look of betrayal on her face. But, having begun his confession, he could not stop now, nor would he justify it with any tales of being a German sodbuster's son who sought to create an alternative world in which he was the hero.

"Dad Everett and I are con men. Flimflam men. The oil well scheme is our scam. We've done it dozens of times."

"You…you prey upon widows?"

Bumstetter hung his head in shame. He wished he had died before he uttered the words: "Yes, ma'am. But all the lies I told before, every word, was true when I spoke them to you. And I swear to you, I thought, I prayed, I hoped with every fiber of my being that if the words of my affections had come true, that perhaps this time, we *would* strike oil, and *that* would be true as well!"

"It was all a lie?" she said, and the veil was finally lifted and her sight restored. What she saw was no fairy-tale knight but the worst villain she could have imagined.

"Not the endearments I spoke to you, Flora May," Bumstetter insisted, pleading with her to believe. "No words ever spoken were truer than the affections I expressed to you. After we left Oklahoma, Dad and I went to Texas, and this time, we really *did* strike oil! All of *those* lies finally came true as well. And I only wish it had happened when I was here with you. And now, I reckon, Dad and I will both be arrested. We could have capped that well and declared it a dry hole, but we couldn't walk away from it. This time, too late, all those lies have turned out to be true."

Flora May shook her head in disbelief. "Why have you come here to tell me this, after you have deceived me so cruelly?"

"Because," said Bumstetter, "I care about you, Flora May, more than I've ever cared about any living soul. I traveled across two states because I want to be square with you, ma'am." So saying, he withdrew from his vest pocket the ten one-hundred-dollar bills he had brought with him. "This is the thousand dollars I took from you." He put the money on the coffee table there before them.

Flora May looked down at the money as if it were the vilest thing she had ever beheld. "Money that you swindled from other widows, the same way you swindled me?"

"I wanted to be square with you," was all he could lamely say, once again.

"You didn't just deceive me out of money. You broke my heart, Horatio. What am I saying? I don't even know your real name!"

Bumstetter was about to pronounce the name he had run from all his life, when the Widow Simms held up her hand to stop him. "And I don't want to know your name. I don't want that money!" she exclaimed. "You take it back! I just want you out of my life and out of my house!"

"Flora May..." Bumstetter said, fighting back the tears he felt stinging in his own eyes.

"Don't you speak my name. Don't you *dare* speak my name. Get out of my life and out of my house, now. *Now!* Or I swear by all that's holy, I will call the law on you myself this very instant. And when they *do* come to arrest you, I swear, I will crawl across broken glass in order to testify as to your villainy." She picked up the money and stretched it out toward him. "Take it!"

"No, ma'am," he said. "You're right to feel nothing but revulsion for me. But that is your money, and I have returned it."

"I don't want it," she said, throwing it against his chest and then, suddenly, slapping his face.

Doc could say nothing, felt the sting upon his cheek, then simply nodded his head, picked up his derby, walked across the parlor, with the sound of her sobs echoing behind him, and out the door.

Once on the porch, he did not look back but walked to the Model A. He heard her running after him but didn't turn to face her.

"I don't want this!" she screamed and threw the money at him as the Oklahoma dry wind swept it up and scattered it, like mammon, across the prairie, like an evil cloud blowing across the land.

Doc could hear her sobbing as he got into the Model A and cranked up the engine to drown out the sound, watching her recede in the rearview mirror and her laundry waving, like a fortress flag, against the horizon.

Doc did not stop to eat but drove, retracing his steps to McAlester, southward to Route 70. He had but to turn right at Durant and keep on driving until he hit the place they called the promised land, of orange groves and ocean sunsets, of fabled beauties and black gold bubbling up from the earth at Signal Hill.

It was the smart move. It was the *only* move. It was the way that led to freedom. Only a fool, a chump, a sucker, a country bumpkin *mark* would continue south to bring in that well, which he knew would be his doom, which he knew would lead to the rest of his days rotting behind bars. There were bathing beauties to the west, and the only thing down south were the Texas Rangers, if he and Dad were stupid enough to bring in that oil well. If they made that set of lies come true.

It was the sucker move, and he knew it. But as he crossed Route 70 in Durant, ignoring the sun sinking toward the ocean in the west, he reckoned as how he could make it to Cornville before midnight.

Chapter 18

On the day that Doc Boyd had traveled to make amends with the Widow Flora May Simms, Dad Everett had gone about his usual labors.

These were the fleeting moments when he knew self-respect: overseeing the drilling operation, watching the cable dance as if it telepathically transmitted to him the efficacy of the drill bit more than three thousand feet below the surface of the earth. He supervised his crew of amateur oilmen, store owners, and sharecroppers who had never worked a rig a day in their lives, and Dad made sure that their lives did not end on the rig for which he was responsible.

It was a dangerous business, and Dad took as much pride in keeping his crew safe as he did in the fact that he knew, with a hundred percent certainty, that this would be no dry hole. That he would bring in a gusher at last and be a joke no more.

Those hours spent out on the rig, where men looked at him with respect, were his saving grace—the antidote to the self-loathing he felt at what he would have to do when the sun set. Because a drilling operation took money. It took money to make money. It took money to chip away at the earth. It took money for sections of pipe and cable and rope, firewood, and the wages he paid to the few skilled cable-and-tool men he had, without whom he could not bring in the well.

It took money. And the only source of that money, Dad knew, was not just the widders but specifically the widder for whom he had come to care so deeply.

It was all on him now, and he knew it. He hadn't seen hide nor hair of Doc in well over twenty-four hours and reckoned he was halfway to California by now, absconding not only with the automobile they jointly owned but, he discovered to his dismay, with part of their poke.

They kept their kitty in a Maxwell House coffee tin wedged in behind a loose board in the wall of the room they shared above the Dials' general store. He had examined it shortly after Doc had left and found it was two thousand dollars lighter than it should have been.

So now, the burden was even greater than before, and only Dad could shoulder it. The only way he could bring that well in was to get part of it from Martha Jean Tyler, who was the most well-heeled of the crop of widows they had harvested in the vicinity between Cornville and Mule Chute, Texas. There was nothing else for it.

He would have to shower, shave, dress in what passed for his formal attire and would even dab a bit of brilliantine into his unruly shock of white hair. And yet, at the same time, he knew he could not do it. He could not continue even one more day in the image Doc and he had created. He was caught betwixt the devil and the deep blue sea, between a rock and the hardest place he had ever known. He needed money, and yet he loved the Widow Martha Jean and could not lie to her.

So there it was. He could either continue to deceive her, which was to betray the object of his affections, or confess his sins and not only lose the money he could and should have pulled from her but lose *her* as well.

To add to his dilemma, there was always the slim possibility that Boyd would return, that he had, indeed, set out to shake down a new or old prospect, perhaps even the chestnut-haired Widow Simms. And if Dad had not pulled his share of the weight, having convinced Doc Boyd that they had to bring in the well, he would then have betrayed his partner.

Even if that partner was the devil himself, Dad had a moral code of sticking to his word. It stuck in his craw that there was, indeed, honor among thieves, and he now counted himself as one of their ilk.

Dad was, in essence, a simple man, and the intricacies of self-delusion were too much for him. He felt as if his brain were about to explode and knew, as he knocked on the Widow Martha Jean Tyler's door, that it was not only his brain that was in jeopardy but his heart that was about to break.

She opened the door, and the smells of her home cooking greeted him warmly. He felt all the more the cad because of it. She had prepared a baked ham worthy of a Christmas dinner, along with potatoes and cheese and okra fried to perfection. The table was set with her finest china and linen napkins, and there were fresh flowers cut from her garden, made even lovelier in the glow of candlelight.

Dad picked at his meal, obviously uneasy. They had been talking about the progress of the oil well, and Dad had assured her that the quality of the Woodbine sand they had pulled up in the cuttings bucket would fulfill the promise first indicated by the dip of his divining rod as well as the petroliferous chart indicating the salt dome, Sabine Incline, Rusk Depression, anticlines, and Yegua and Cook Mountain formations. The prophecy foretold was about to be realized. It lacked only one thing to bring it to fruition.

"And so you see, dear lady," he said, holding Martha Jean's hands and looking into the mountain brook pool of her eyes, "all we need now is for each of our shareholders to chip in another five hundred dollars and…"

That was it. He had come to the fork in the road. He was standing before the abyss. One more step, and he would fall off the edge and sink into the very depths of hell, never to rise again. He stood at the banks of the Rubicon and dared not cross.

The Widow Tyler, noticing his distress, squeezed his hand and said, "Why, David…"

She had long since ceased referring to him as Mr. Everett, and she was not as raucous a type as Lou Della had been, for whom Dad had been "My Davey." No, the Widow Martha Jean Tyler preferred the biblical dignity of David, progenitor of the Messiah. "Why, David," she said, "whatever is the matter?"

"I can't do it," Dad said, pulling away the napkin he had tucked under his shirt collar. "I simply can't do it!"

Martha Jean assumed he was referring to the victuals and that he could not take another bite. She had labored long and hard over the baked ham, used her grandmother's recipe. But still, if his stomach was bothering him or, for some reason, if her cooking did not agree with his system, she certainly would not force the issue. "Well," she said, "if you're not hungry, you don't have to…"

Dad took her hand in his and looked directly into her eyes. "I *am* hungry, madam, but not for food. For the warmth of human companionship that, for once, is not based on a lie."

"I do not know what you mean," said the Widow Tyler.

"I came here tonight to swindle you, Martha Jean."

The Widow Tyler stared at him in shock.

"That oil well you own a part of," Dad said, "we've already sold more than five hundred percent. Your shares are worthless."

It took her what seemed like a misspent lifetime to fully comprehend what the ancient wildcatter had just said. But when the penny dropped, she exclaimed, "You scoundrel!" and withdrew her hand from his as if bitten, suddenly, by a serpent. "You lowlife! You…you…" She searched her vocabulary to describe the conniving, ancient lothario she now realized sat opposite her.

"Two-bit flimflam man," Dad offered.

"You two-bit flimflam man!" the Widow Tyler agreed.

"The only true things I've said," Dad continued, "concern my affections for you. You're the real treasure in life. The tender mercy. And the urgent prayer of the heart."

Martha Jean looked at him in wonder and bewilderment. How could a man admit in the same breath to being a swindler and a liar and then confess with such eloquence his affections for her? Her anger toward him softened at his words. Part of her wanted to reach out and assure him that it must all be some sort of misunderstanding.

Then Dad added, "So if you just write me out a check for five hundred dollars, I'll be on my way."

"You *are* a scoundrel!" Martha Jean Tyler exclaimed, looking at him as if he were not only evil but insane. Her cheeks flushed with color as she all but spat out the words, "I wouldn't give you two cents. Now, you get out of my house, before I…I…"

Dad Everett held up one callused, scarred hand, accepting all her insults but pushing on nonetheless. "If you'll allow me to finish," he said contritely, fishing a thousand dollars from his coat pocket, "I'd like you to write me out a check for five hundred dollars in exchange for this thousand dollars cash. I wouldn't want Boyd to think I came back empty-handed."

Martha Jean just stared at him. He put the money into her hands, gently closing her fingers around the bills. Now it was her turn to be overcome with emotion. If he was a scoundrel, he was a repentant one. And if that were true, perhaps his professed words of affection were not flimflammery nor folderol after all.

The two were silent for a moment. She didn't know what to think, whether to believe him or not, and he didn't know what else he needed to say except to squarely face the practicalities of the matter.

"When we bring that well in," he said, "we'll most likely be arrested for fraud, and I expect they'll send us both up to the big house for the rest of our days. But I want you to know that the last thing I'll whisper on this earthly plane will be your name, Martha Jean, and my last memories will be of the few precious hours I've known in your sweet embrace. I need you to write me out that check now. And I'd appreciate it if you didn't sic the law on us till we bring that well in."

It seemed to Dad Everett and Martha Jean Tyler that they had both found and lost true love in the same instant. A ship had sailed; one of them was left standing on the shore, and the other had a ticket-of-leave, embarking upon a journey that was doomed to end in tragedy.

Later that evening, around about midnight, Doc Boyd wearily climbed the rickety stairs leading up to the spare room above the Dial General Store. He could see that the lantern was still lit, which was odd. Dad Everett would generally have been asleep and snoring in bull moose fashion by this time. Instead, the ancient fat man sat up in bed reading the Good Book, which in itself was passing strange as well.

Dad looked up from his Bible and peered over his spectacles as Doc entered the room. "Where you been for the last day and a half?"

"Told ya," Doc said. "I had some unfinished business."

"With that prospect of yours," Dad said. It wasn't a question; it was a derision.

"That's right," Doc said defensively.

Dad Everett belched loudly, emitting with the sound a noxious odor from the depths of his bowels. "And how'd it pan out?"

Doc sat down on his cot and shucked off his high-top boots. "Dry hole," he said. "How'd you do with the Widow Tyler?"

Dad pulled Martha Jean's check for five hundred dollars from the nightstand and handed it to Doc. "Like I always do," he said, with an air of moral superiority. "I pulled the check. Added it to the pile."

"Uh-huh," said Doc. "So why the long face?"

The two aging con men were silent for a bit. Finally, Dad Everett said, "Must be…heartburn. Or somethin' like it."

"Yeah," Doc said. "Heartburn'll do that to ya."

Chapter 19

In for a penny, in for a pound.

There was no turning back now. Not for Doc nor for Dad. Nor were there any more discussions of what was bound to happen not if but when they brought in the well. The widders, as Dad would say, would all come out of the woodwork, each one showing her signed and sealed certificate, proclaiming that she owned ten, fifteen, or twenty-five percent of the Junipera Sue Number One and Cornville Petroleum Corporation.

The saying "Hell hath no fury like a woman scorned" would be nothing compared to the fury unleashed by women who had not only been scorned but swindled out of their share of the riches both men knew would bubble up from the earth in an unquenchable release of pent-up pressure.

With five hundred percent or more having been sold, two things would be assured. Doc and Dad would be arrested, tried, and convicted for fraud and spend the rest of their lives in the state penitentiary. The widders, likewise, would be confined to spending the rest of their lives in court in an unending attempt to untangle the Gordian knot fashioned by the two aging, lothario oilmen. There would be suits and countersuits, and all of them suits would outlive the widders.

Chapter 19

Thus, no matter how rich the oil strike, no deal would be struck for the sale of the petroleum issuing forth from their well because as long as the company was embroiled in litigation among its shareholders, no one would have the authority to sign any offer, no matter how handsome it might be.

In the meantime, word had already gotten out, as is always the case in the world of the wildcatter, that Horatio Daedalus Boyd, PhD in petroleum engineering, geology, and all matters petroliferous, and Dry Hole Everett had, indeed, hit the Woodbine.

Overnight, it seemed, the population of Cornville, Texas (population 495), doubled, quadrupled, and multiplied itself again with alarming alacrity. Every oil company in North America and pretty much every wildcatter on the continent descended upon the dusty little burg of Cornville, snapping up mineral rights to parched land of dirt-poor farms and hardscrabble ranches.

Oil derricks sprung up within days, like mushrooms in a rainforest after a downpour. Roughnecks and cable-and-tool men flocked to the New Jerusalem that was Cornville, all in a desperate, mad rush to see who would be the first to bring in a gusher and what the size of the sleeping black giant that lay beneath their feet might actually be.

At the Junipera Sue Number One, Doc, Dad, Thurman, Junipera Sue, most of their neighbors, everyone who shopped on credit at their general store, and all *their* cousins, friends, out-of-work relatives, and ne'er-do-well relations worked twenty-four hours a day, bound and determined to bring in the well. Black folk, white folk, Mexicans, even Chinese former railway workers showed up at the Dial Ranch in search of any job that might be had. That, on the surface, might seem perverse, since one and all knew that Doc and Dad's drilling outfit was strictly a poor-boy operation and that no one was being paid any wages at all.

But folks knew, just as well, that Dad and Doc had a mile-long jump on all the big boys. The Texaco and Esso and Humble Oil companies had just gotten there, but Dad and Doc had already hit the Woodbine at thirty-five hundred feet. Thus, no matter how rich their competitors, odds were that the Junipera Sue Number One would be the first well in Cornville to be brought in.

Not only roughnecks and cable-and-tool men but folks who had never worked on a rig a day in their lives descended on the once sleepy hamlet in the hopes of finding some kind of job that would pay any kind of wage. And, with them, came the rougher elements, as tent camps sprang up to accommodate the workers who manned the scores of new derricks going up every day.

There were cardsharps and pickpockets since everyone knew that a workingman was prey to games of chance, and despite the Prohibition Act, whiskey was as plentiful, if not more so, than potable water. Thus, if and when money began to flow along with the oil, the pickpockets and the sharpies stood ready to relieve the newly arrived workers of their just-earned wages.

With the tent camps came tent restaurants, cafeterias, and soup kitchens since the few eating establishments in Cornville could not possibly accommodate the new population. There were tent dance halls, and coveys of soiled doves migrated to the southern climes of Cornville, each and every one of them waiting for that first well to be brought in and holding their breaths lest it turn out to be yet another of Dad Everett's dry holes.

Any man who knew Dad's history and was of the least superstitious nature, which meant pretty well near every roughneck there was, knew that a curse had followed Dad Everett all his life; a dark cloud had rained on every parade that he tried to launch, and this one could turn out just the same.

To say that nerves were on edge would be an understatement. Roughnecks were not called roughnecks because they were timid customers by nature. They were hot-tempered, hardfisted men who took out their frustrations at the least provocation, whether stone-cold sober or staggering under the evil influence of demon rum. Arguments quickly descended into fistfights, and fistfights into melees, until the inevitable stabbing or shooting occurred.

The mayor of Cornville, Donnie Joe Durban, who had at his disposal a grand total constabulary of three potbellied, middle-aged men who had not fired a bullet in anger since the Spanish-American War, dispatched a desperate telegram to the governor of the great state of Texas, which read as follows:

Melees in Cornville Texas due to possible petroleum find STOP Urgently request assistance STOP Please send Texas Rangers STOP signed Donnie Joe Durban Mayor and Acting Chief of Police Cornville Texas.

Durban waited at the telegraph office for any news of aid and comfort that state authorities might be able to afford. And then, the telegraph clicker began to rattle off a response from the state capitol.

Ranger detachment proceeding by rail to Cornville STOP Please meet morning train arriving Cornville 11:20AM STOP Signed Daniel Moody Governor.

Cornville did not actually possess a train station. There was a platform at the edge of town where the train from Dallas made a mail drop, and there was a ticket booth where G. D.

Spradlin sat each day playing solitaire, drinking fortified cups of coffee, and smoking Lucky Strikes. If he sold a dozen tickets in a day, he considered it a sign of mass migration.

The mayor, in his capacity as acting chief of police, appeared with his lead deputy, Jimmy Joe Trebek Quattrochi, known to the locals as Jimmy Q. He was the product of the unlikely union between a French Canadian woman and an Italian immigrant and wore slicked-back hair and a thin mustache of which he was inordinately proud. Donnie Joe and Jimmy Q. checked their pocket watches. It was already past 11:45 when they saw belches of smoke billowing in the distance and then heard the steam whistle blow, announcing the arrival of the 11:20 from Dallas.

The train consisted of an engine, two passenger cars, three boxcars, one flatbed loaded down with building materials, tools, and hoboes, and a caboose. As the engineer applied the brakes and steam blew out in every direction like an erupting Vesuvius, a scruffy-looking horde of humanity poured out of the passenger cars—folks obviously in search of work in the new boomtown. They and the nonpaying passengers who rode the flatbed soon crowded off the platform and melded into the throngs clogging the narrow main thoroughfare of Cornville. Finally, there stepped from one of the passenger cars one of the handsomest men Durban, Jimmy Q., and G. D. Spradlin had ever beheld.

He must've been six foot five and looked to have a muscular build of probably 230 pounds—and not a bit of it fat. He had an olive complexion and jet-black hair, slicked down and parted in the fashion of Rudolph Valentino and certainly was his equal, if not his superior, in his countenance. He wore the khaki uniform and badge of a Texas Ranger, with two crossed, pearl-handled Walker Colts strapped to his sides and a case the size of a viola, which carried a Thompson submachine gun. He was courtly in his appearance and, alighting from the train, put on the Stetson, which he had taken off as a chivalrous mark of respect for the ladies in the passenger car.

Durban and his deputy eagerly approached. If this man was the captain, as they assumed he surely must be, he must have commanded a detachment of rangers to match any of the mighty men of Israel, the warriors of King David himself, come to save their town from certain riotous destruction. The mayor introduced himself, and the ranger looked him straight in the eye.

"I am Captain Enrique Rodriguez."

Jimmy Q. looked as if he recognized the name. "You the one they call 'Lone Wolf' Rodriguez?"

"I don't put much stock in what others call me," answered the ranger captain, returning Jimmy Q.'s gaze.

"I cannot tell you," said the mayor and acting chief of police, "how relieved I am that you and your detachment have arrived. Where are the rest of your men?"

Rodriquez turned his gaze back to the mayor, looking him squarely in the eyes. "I *am* the detachment, Mr. Mayor."

"You've got to be joking!" said Donnie Joe.

"I am not known for a humorous disposition," answered Captain Rodriguez.

"'Lone Wolf,'" whispered Jimmy Q. in a hushed tone of awe.

The mayor and acting chief of police was outraged. "Shut up, Trebek!" He turned back to Captain Rodriguez. "I informed the governor that we have a *riot* here in Cornville! I requested a *detachment* of men, and he sends me only one ranger?"

"You only got one riot," said Rodriguez.

With that, he walked down the platform, spurs jingling against the sound of his footfalls on the wood planks, to one of the boxcars, from which he led a truly magnificent black stallion named Lucky, who not only was festooned with the usual saddlery but, where a Winchester might usually be found, sported a scabbard large enough to encase the Thompson submachine gun. He led the magnificent charger to the mayor and handed him the reins.

"If you will see to the stabling of my horse, I will be much obliged. In the next few days, you will not see me at all. After that, when I deem the moment proper, your troubles in this town will have come to an end."

Having thus spoken, the courtly Spaniard descended from the platform and, within moments, as if by magic, disappeared from sight.

"Lone Wolf," said Jimmy Q. again. "*El Lobo Solitario.*"

"Shut up, Trebek!" Donnie Joe exclaimed, clearly unimpressed with the lawman's moniker.

By the time Captain Rodriguez had arrived by train in response to Donnie Joe Durban's urgent request for assistance, close to a thousand people were turning up on a daily basis at the Dial Ranch, their Model A and Model T Fords lining the dirt road leading to the ranch for a good country mile, waiting, *hoping* that, in the midst of drought and depression, in the vast desert of despair in which most of America was wandering, there would suddenly be a spring of hope.

Now, it will be remembered that pumpjacks of the day were steam powered, which meant boilers, and that meant wood. And that's where the big boys stood the chance of eliminating the competition that Dad and Doc so clearly represented. They simply bought up every last stick of firewood available from Mule Chute all the way to Dallas and everything in between. Those were the sad tidings that Tanner Irving Sr. delivered from his empty Model A truck.

"Doc," he said, "Dad, there's not another stick around to be had for love or money. I'm sorry. I don't know where y'all are gonna find any more wood. The big companies done went and bought it all up."

"Jehoshaphat!" said Dad Everett. "Why didn't ya hide some? Squirrel it away, or…If we can't feed that boiler, this rig shuts down!"

"I'm sorry, Mr. Everett. There just ain't no more wood, and that's all there is to it."

Dad threw his well-worn fedora to the ground and kicked it, as if it were the mangy dog responsible for the recurring nightmare of his life. "We're this close to bringing this well in," said Dad, "and you're gonna tell me for lack of firewood, we're gonna shut down? This is Burkburnett and Spindletop all over again!"

At the mere mention of those names, a gasp of terror arose in the crowd among all those who knew the legend and curse of Dry Hole Everett.

Just then, however, Horatio Daedalus Boyd fell back on his exalted medical career as the inventor of Dr. Enrique Alonzo's Miracle Elixir of Life. He leapt up onto the oil rig with an alacrity belying his years and, half country preacher, half snake oil salesman, called out to the crowd: "Now, y'all listen to me! If we bring this well in, it'll blow black gold out over each and every one of us. And there'll be more jobs paying good wages here than you can shake a stick at, and your general store will rival Sears an' Roebuck," he said to Thurman and Junipera Sue. "But none of that's gonna happen if this rig shuts down."

"But we can't make wood appear by magic, Doc," Thurman protested. "There just ain't any!"

"There's no wood," Doc answered, "but I see some rubber out there, and that burns just as good!"

"Whatever are you talkin' about?" Junipera Sue asked plaintively.

"I'll tell you what I'm talkin' about," Doc cried, falling into the familiar patter that had sold countless caseloads of Dr. Enrique Alonzo's Miracle Elixir of Life. "You got tires on your cars and on your trucks, don't ya?" he called out to the gathered throng. "Well, if we don't bring this well in, you're not gonna have any place worth goin' to nor any money to pay for gasoline to get you there. You want this well to come in, don't ya?"

A mighty roar of affirmation went up from the crowd.

"Well then," Doc continued, beginning to strut back and forth across the rig, like a country preacher searching out lost souls to save. "The fruit that the good Lord has provided for us isn't gonna just fall off of the vines into your mouths so you can lap it up. You've got to get up off your backside and *work* for it. That's right! You gotta sacrifice, just like the Israelites of old did in the holy temple of Jerusalem. And this rig right here is the altar, and I'm grabbin' hold of the horns. The tires on your automobiles are the lambs and bullocks and sheaves of wheat. And it's time to tithe, by heavens! Because the good Lord, in all his good grace and mercy, will help only those who help them*selves*. Now, I want every man, woman, and child within the sound of my voice this mornin' to get down on your hands and your knees and not only pray for his grace and his love and his mercy and his guidance but pull out those jacks and lug wrenches and strip those tires off those Model As and

Model Ts. Because we bring this well in, and you'll all be drivin' Cadillacs and Doozies!"

No one in the crowd moved.

"What are you lookin' at me for?" Doc said. "Are we gonna bring this well in? Or turn our backs on the bounty that the good Lord has laid out before us and risk his almighty wrath and righteous indignation? Ezekiel 25:17 says, 'I will execute great vengeance on them with wrathful rebukes. Then they will know that I am the Lord, when I lay my vengeance upon them.' You willin' to risk that, brothers and sisters?"

"*No!*" shouted the crowd as one.

"Then, somebody, please give me an amen and start strippin' off them tires!"

"*Amen!*" shouted the congregation of farmers and shopkeepers, the homeless and the out of work. And, as one, almost a thousand people began stripping the rubber off their automobiles, and a kind of assembly line was formed of tires tossed up and passed hand to hand, up to Doc and Thurman and Tanner. Dad and Tanner took a hacksaw to the tires, but big Thurman just ripped them in two with all the fury he felt at the cruel banditos who had so cowardly attacked him outside of Juarez and the cloud of confusion that buzzed about his brain like so many noisy swarms of flies every time he tried to retrieve a memory of Doc or Dad or the gypsy fortune teller who prophesied riches fifty paces from the lone cottonwood tree.

As the men fed the sections of tire into the boiler, black smoke belched forth, and the flames licked higher. As the boiler heated up and steam poured out, the flywheel began to turn, and the oil rig began to pump once more.

Black folks, white folks, Chinese, Mexicans—all working together. And some might have thought it was greed that united them, but it was more like a tiny window had opened in the heavens. And, led by the Reverend Doctor Boyd, they realized that they were all gonna sink or swim together.

Chapter 20

In the two days following the arrival of El Lobo Solitario and the almost miraculous tithing of automobile tires by the throngs who had crowded around the Junipera Sue Number One at the Dial Ranch, no one in Cornville saw a trace of the tall and handsome captain of the Texas Rangers, Enrique Rodriguez.

A veritable tent city had sprung up on the outskirts of Cornville. There were tent dormitories, tent bawdy houses and dance halls, tent barbershops and Chinese laundries, tent bath houses, tent eating establishments for every taste—from chop suey to T-bone steak. There were tent purveyors of dry goods. Work gloves and boots were at a premium.

The tent city now dwarfed the clapboard storefronts and raised sidewalks of the original town. It was here that the newly arrived masses of workingmen congregated, in search of news of who was hiring and where and to blow off steam, engage in games of chance, drink illicit hooch, and carouse in an ill-mannered fashion throughout all hours of the day and night.

Pickpockets flourished and newly robbed men swore vengeance, searching out the perpetrators and, more often than not, assaulting some innocent soul who simply conformed to their image of an itinerant thief.

Racial tensions flared, but it was more the tension of single men, lean and hungry, without the civilizing influence of hearth and home, church, or any of the other trappings of civilization to gentle their behavior. No respectable woman ventured into the new tent-and-shanty town. More distressing still to the citizens of Cornville, the rougher elements spilled out from the confines of the tent city and made them feel like strangers, unsafe in their own little town.

Drunkards staggered about, openly inebriated, insulting womenfolk and men alike with their rude behavior. Hidden within this powder keg waiting to explode, this veritable pot of seething humanity waiting to boil over, were various bums and panhandlers, passed out or pleading for alms, some within their own filth; the flotsam and jetsam of humanity washed up on the hitherto welcoming shores of Cornville.

Now nothing in life is as invisible as a bum: a drunken panhandler passed out on the street or stretching forth an upturned palm in search of a handout. It is almost instinctual that men and women of every ilk, respectable and disreputable alike, avert their eyes from such creatures. In Cornville, some avoided the pleading stare because they saw in their visage a portent of what they, themselves, might become. Others simply looked the other way so as not to be bothered by the raggedy beggar who pleaded for a few coins, a shekel or two, a few pence with which to hold body and soul together for but another day.

When the vagrant reeked of whiskey mixed in with the malodorous stench of hopeless poverty, the passersby, whether townsfolk or roughnecks, averted their gaze all the more readily, for they knew that any donation they might offer would only end up going for drink.

Chapter 20

Thus, when a new bum in ragged clothes, mud-caked as if he had drunkenly pitched face-first into the muck and mire of the tent city or, worse still, soiled himself after a night's carousing fueled with bathtub gin or moonshine, stumbled along the dusty streets of Cornville and the new tent sin city that metastasized around it, not a single soul noticed. The lanky bum panhandled from this person or that, then tripped over his own feet, then seemed content to lie there, where he had fallen, until he had sufficient strength to rise again in search, perhaps, of a new street corner on which to beg.

Despite the man's stature and because of the fact that he seemed to lean into the wind as he walked, thus dwarfing himself, he was, as all bums are, nearly invisible to those around him. In the next forty-eight hours, he traversed every inch of every street and alleyway, each dusty corridor of old Cornville and new, all the wooden storefronts and those that sprouted up cloaked in canvas.

Though no one noticed him, he made note of every person he saw. His torn and dusty hat was pulled low over his eyes, masking the fact that he marked each passerby with an expert and steely gaze. This one was a cardsharp; that one, a thief. This, a pickpocket, and that, his accomplice. Such miscreants worked in teams, with one relieving the unsuspecting worker of their wallet and then slipping it, in a lightning flash, to the accomplice, who passed in the opposite direction.

The raggedy bum saw them all and made mental note.

After forty-eight hours, the bum was nowhere to be seen. He no longer staggered along the raised sidewalks nor wallowed in the dirt outside the tented gambling parlors. He had vanished as suddenly as he had appeared, and having been invisible the entire time, his absence went as unnoticed as his presence had been.

In the wee hours of the night, before dawn was breaking, when the last of the carousers were headed to the newfound dormitory or open field to sleep it off and before the morning shifts appeared for early breakfasts and the day's labors began, the bum was there once again, only this time engaged in a new occupation that, as before, went completely unseen.

He affixed a steel cable to a hitching rail and, walking as if made unsteady by drink, ambled his way down the long stretch of what passed for road extending from the old Cornville to the new. Every twenty yards or so, he secured the length of cable to a new hitching rail or pillar, until he had anchored this thin line of steel braid, which stretched almost a quarter mile from one end to another.

Despite his stumblings, it took no more than half an hour before the steel cable was in place and immovable. Those who encountered it, most of them inebriated themselves, simply cursed it as a nuisance and crawled under it or hiked themselves over it, never questioning for an instant what utility it might serve.

That evening there appeared on the outskirts of the tent city a new figure of a man who was far from invisible. He was a khaki-clad captain of the Texas Rangers, and at six foot five, atop his black stallion, he appeared to be the Lord's vengeance come to earth.

He trotted out into the middle of the street, a billy club dangling from his wrist, and, with an eagle's eye, identified those he had marked and committed to memory during the previous two days. Without a word, he wheeled his horse down upon them and felled them with his billy club. Within minutes, there were literally dozens of unconscious miscreants scattered about the streets. He chased some into a tent gambling den, where easily a hundred men had crowded around the illicit gaming tables, openly imbibing the outlawed hooch.

"My name," he shouted to one and all, "is Enrique Rodriguez. I am a captain in the Texas Rangers. And this all ends—now!"

So saying and without a moment's warning, he spurred his horse inside the canvas gaming house and felled three men, then wheeled around and pointed at half a dozen more.

"On your knees, hands locked behind your heads!" he said to the men he was pointing at with the billy club, simultaneously shifting it to his left hand.

"Or what?" said a drunken giant of a man, reaching his hand for the .45 tucked inside his belt.

In a lightning move, the Lone Wolf had but to apply his knee to the stallion's flank to turn him into position, and then he drew out, from one of the crossed holsters, his Walker Colt and shot the man's kneecap, exploding it and sending him crying to the floor.

"Or that," the captain said. "Any other takers?"

The bad men in the canvas den of iniquity looked at one another and then at the lone lawman astride the horse.

"There's a hundred of us and one of you, you tinhorn! You think you can take us all on?" shouted a drunken, redheaded ogre, brandishing a bowie knife.

With that, the drunken crowd seemed to gird up its loins as one and surge forward, surrounding the Lone Wolf. But he hesitated not a moment, returning the smoking Colt to its holster and pulling the Thompson submachine gun from its scabbard like a knight of old brandishing his sword. Though none could see it, its wooden stock was engraved with the balanced scales of justice. He thumbed the safety off and let go a burst that stitched through the canvas rooftop and shattered the air with its roar of rapid fire, then leveled it at the surging crowd around him.

"I reckon I can," he said.

Then he spurred Lucky, who leapt up over a craps table. Men flung themselves to the ground in terror of the almost fire-breathing steed. He bore down upon the ginger-haired ogre and swung the Tommy gun like a polo player's mallet, ripping open his chin, lifting him up off his feet, and sending him crashing back to earth unconscious. He gazed down at the bleeding man who lay there twitching in the mud, his blood, and the beer soaking into the dirt floor. Then he turned to address the ginger ogre's comrades.

"I don't tolerate coarseness in a man," he said.

So it went, throughout the night.

The Lone Wolf had packed hundreds of pairs of hand-cuffs into his saddlebags. And, as dawn broke, 123 criminals awakened with aching heads and gaping wounds to find them-selves shackled to Lone Wolf's trotline.

He rode down the street, addressing one and all.

"These criminal elements will spend twenty-four hours on my trotline with neither food nor water. At the end of that time, they will be set free. If I ever see them again in this town, they will live to regret it, I promise you. If you are a miscre-ant, there is no place for you here. You have four hours to leave Cornville. Use it! Or you will meet the business end of one of the tools of law enforcement at my disposal. There will be no blessing in it for you. If you are an itinerant, get a job or get out of town. The gin joints and bawdy houses exist no more for you.

Chapter 20

Any person who offers one of the criminal elements on my trotline food or drink will be arrested by me for interfering with a peace officer. You have all been forewarned! Govern yourselves accordingly."

Donnie Joe Durban and Jimmy Q. looked on in horrified silence.

Finally, Mayor Durban spoke. He was a churchgoing man, familiar with the Scriptures, and he spoke from Revelation 6 as if seeing prophecy unfold before him. "And I looked, and behold, a black horse! And its rider had a pair of scales in his hand...And I looked, and behold, a pale horse! And its rider's name was Death, and Hades followed him."

As Mayor Donnie Joe Durban beheld the black horse and he who held the pair of balances in his hand, black smoke billowed out of the boiler that fueled the oil rig at the Junipera Sue Number One.

A thousand men and women had worked for two full days and nights straight in a kind of delirium. They had stripped the tires from hundreds of automobiles, cut them up, and fed them into what looked like the fires of hell. All of them were besmudged in black soot, their hair and faces covered in a kind of tar. Their eyes were bloodshot, and when they coughed, their spittle and phlegm was thick and black.

The big arm on the drilling rig moved relentlessly up and down, the drill bit driving farther and farther down into the crusty core of the earth, which would not yet yield its treasure, it seemed, without a mighty struggle.

After two days and nights, the men felt as if their arms could lift no more. They were beyond needing sleep. Their bodies shook with fatigue and hunger.

Junipera Sue Dial had gone back and forth to the general store and emptied it of every edible provision she had. She and the other women had made endless plates of griddle cakes, fried eggs, and sandwiches of hardtack and jerky. Every can of beans had been boiled and eaten, every sack of cornmeal baked into cornbread and consumed.

And still, there was no sign of the prophesied oil. All eyes drifted toward Dad Everett, as if he were the cursed Jonah on the boat bound for Nineveh, who had incurred the wrath of the Lord. He was the Ancient Mariner, with albatrosses slung about his neck, and their names were Spindletop and Burkburnett.

The stench of burning tires was the smell of despair and failure. Even Doc had run out of words with which to urge his followers forward. The pile of cut and chopped tires, which had stood almost as tall as the derrick itself, had dwindled down to but a dozen pieces.

It was midday, and the late-summer sun beat down on broken bodies without a hint of mercy. Junipera Sue and the other women had made lemonade and coffee, and that, too, was gone. But half a glass remained of sooty water, resting atop an oil drum next to the derrick. Sullen men smoked what cigarettes they had left, covered in the smoke of burning tires and defeat and hopelessness.

And the well pump, as if to mock them, continued.

Up and down.

Up and down.

Up...and...down.

It was Junipera Sue who saw it first. Her beloved husband, Thurman, the modern-day Lazarus risen from the dead, who had wandered five years through his own personal desert of the Sinai toward his promised land of Cornville, had spent all the wrath and fury in his giant's body that he had felt toward the banditos who had robbed him of half a decade of his life with his beloved Junipera Sue ripping tires to shreds barehanded until his hands, as well, were shredded, bleeding, and black as coal. Junipera Sue lovingly tended them. He was too tired to even wince in pain as she cleaned and bandaged his wounds.

And then, she saw the half-full glass of smoky water atop the oil drum, beside the derrick. It shook, ever so slightly, as if someone had merely bumped into the oil drum upon which the glass now rested. There were ripples on the surface at first.

Tanner Irving stood next to her and saw it as well. She reached out and touched his hand and pointed, and Thurman saw it too. Saw the water begin to vibrate. And Tanner Irving Sr. recalled the spiritual of his youth.

> Waaade in the water.
> Waaade in the water, children!
> Waaade in the water!
> God's gonna trouble the waaater!

The shaking grew more violent still.

The water in the glass tipped to and fro and spilled out its contents as if on a ship overcome by stormy and troubled waters, and they all began to feel it. The earth trembling beneath their feet. The low rumble, building into a roar.

Doc and Dad looked at one another. Doc had never beheld such a thing before, but Dad knew it well. And suddenly, the old, fat man was on his feet. "Put out those cigarettes!" he shouted. "Put 'em out now! Seal that boiler up, unhook it, and detach it from the rig! Get it out of here! She's gonna blow!"

Instantly sensing the danger that could, quite literally, explode and blow them all to fiery smithereens, the seasoned roughnecks sealed the boiler, cut the canvas belt, lifted up the hitch, and pushed the boiler's wagon wheels as far and as fast as they could away from the rig, whose rickety boards began to splinter now.

And with that, blow she did, like the most monstrous leviathan spouting up from the deepest, darkest seas in fury! First, the gas, which blew open the seal and cast the drilling platform into the air as if it were a pile of matchsticks. And then, suddenly, the black gold spout that shot, like a volcano, Dad would later say, at least 250 feet into the air, as men and women fell on their knees to pray and others danced. Doc himself simply stretched out his arms, looked into the sky, and allowed himself to be washed, baptized, bathed, and anointed in holy oil.

Chapter 21

"Secrecy, my dear," whispered Doc Boyd to the Widow Clara Fern Cochrane, who had purchased what she thought amounted to fifteen percent of the Junipera Sue Number One and the Cornville Petroleum Corporation.

"Whyever so?" Clara Fern asked, with wide-eyed wonder. "Horatio, I should think you would want me to shout it from the rooftops." Then, she lowered her voice into equally hushed tones and continued. "I don't know if you are aware of it or not, but there have been vicious rumors, baseless gossip I am sure, spread by virtueless busybodies, jealous, I am certain, of the affections you have shown me, that you are some kind of flim-flam man and not any kind of doctor of geology at all."

"No!" Doc said in disbelief and horror.

"*Yes!*" she replied. "Wicked tongues, trying to vilify and defame your name, have tried suggesting that you are not all that you appear to be."

"I am shocked to my very core, madam, to the very core of my innermost being, that anyone might suggest such a thing! And if ever there was the *slightest* concern on your part that there was the *tiniest* iota of truth to such scurrilous accusations, then the bringing in of the Junipera Sue Number One will have laid all doubt—"

"Oh," said Clara Fern, "I could never doubt you! You are so forthright and, if anything, too modest."

"No one abides a braggart," Doc said with pious and solemn modesty.

"Which is all the more reason I should think you should want me to trumpet your virtues to the heavens. To stop those wagging tongues."

Doc held the Widow Clara Fern Cochrane's hands, looked into her eyes, and said, "You are too kind, madam. But secrecy and discretion are what are called for now. For your own good, not for mine."

"I don't understand," said the Widow Cochrane.

"My dear," Doc gently explained, "it is one thing to discover oil. And, from all appearances, we have discovered what may well be one of the single greatest oil strikes in the history of our fair land." (Indeed, what Doc did not know and would learn only in the months to come was that he and Dad had, in fact, spudded in the single greatest oil strike not only in the history of the continental United States but in the entire world.) "But," he continued, "it is one thing to discover oil and quite another to make the most profitable deal for all our shareholders."

"I am afraid," said Clara Fern, "that I am completely untutored in the ways of commerce."

"And that is why I am here to advise you, dear lady. I'm an oilman. I like to think of myself as an oilman who looks after his family. And our little company, and you in particular, are family indeed. Despite the size of our oil strike, we are a small company. More like…a family business."

"I feel as if we are family, Horatio! The dearest of families."

"As do I," said Doc Boyd, reassuring her with a pat on her plump hand. "But we lack the wherewithal to market our petroleum ourselves. We have not nor can we afford to build, at this stage, a pipeline with which to transport our black gold to ports of call. Deals must be struck with railways. It would be more profitable for us, by far, to wait for the large oil companies to come to us and make us an offer. We must act the part of kings even though, compared to the Rockefellers and robber barons of the world, we are but paupers. That, of course, will all change. But only once we have succeeded in making the most profitable deal. However, if you began to trumpet the fact that you own fifteen percent, soon enough, someone else who owns ten or fifteen percent will begin to brag about their success as well."

"What's the harm in that?" Clara Fern asked innocently. "I couldn't be prouder of what you and Mr. Everett have accomplished."

"The harm, dear lady," said Doc, "is that our strength lies in our anonymity. Right now, if John D. Rockefeller himself wants to make a deal with us, he has to come to me. And though I cannot match his fortune, I assure you, I am every bit his equal when it comes to business acumen. But if he or his nefarious agents were to know the names of individual stockholders, they could go to someone who owns ten, fifteen percent and pick it up for mere peanuts, which, I assure you, is what they'll try to do!"

"Mere peanuts," Clara muttered to herself, mulling over the prospect of some virtueless busybody underselling that which might make her a fortune.

"If that were to happen," Doc continued, "heaven forbid, they could pick up a controlling interest in our company, and you would be offered pennies on the dollar. That is why secrecy and discretion are our crucial allies at this most sensitive juncture."

Dad and Doc would repeat this sage advice to all the widows, almost word for word, over the next twenty-four hours. Their greatest fear was not John D. Rockefeller or the robber barons; their greatest fear was the Texas Rangers and, especially, the six-foot, five-inch captain who was now the law in Cornville. They knew that, if the widows began blabbing, they would soon discover that Doc and Dad had oversubscribed not only their shares but also their affections.

Both men were also wise enough to know that, despite their admonitions, human nature being what it was, it was only a matter of time before the widders did begin to come out of the woodwork, waving their stock certificates like banners on a marble arch, and with that, the law would soon follow.

They were under no illusions that they would be able to strike any deal with anyone. What they needed, and needed fast, was getaway money. To say that it was frustrating that they were penniless when they were sitting atop a fortune was to understate the obvious. They figured they had fewer than forty-eight hours in which to make their getaway, and though any restaurant or store in town would extend them credit, the truth was that the two men could not rub two cents together.

Having spent the bulk of their day trying to keep the widders in line and silent, Dad and Doc retired in the late afternoon to New Dugan's for cups of fortified coffee, which the proprietor, one Timothy Sean Michael Ignatius Miguel Joaquin Emiliano Reilly O'Sullivan, offered up on the house.

Timothy O'Sullivan was the child of an Irish immigrant from County Clare and a Mexican Irish descendant of a union reputed to have been between a Spanish maiden and John Reilly himself, founder of the Saint Patrick's Brigade of the Mexican army, which consisted mainly of Irish deserters from the American army during the Mexican-American War of 1846. Reilly most famously commanded the battalion at the Battle of Churubusco, where he was captured, court-martialed, and branded with the letter *D* for Deserter on his cheek. Though vilified in the United States, he was a hero in Mexico and fell in love with the beautiful, dark-eyed, virtuous lass, who bore him a child before they could marry. Thus, O'Sullivan could proudly claim a distinguished family lineage from four different sources: Irish Catholic and Mexican immigrants, an American deserter, and a Mexican national hero. As far as O'Sullivan was concerned, it didn't get more American nor more Texan than that.

There were, of course, those who disputed that interpretation, as Texas memories run long. All of that endeared him even more to Doc and Dad. Being con men, they had a natural affinity for mutts and underdogs. Like his establishment, they referred to him as New Dugan. O'Sullivan's philosophy was he didn't much care what you called him so long as you paid in cash. He did not carry tabs or extend credit.

"Your money is no good here," O'Sullivan New Dugan said in his exaggerated, counterfeit Irish brogue. "Sure, and you men have made me prosper a hundredfold. Order anyt'ing you like. It's an honor to be able to serve yas, squires."

Dad and Doc had T-bone steaks and what New Dugan assured them was a sampling of his private stock of Canadian whiskey in their coffee cups and Cuban cigars rumored to have been hand rolled on the thighs of virgin maidens in far-off Havana and offered only to New Dugan's finest customers.

While it was true that the two men had enjoyed the meal, the libations, and the smokes, they were in desperate straits as to what to do next.

That is when they noticed the saddest of caravans passing by on the street outside. Scores of Black sharecroppers, with their belongings piled high on rickety wagons drawn by horses more accustomed to pulling plows than wagonloads of goods, made their way down Cornville's main street and headed out of town. Among them, Dad and Doc recognized Tanner Irving Sr. While Dad beheld what was evidently human tragedy, Doc smelled opportunity.

"Come with me," he said. And the two men walked out the swinging saloon doors of New Dugan's, tipping their hats to the gracious proprietor, who waved them happily on their way and thanked them again for the honor of their patronage.

Doc approached Tanner Irving and said, "Well, what's goin' on here, Tanner? Where you folks all headed?"

The wood carter and fellow shareholder in Cornville Petroleum shook his head in sorrow and stared momentarily at his shoes. He knew that he, personally, was about to make a fortune and did not relish having to say the words he knew he was about to speak. But, at the same time, he was overcome with grief at the fate that had befallen the other members of his race and, by association with Doc and Dad, for which he felt no small amount of guilt himself. He looked up from his shoes, first at Dad and then Doc, and spoke directly to the two men. He spoke not with recrimination, but there was nonetheless a streak of ill-hidden bitterness in his voice.

"You said the oil strike would be a blessing."

"Well, it will be," Dad said, "just as soon as we conclude the business deal for the disposition of our petroleum."

Chapter 21

"And," said Doc, "that's just the *first* well. Why, we'll be spudding in *dozens* of wells on the Dial Ranch! And that'll be just like owning our very own bank or, better yet, your own printing press, spitting out nothing but greenbacks. Now, if you don't call that a blessing, I don't know what you'd call it."

"Well," said Irving, "it's a fact that my missus and me will make out just fine because of those stock certificates you paid me with."

"Smartest deal any man ever made," Doc said. "Trading firewood for gold!"

"Yes, sir. And don't think my missus and me aren't thankful for it. We're gonna be able to give our son things we never dreamed of. He and his children are gonna have better lives because of it too." Then Tanner looked at the sad caravan making its way out of town. "But for the rest of these Black folk around here, this whole thing has been a curse."

"A curse?" said Dad.

"You call prosperity a curse?" Doc asked. "What do you mean?"

"Not a one of them is sharing in that prosperity," Tanner said. "All these folks were sharecroppers. Worked the land for as long as anybody can remember. But now the oil companies come in, bought up all the mineral rights, and instead of crops, they're plantin' derricks. And all the jobs are goin' to white folks. White folks who just got here and never lived a day of their lives in Cornville until this strike came through."

Dad and Doc looked at the sad procession of the dispossessed that paraded before them, having made their way from their side of town to its extremities. Where they would go from here was anybody's guess. By all appearances, all they had left in life were the meager belongings piled high on their rickety wagons pulled by their beasts of burden. Tanner followed their gaze and said, looking at his people, "I thought it was hard times before. But these folks got nothin' now."

"Well, that's a downright shame," Dad said. "But you can't blame it on us."

"Ain't nobody blamin' nobody," said Tanner Irving. "Just tellin' the truth."

Horatio Daedalus Boyd knew only too well that one man's misfortune could be another man's salvation. And he was determined, at all costs, to always be that other man.

"Tanner," said Doc. "Give me a second to have a chat with Mr. Everett, here. I've been struck by your remarks, sir, and by the sight of this...this tragic migration. If Dad and I have, unwittingly, been the cause of these folks' tribulation, there may be a way that we can contribute to a solution to all their problems."

"I don't rightly see how that could be," said Tanner Irving in despair. "These folks worked the land, and the land around here's fillin' up with oil rigs, not crops to harvest. They're gonna have to go a good long ways from the only home most of 'em have ever known. Hard enough tryin' to be a farmer with this drought. Now they gotta move on. Hard times. Harder than ever now."

"Maybe yes and maybe no," Doc said. "Let me and Dad have a chat."

With that, Doc put an arm around Dad's shoulder and led him to the opposite side of the street, where white shopkeepers, here and there, watched in stony silence as the sad parade of Black refugees passed them by. Doc led Dad into the shade of an overhang in front of the Chinese laundry. He spoke in hushed tones so that none might hear.

Chapter 21

"These Black folks might just be the answer to our prayer."

"How so?" Dad asked.

"They just might be the getaway money we need."

"What are you talkin' about?"

Doc patted Dad on the back. "Just back me up."

Doc knew that he didn't have to say a word more than that. He and Dad had been working their con for so many years that one man had but to begin a sentence and the other could finish it. One would lie, and the other swear to it. Doc led Dad back across the street to Tanner Irving. And now he spoke with a loud enough voice that the other Black folk could hear him as well.

"Well, Mr. Irving," Doc said, his voice booming for one and all to hear. "This is an abomination!" He looked around as if there were a crowd he could gather to whom he might be able to sell a bottle or two of Dr. Enrique Alonzo's fabled Miracle Elixir of Life. "That's exactly what this is, sir. An abomination! Your people are being driven off their land just like the ancient Israelites being taken into the Babylonian exile."

Tanner Irving couldn't figure out why Doc had begun to preach in the street on a weekday, and he was a shrewd enough man to know that Dr. Boyd was something more complex than he had heretofore encountered. Nonetheless, he said, "Yes, sir. That's just what it's like." And, as he said it, as if they were congregants in the First Church of Horatio Daedalus Boyd, several of the passing sharecroppers mumbled, "Amen."

Doc put an arm around Tanner Irving. The gesture did not go unnoticed by either the white or the Black folk whose attention was being drawn to the man who had just brought in what they all knew was the secret to their future prosperity.

Some of the white workers took offense at the familiarity with which Doc treated his wood carter partner. Tanner Irving took neither offense nor comfort from the gesture. He instinctively reached his hand back to see if he still had his wallet.

"Now, let me ask you something, Mr. Irving," Doc said loudly, addressing his partner with the greatest respect. "As I recall, you folks have a little church on the edge of town. Is that right?"

As he spoke the words, Doc snuck a look at Dad. Dad smiled the softest of smiles, not broad enough to betray himself to Tanner Irving or any of the onlookers, but simply to let his partner know he now comprehended which way the wind was blowing. The two men had a psychic Morse code, and the message had just been sent and received.

For his part, Tanner Irving was now wary of both men. Something just didn't seem right. But then, he recollected, neither did the lady on Doc's diploma, whom Doc had sworn was the Greek goddess Petrolia. He and Della May had their doubts about the authenticity of that degree, but there was absolutely no doubting the gusher that Doc and Dad had brought in, exactly as they had predicted. Thus, Irving was torn between an innate feeling in his gut and the memories of the black gold that had spouted 250 feet high and promised his wife and son a better life than anything they could ever have hoped for.

"That's right," Tanner said. "The Beth El Baptist Church is on our side of town."

"Mm-hmm," Doc said. "And I'll bet that's where your son goes to Sunday school."

"Yes, sir. Della May makes sure of that."

Doc nodded vigorously, in approval of the religious guidance Mr. and Mrs. Irving were providing their firstborn child. That's when Dad instinctively picked up his end of the routine.

Chapter 21

"Now let me ask you a question, Mr. Irving. Do you folks own that church?"

"We do," said Tanner Irving.

Suddenly the procession of refugees came to a halt. Doc and Dad had proved themselves, at least insofar as bringing in the well was concerned. The law of unintended consequences had forced the refugees off their land, but there was no denying the expertise of the two white men with whom Tanner Irving was now engaged in conversation.

"Now, when you say *own*," Doc asked, "does that mean that you've got a formal deed to the building?"

"I know what *own* means, Doc. And the answer is yes. We do."

"And," asked Dad, "does the deed cover the land that's *under* that building?"

"It does," replied Tanner.

"Any bank loans?" Doc asked.

"You know of any bank around here that would make a loan to Black folks?"

"Can't say as how I do," Doc responded evenly.

"We own it, free and clear."

"No mortgage and no liens?" Dad persisted.

"Free and clear," Tanner answered again.

He had no idea what these two were getting at. But Doc and Dad exchanged subtle glances. They both now knew that they were onto something, and that something was getaway money.

"Well, that's all I need to know, Mr. Irving," Doc said, with a lilt in his voice that betrayed the preacher in him. "If you organize your congregation to meet with us there tonight,

I promise you, we're gonna have us the most sensational prayer meeting you ever did see."

It was now Tanner Irving's turn to speak in hushed tones. "Doc, I gotta tell ya," he said, barely over a whisper. "Most of the Black folks in this town hold you and Dad to blame for what's happened to them. Whether that's fair or not, they say if that well hadn't come in, they'd still be on their land. You might want to think twice about that prayer meeting. Folks are feelin' bloody."

Dad and Doc simultaneously felt a shiver run down their spines. It was a bold statement to make, but Tanner Irving felt compelled to impress upon Doc and Dad the seriousness of the situation and the very real danger to which they might be exposing themselves. It was not merely out of concern for them; the repercussions that his community would suffer if things got out of hand were too awful to contemplate.

But Doc Boyd was undeterred. Indeed, he smiled now like the cat who had caught the canary. "You just get that congregation in the pews, Mr. Irving. The Lord is my rock and my shield, and yea, though I walk through the valley of the shadow of death, I will fear no evil."

This time none of the people within earshot answered amen.

Chapter 22

The Beth El Baptist Church was a ramshackle, slat-board affair in the Black part of town. It had been built with the sweat and toil of its congregants, and the love with which they had constructed it belied the lack of funds and expensive building materials. It was a construction made entirely of wood, not just the floor, walls, and ceiling but the pews and pulpit. Moreover, the wood that they had chosen they picked not for its durability nor for its aesthetics.

The Right Reverend Reese, founding pastor of the Beth El Baptist Church, was a large man with a booming baritone voice who had been raised as a Pentecostal at the Church of God in Christ, which had been founded some thirty years before, give or take, by Bishop Charles Harrison Mason, who believed in making a joyful noise before the Lord and was remarkably progressive for the time in allowing women to both sing and teach and preach in church. Indeed, singing and dancing in praise were as integral to the Church of God in Christ as speaking in tongues while feeling the Holy Spirit.

Now, it so happened that, at the time of the petroleum strike, Mother Katie Bell Nubin, one of the best-known evangelical gospel singers of the time and a mandolin player of some renown, and her daughter, Sister Rosetta Nubin, had been playing a Pentecostal revival in Dallas. When word got out that the largest oil strike in the history of the country had been found in Cornville, Reverend Reese, who had known Mother Katie Bell for years, asked her and her daughter to make the trip to the Beth El Baptist Church in order to lift the spirits of the sharecropper congregants who were being forced off the land to make room for a different kind of crop: a crop made out of oil derricks.

Sister Rosetta Nubin had been performing since the age of six. She was a child prodigy: a singing and guitar-playing miracle in an age when women hardly played the guitar at all. Rosetta had started out as Little Rosetta Nubin, but now, as a young woman of fourteen, she performed as Sister Rosetta Nubin alongside her mother, and she had made a joyful noise before her Lord and Savior and made the congregation of the Beth El Baptist Church forget their troubles and remember their Creator.

Thus it was that, on the night that Brother Irving had requested of Reverend Reese that Dr. Horatio Daedalus Boyd be allowed to address the congregation, Mother Katie Bell and Sister Rosetta were still in residence.

Reverend Reese held no truck with Doc Boyd. He regarded him as the spawn of the devil and the progenitor of all the misfortunes of his congregation—and himself because as the congregation shrank, it could no longer support a preacher. So if Doc Boyd was looking for a friend that night, he would not find one in the Right Reverend.

Reverend Reese had agreed to allow the so-called doctor of all matters petroliferous to address his congregation on the condition that he would be the one to introduce him. And he intended to give a proper introduction at that.

He turned to Sister Rosetta and said, "Child, I'm gonna ask you to do something you ain't never done before. You play and you sing and you play to accompany other peoples' singin'. But tonight, Sister, I want you to play what I preach. You listen to me and let the sound of my voice be like one of the bass strings of that L-5 Gibson guitar of yours, and you pick up the lead."

Sister Rosetta was delighted at the prospect. There had been piano players who had accompanied preachers, but she had never seen a guitar do it in her life, not even at the giant Church of God in Christ temple in Chicago. So when Doc Boyd and Dad Everett pulled up in their Model A convertible and stood in the entryway, Reverend Reese took to the pulpit and nodded at Sister Rosetta.

A hush fell over the congregation. It was a hot, humid night in East Texas, the sultry kind in which the sweat just seems to roll off you no matter how much you fan yourself. Reverend Reese took out his handkerchief and wiped the sweat away from his brow, held the handkerchief in his hand, closed his eyes, and let out a low, long moan, like a man in mourning. Like someone who had lost the dearest thing that life had to offer.

"Mm-hmm…"

His baritone vibrated off the walls and through the pews. Sister Rosetta could feel it resonating against her body as she held that Gibson L-5 close to her and played lead. She didn't play a lot of notes, but the ones she played, she made count. She went straight to where the neck frets of the guitar met the body, in the highest register she could play, and made that guitar whine a warning to counter Reverend Reese's baritone.

Now, Sister Rosetta was what people called a "foot-stompin' Christian," so in between those licks, she stomped her foot twice to set the rhythm to match Reverend Reese. When he moaned and she played lead, it sounded like, "Mm-hmm..."

Stomp. Stomp.

Doc and Dad could feel it through the floorboards—that baritone voice, the whining guitar licks, and the *stomp stomp* that traveled from the floor through their boots and straight up into their spines, like a whipcrack and the pitiful moan of one whose flesh was seared and called out in pain.

"Mm-hmm..."

Stomp. Stomp.

"Mm-hmm..."

Stomp. Stomp.

It was the kind of music meant to scare the devil himself. Meant to say, "Sinner, get thee behind me!"

Stomp. Stomp. "Now, Brother Tanner Irving is a good man," the Right Reverend Reese intoned. Sister Rosetta played the gospel lick, and when the Amen Corner weighed in its chorus, she added her *Stomp. Stomp.* And Doc Boyd started feeling downright uncomfortable.

"I know Brother Tanner."

Stomp. Stomp. "*You* know him."

Stomp. Stomp. "And we all know he is a righteous man."

"Amen!" someone shouted.

"Who walks with the Lord."

"Preach it this evening!" Mother Katie Bell shouted.

"But even a *righteous* man," preached the Right Reverend Reese, "can be misled."

Stomp. Stomp. "Now, I ain't sayin' that there's a white devil...or two..."

Stomp. Stomp. "…that done took Brother Tanner and bamboozled him, hornswoggled him, hustled, and flimflammed him."

Stomp. Stomp. "Nobody heard me say that!"

"Uh-uh!" said Mother Katie Bell.

"But I'm sayin' all the blessings that were supposed to rain down, like manna from heaven on the children of Israel…"

Stomp. Stomp. "…turned out to be a curse!"

"Preach it!" shouted the Amen Corner.

"Now, Brother Tanner…"

Stomp. Stomp. "…has asked that we come together and listen to 'Dr.' Boyd." And at the mention of this name, Sister Rosetta bent that string, played that high note, and made it twang and turned the guitar licks into licks of flame that would consume all sinners and all sinners' sins and leave them charred in fire and brimstone, *hellfire* come to earth.

"And because Brother Tanner is one of our own, I said, 'All right let's hear what he has to say.'"

Stomp. Stomp. "And then we'll be the judge of whether it is fish or fowl."

Stomp. Stomp. "Angel or devil."

Sister Rosetta played that Gibson and made it moan, made it shout out a warnin', made it cry to the heavens, and made Doc Boyd turn to Dad Everett and say, "Just in case it doesn't go as planned, I'd have that Model A runnin' around back."

"You got it," said Dad.

And with that, Reverend Reese turned his coal-burning gaze on the con man and said, "Well, what are you, brother?"

Stomp. Stomp. "Are you an angel?"

Stomp. Stomp. "Or are you the devil?"

And Rosetta let go with one last, long riff that cut down to the marrow of your bones and held it there, bendin' that string till everybody in that church believed that girl could make the walls of Jericho themselves tumble down before her.

Doc swallowed hard, and one of the sisters of the congregation stood up and pointed an accusing finger.

"Where's all the jobs you promised?"

"Yeah!" said the Amen Corner.

There were no more guitar licks. No more foot stomps. Just the sound of people fanning themselves on this sultry night and the feeling of anger welling up instead of a joyful noise rising up before the Lord, as another woman stood up and declared, "You said we'd all be anointed in black gold. All we've got is a swift kick in the backside! No jobs, no land, no nothin'. Because of *you*!"

"That's right!" shouted a huge man, with fists as big as ham hocks. "Get thee behind me, Satan!" he said, pointing straight at Doc.

And then suddenly all was silent as all eyes turned to the tall man who stood in the back of the church—the man who had promised salvation in the form of black gold and brought with him nothing but curses and misery and was come now to face his judgment.

It was so quiet, Doc Boyd thought he could hear himself sweat. He took a step inside the church, and the sound of his high-top boots echoed across the floorboards, almost like his own Amen Corner.

"From the book of Daniel," he said, holding his own worn copy of the Good Book before him like a shield. "Chapter six, beginning at verse sixteen."

Another step that echoed up, "Amen!"

Chapter 22

"'Then the king commanded, and Daniel was brought and cast into the den of lions…And a stone was brought and laid on the mouth of the den…Then, at break of day, the king arose and went in haste to the den of lions.'"

Doc stepped up to the man who had said, "Get thee behind me, Satan," and locked eyes with him.

"'As he came near to the den where Daniel was, he cried out in a tone of anguish…, "O Daniel, servant of the living God, whom you serve continually, been able to deliver you from the lions?"'"

Doc maintained his eye contact with the man as he took two more steps toward the pulpit.

"'Then Daniel said to the king…, "My God sent his angel."'" And, with that, Doc stepped up to the pulpit and held his Bible up before the Reverend Reese. "'"And shut the lions' mouths."'"

Then Doc turned and looked at the congregation, holding his Bible aloft to them, and continued. "Hath shut the lions' mouths on this Lord's Day evening. And why? What does the Bible say? What does the Bible teach us? Why was Daniel not hurt in the lions' den? 'Because I was found blameless before him; and also before you…I have done no harm.' That's what Daniel said. 'I have done no harm.'"

Reverend Reese backed away a bit, and even the sound of the fanning had stopped, as Doc's voice sank barely above a whisper that told each and every one of them that their pain was his and that he felt it down in the marrow of his bones, in the depths of his soul.

"But somebody's harm'd tonight," Doc said. "Somebody's in pain tonight. Might be a mother who can't feed her child."

"That's right," said Mother Katie Bell.

"Might be a father who can't support his family."

"Mm-hmm," said Sister Rosetta, and her fingers moved along the frets of her guitar, directed by a higher source, it seemed, playing a soul-wrenching lick as Doc said, "Might be a son who's heartbroken to see the look in his father's eye."

"Preach it!" said the giant of a man who, only a moment before, had said, "Get thee behind me, Satan."

Doc's eyes filled with tears as he thought of Flora May Simms and the treasure he had found in her embrace and forfeited with his lies so that, when he spoke, it was with the voice of the brokenhearted, the wounded of spirit and soul. "Might be a man who's lost the woman he loves."

Sister Rosetta couldn't help herself but called out, "Amen!" while her fingers still pulled licks from the strings of her Gibson.

"Somebody's in pain tonight. And that's a fact."

"That's true!" said a voice from the Amen Corner.

Doc's voice rose, and now it was *his* baritone that vibrated, resonated through the pews, accompanied by the licks on Rosetta's guitar. "Well, I say to you here and now, from the pulpit of the Beth El Baptist Church...Amen! *Beth El*, you know what that means?"

Stomp. Stomp. "It means 'house of *God*'!"

Stomp. Stomp.

"So, I say to you, from the pulpit of this church in the house of *God*—!

Stomp. Stomp. "—that *Jeeezuuuss* will not let this injustice stand!"

"*Amen!*" shouted the congregation.

Which prompted Dad Everett to mutter so that only he could hear it, "That man is the devil himself."

Chapter 22

"I say to you," Doc said, "here and now, from the pulpit of this church on this Lord's Day evening..."

Stomp. Stomp. "That if the only thing you own in life is this church, right here?"

Stomp. Stomp.

And Sister Rosetta's Gibson spit fire.

"Then I say you form a company with whatever you got left, and we drill a well right down through the middle of this *pulpit* and leave the rest up to *Jeeezuuuss!*"

Doc threw his arms out wide to the heavens as his voice echoed and reverberated through the church built to sound like the inside of a Gibson guitar, and all the saints and brothers and sisters and mothers of the church *and* the Right Reverend Reese himself shouted out, as the Lord's own mighty host, "*Amen!*"

Reverend Reese let Doc and Dad set up a little table near the back of the church. The members of the congregation stood in line, dropping what little money they had left into the collection bucket.

"That's it. Thank you kindly. Thank you kindly," Doc said to each of the congregants, who now treated him like family, as Dad Everett explained the nuts and bolts of the venture they had just entered into.

"Every member of the congregation will have an equal share in the Beth El Petroleum Company. And Doc and I will just take a simple fee for drilling the well. One thousand dollars."

Just then, Tanner Irving stepped up and took possession of the collection bucket. He still had that "watch your wallet" feeling he got whenever he was around Doc and Dad of late. More than that, his reputation was now on the line as well. If Doc turned out to be a blessing, he had been the intermediary. But if Doc turned out to be a curse, he would have been the cause.

"Ain't no offense, but just to make sure you don't skip town with it, we're gonna hold on to the money till you drill that well. And then, dry hole or gusher, you'll get your fee."

"Skip town?" Dad Everett said in shock, as if the very thought of it had wounded him to the quick. "Mr. Irving, why would we skip town? We brought in the gusher over at the Junipera Sue. You saw that."

"Mr. Everett," said Tanner, passing the bucket to the Reverend Reese for safekeeping, "you'll get the money when you drill the well down to at least thirty-five hundred feet. Then, whichever way it turns out, gusher or dry hole, you'll get your pay."

The Right Reverend Reese looked at Doc Boyd and said, in his mellifluous baritone, "Amen, Brother Boyd. Amen."

Chapter 23

Doc and Dad's plan was pretty straightforward: keep stalling the widows long enough to spud in a well through the pulpit of the Beth El Baptist Church and then declare a dry hole, collect their thousand dollars, and get outta Texas before the law could get to them.

It was the most incredible thing anyone ever did see. First of all, once all the white folks who had worked bringing in the Junipera Sue Number One heard that Doc and Dad were gonna try to spud in a well to help out the Black folks who had helped them, they decided to return the favor. Nobody asked them. Nobody put out a call. They just showed up with their work gloves.

Not just roughnecks, either, but some of the same shop owners and farmers who had never worked on an oil rig in their life simply showed up, walked up to Doc or Dad, and said, "What do you want me to do?"

And, because they had already had the experience of bringing in one well, they weren't total greenhorns. While they were far from capable cable-and-tool men, when it came to erecting the derrick, they could bore a hole, saw boards straight, and be trusted not to drive a nail through their own finger but through the wood instead.

Second thing, no less remarkable and certainly more dramatic, was the fact that this was the first oil well in history, so far as anybody knew, that was being drilled straight through the pulpit of a church. Doc and Dad didn't want to waste any time dismantling the pulpit, so they just cut a hole through it and sank their drill bit. They sent some of the volunteers up on the roof and had them tear a hole through that as well, right behind the steeple, to make room for the top of the derrick and give the imaginary gusher someplace to spout.

Both white and Black people alike were impressed with Doc and Dad's zeal. The men never took a moment's respite. They worked round the clock and divided up their crews into eight-hour shifts so they could get to those thirty-five hundred feet as soon as possible and skedaddle.

They had that derrick up inside of twenty hours. The boiler was set, fired up, the flywheel started to turn, and that drill bit started biting into bedrock twenty-five hours after they had begun the task that seemed, to the parishioners, something as mighty as the children of Israel building Pharaoh's pyramids. When dawn broke, they looked up and, right behind the cross of the steeple, poking its head out a little bit higher, was the top of the derrick.

There were some elders of the church who disparaged the efforts, and Brother Sonny Irby said it was blasphemous to try and drill a well and prospect for oil in the tabernacle of the Lord. Reverend Reese replied, "When that gusher blows in, I guess you won't take your share, then, will you."

And then, suddenly, Brother Irby remembered his Bible. "Exodus forty, verse nine. 'Then you shall take the anointing oil and anoint the tabernacle and all that is in it, and consecrate it and all its furniture, so that it may become holy.'"

Chapter 23

"Amen," said Reverend Reese. "Any oil that comes outta this church is gonna be *holy* oil. And this tabernacle is gonna get consecrated!"

To which Brother Irby answered a pious amen, put on a pair of work gloves, and started tightening up the bolts that held the crosspieces of the derrick in place.

Junipera Sue worked with some of the sisters and mothers of the church, cooking dinner and making sandwiches and pots of coffee for the crews who worked in eight-hour shifts both night and day.

No one could remember such a thing: white folk pitchin' in to help Black folk simply because they figured it was time to return a favor. Dad got positively misty-eyed at the fact that they had built a bridge across the racial divide, but Doc couldn't care less whether his crew was white or Black or little green men from Mars. All he wanted to do was get down to thirty-five hundred feet, collect that thousand bucks, and get out of Dodge.

There was only one problem with his plan. At 10:52 in the morning, at exactly twelve hundred feet—they hit oil!

The earth began a mighty shaking, like the earthquake that struck Golgotha when our Lord and Savior was on the cross and the veil in the temple was rent.

Doc didn't have to shout out, "Put out those cigarettes and unhook that boiler!" this time. The folks who had been at the Junipera Sue Number One knew exactly what to do. They sealed up that boiler, unhitched it, cut the belt that went from the flywheel to the drill bit, and wheeled that thing out the front of the church as, all the while, the earth roared like a volcano about to erupt.

And blow she did exactly, in the words of Brother Irby, anointing the tabernacle and all its pews in holy oil that shot up, through the roof, high above the steeple, some said, as much as two hundred feet in the air, and rained down black gold like manna from heaven, drenching white and Black people alike. And right there from the pulpit of Beth El Baptist Church, the house of God, they brought in the second largest well in the history of the world. Everybody embraced, danced, clapped each other on the back, raised their arms to heaven, and praised their Lord in hallelujahs.

Once they had the gusher capped, Doc walked up to Reverend Reese and Tanner, stuck out his hand, grinning from ear to ear, and said, "Reverend Reese, Mr. Irving, give me my thousand dollars!"

Reverend Reese nodded, then said, "Before we do, I think we should all get down on our knees in prayer and thank the Lord." Reverend Reese, all the congregants, Dad and Doc, and all the white volunteers, anointed in the holy oil, knelt down in front of the Beth El Baptist Church as the reverend's baritone voice boomed out, "O Lord, in your grace and mercy, you sent two angels whom we mistook for devils and showered us with your merciful bounty. How mighty are your works, O Lord! And in Jesus' name, let us say amen."

Doc looked up and saw the sun glinting off the cross, drenched in oil atop the steeple. He felt as if perhaps this unintended good deed had placed him in what he could only think of as a state of grace. He had twice meant only to swindle people, and, not once but two times, every lie he told about striking oil was gospel truth. And now he had getaway money to boot!

Just then, he heard another baritone voice, booming out behind them. It belonged to Captain Enrique "Lone Wolf" Rodriguez.

"Which one of you is Everett?" he demanded.

Doc, Dad, and all the parishioners were still on their knees, and thus, Lone Wolf Rodriguez looked even taller than his six-foot, five-inch frame.

"Everett?" Rodriguez called out again.

"That's me," Dad said.

Lone Wolf turned his gaze on Doc and said, "Bumstetter?"

In reply, Doc looked around in all innocence to the people gathered round about and said, "Any of you folks named Bumstetter?"

Then Captain Rodriguez put in, "A.k.a. Horatio Daedalus Boyd?"

Doc arose graciously, trying to put on as good a face as possible. "I am he, sir. To what do we owe the pleasure?" he said, sticking out his hand to shake that of the Texas Ranger, who, instead, in a lightning move, slapped a handcuff on it while Deputy Jimmy Q. put cuffs on Dad.

"You're both under arrest," said Rodriguez.

Doc just looked at Dad and said, "I told you we ought to go to California."

***

There was no courthouse in Cornville. There was a circuit judge who, in normal times, visited once every ten weeks. But this was far from a normal time, and the trial not only was the biggest that anyone in Cornville had ever seen but drew national attention, with newspapermen from as far off as New York City arriving to cover the trial, which promised to detail the saga of the libidinous, aged con men colorfully described as the Love Bandits of East Texas and the Merry Widows of Cornville.

The trial would be held in the schoolhouse, which had been set up as a temporary courtroom. All the little school desks with their inkwells and folding desktops had been removed, replaced by folding chairs for the gallery of white folks, benches for the Black spectators in the back of the court, two rows of church pews for the all-male jury, tables for the defense and prosecution, and a truly magnificent mahogany desk, which had been commandeered from the bank manager, for the judge.

The makeshift courtroom was packed to the rafters not just with citizenry but also with photographers and reporters from across the continent. A live radio feed had actually been set up just outside the courthouse, where a reporter named Jerry Houlihan was describing the events within.

Inside, Doc and Dad sat at the defense table with their attorney, a court-appointed public defender by the name of William Wimple. He was fresh out of law school and had never tried a case before in his life. Opposite him was the aptly named prosecutor Mr. Grimm, a man who made the infamous reaper look positively cheerful. Behind them were the widows, for whom Dad had advocated so eloquently and who now seemed bent on nothing but revenge. Deputy Jimmy Q. was acting as the bailiff and relishing his moment in the spotlight.

"You think they can hang us for fraud?" Doc asked Dad.

"If the judge doesn't, I reckon the widders will," Dad answered.

Mr. Wimple, their attorney, turned to them. "Never you mind, gentlemen. I intend to mount a vigorous defense. Even though, as a public defender appointed by the court, I receive no remuneration. I assure you, you'll get your money's worth."

Just then a black-robed man, whose truly biblical beard molded his visage into that of an Old Testament prophet, entered the schoolhouse. Jimmy Q. stepped forward, sucked in

Chapter 23

his gut, and struck a manly pose for the photographers whose flashbulbs exploded to record the historic moment.

"All rise!" he said. "The Superior Court of Cornville County is now in session. The Honorable Judge J. J. Watson presiding. God bless this honorable court, the great state of Texas, and the United States of America."

Judge Watson took his seat at the bank manager's desk, turned to Cornville's version of the Grand Inquisitor, and said, "Mr. Grimm, the prosecution may proceed."

The prosecuting attorney, a man obviously with many years of experience, arose from his table and began his address. "Your Honor, ladies and gentlemen of the jury, this case is as sad and tragic as it is open and shut, for the victims are but little old ladies, widows, sainted silver-haired angels not only from our fair state of Texas but from as far off as the exotic climes of Oklahoma."

He turned and pointed at Doc and Dad. "These two villainous, aging lotharios left a swath of human misery behind them, like a vast, thundering tornado of *amore* run amok."

It was clear that Mr. Grimm was running for higher office.

Dad simply nudged Doc and said, "We're dead."

Grimm stalked back to the jury and continued. "The witnesses who will come before you will not seem like strangers, but rather, with their wrinkled eyes and weathered brows, they will seem like your own mothers and grandmothers."

He let that sink in for a moment, letting each jury member conjure up the image of his own sainted mother or grandmother being defiled before his very eyes by the villainous lotharios seated at the defense table. Mr. Grimm allowed his voice to rise in righteous indignation.

"In what should have been their golden years, they were *twice* victimized, I say! For it was not only their life savings that these men stole from them but also their hearts' affections as well. And the prosecution will present evidence in black and white—from out of the accused's very mouths—that will prove their guilt beyond any doubt."

"What's he talking about?" Dad asked as Grimm dramatically pointed his accusatory finger at the defendants.

"Therefore, the state will feel no compunction whatsoever in asking for, nay, in *demanding* that justice be served by exacting the maximum penalty possible for those who would prey upon… upon our very own mothers and *grand*mothers so that they serve out the rest of their days in the prison of their own devices."

"He's very good," Doc said.

"Heck, I'd convict us," Dad agreed.

"Thank you, Mr. Grimm," said the black-robed Old Testament prophet. Then, nodding at the public defender, he continued. "For the defense, Mr. Wimple."

Wimple nervously straightened his tie, slicked back his hair, pulled down on his coat, took a long drink of water, cleared his throat, took another sip that dribbled down onto his necktie, bumped his knee against the defense table as he stood up, and then declared in a high-pitched, squeaky voice as though just arriving at puberty, "Your honor, gentlemen of the jury, though there is no doubt about my clients' moral turpitude, we do not accept Mr. Grimm's characterizations of the defendants." With that, Wimple sat down.

Doc gave him a friendly pat on the back and said, "That's tellin' 'em, Wimple."

"For a second," Dad said, "I was nervous. But you threw 'em for a loop with that one."

Wimple nodded with false modesty, for he was bursting with pride at his opening statement. He gave a broad smile and said, "Ever faithful!"

"Call your first witness, Mr. Grimm," said the judge.

Grimm stood up and said, in his sonorous tones, "Your Honor, the prosecution calls Mrs. Flora May Simms."

Deputy Quattrochi repeated, "Call Flora May Simms!"

Doc turned around in shock. She had come all the way from Oklahoma to testify against him. The one woman he had truly loved.

He watched her, tall and slender, as she rose from the back of the courtroom and walked determinately to the makeshift, wooden witness stand. As she passed, Doc swore he could smell the scent of lilac in the air. She did not return his gaze. In her hand was a bundle of letters.

Flora May approached the witness chair and turned to face Jimmy Q., who proffered a Bible.

"Place your hand on the Bible," he said. "Do you swear to tell the truth, the whole truth, and nothing but the truth in the matter now pending before this court, so help you God?"

"So help me God," said the Widow Simms. Then, she locked eyes with Doc and continued. "I will tell the truth."

"Our goose is cooked," Dad whispered.

"You don't know the half of it," Doc muttered back.

"What do you mean?" Dad asked.

Reluctantly, Doc leaned in and whispered into Dad's ear, "I admitted to her that we swindled her, and I tried to give the money back to her. That didn't go over exactly as I planned."

"Gave the money back?" Doc hissed. "Admit you swindled her? Why'd you go and do a fool thing like that!"

Doc merely shrugged his shoulders and said, "*Amore.*"

"Mrs. Simms," said Mr. Grimm, "what is your marital status?"

"I'm a widow."

"My condolences, madam," said Grimm, as though her husband had only passed away just the day before. "And I appreciate what you must be going through. You notified me, did you not, that you were one of the victims of the accused, Bumstetter, a.k.a. Doc Boyd, in the fair state of Oklahoma. Is that true?"

"It is," she said.

"And the accused found your name in a death notice announcing the demise of your beloved husband, is that correct?"

"It is," confirmed the Widow Simms.

Grimm stalked back and forth like a junkyard dog straining at its length of chain, frothing and waiting to pounce.

"And then he paid a call on you and said that your late husband had agreed to enter into a scheme to back his oil venture. Is that also correct?"

"Yes, sir," she replied.

"And then, I shall simply say, he wooed you, made you believe he was romantically inclined toward you, and then abused your affections by having you invest in his worthless oil well."

"Yes, sir," said Flora May, "that's true."

"You have told me, in fact, that he wrote love letters to you. And I have asked you to bring one of them with you. So that all may hear not only the extent of the depravity of the accused but also a confession—in his own hand—of the crime he committed in wresting away your life savings and your affections."

"Was that a question?" asked the Widow Simms.

Chapter 23

Dad punched Doc in the arm. "You were stupid enough to put it in writing?"

"'Tis true, 'tis pity. And pity 'tis, 'tis true.' *Hamlet*. Act two, scene two," said Doc.

Dad simply looked to the heavens, hoping that the earth would open and swallow him whole to end his misery.

Grimm turned to Flora May and said, "Would you read aloud from the letter?"

Doc put his head in his hands and groaned, "Oh Lord. Here it comes."

Chapter 24

The Widow Flora May Simms set the bundle of letters she had carried with her in her lap. They were still tied together in a neat stack with the same blue satin ribbon, which she had tied in a bow. Doc recognized the letters as being the ones he had sent in what he preferred to think of as their courtship and what others might refer to as the period of time in which he was swindling her, as well as those epistles he had forwarded to acquaintances in various parts of the land, whom he used, he liked to think, as Cupid's messengers, allowing him to send endearments to the Widow Simms but leave no trail which the law could follow.

She pulled the first letter from the bundle without untying the bow, and he recognized it easily. This one did, indeed, have a return address—the Cornville County Jail. It was the last letter he had sent.

Once they had been arrested, he saw no point in hiding his whereabouts or in not confessing his deepest emotions. He now realized that that well may have been a strategic error.

Doc and Dad's arrest for defrauding the widows of Cornville and for bringing in the largest oil strike in the history of the world had made national and, some even said, international headlines that one could imagine had reached even what Mr. Grimm once referred to as "the exotic climes" of Oklahoma.

Flora May had evidently gone to considerable lengths to notify the prosecutor and thus fulfill her own vow to be the first to stand in line to testify against him.

The prosecutor had asked her to read the letter aloud, to show the members of the jury the confession to the crimes of which he was accused, that he had written in his own hand, and the depths of his depravity.

"My dearest," the Widow Simms began reading aloud. She pronounced the words with so much disdain, Doc literally felt his heart ache. There was no doubt he would end his days in prison, but he believed there was no pain greater than the one he now felt, hearing Flora May Simms's bitter disdain for his deepest, most heartfelt emotions. She read the words mechanically, to intentionally denude them of the warmth of his heart and the tears he had shed as he wrote them. Indeed, there was a mocking tone to every word she pronounced.

"You once protested to me," the Widow Simms intoned, with no small amount of sarcasm and rancor, "that we were too old for such foolishness as love. And fool I know I was to hope that such a one as you could ever smile kindly upon such a one as I."

She paused. And it occurred to Doc that it may well have been the first time she had read the letter in more than a purely perfunctory way. When she'd first received it, she must have skimmed through it for proof of his guilt, found it, and then raced to volunteer to testify against him. But now, reading it aloud for the first time, it was as if she were finally hearing the words he had poured out onto the page.

"For I have become, as King David said about himself, in old age, a song for drunkards that sit at the village gate. An object of scorn and derision."

She looked up from the letter, for the briefest of instants, to Doc Boyd, and the moment their eyes met, she looked away and began reading again, slower this time, as if hearing his words at last.

"An object of scorn and derision. Always chasing rainbows and never finding the pot of gold. And now, in a prison of my own making, I know how wounded you were by my deceit."

She paused again and looked up at him from the letter. There was no longer hatred in her gaze. Though he spoke not a word from the defense table, they were now engaged in the most intimate of conversations, which she was being forced to share aloud with strangers.

"You have demanded never to see me again because of my disgraceful conduct in swindling not only you but others as well."

Grimm could not restrain himself; the mouse had just eaten the cheese, and the trap had sprung and broke its neck. He pumped his fist a few inches, as if his home team had just hit one out of the park in the bottom of the ninth and clinched the pennant.

"And of course," Flora May continued, "you were right to do so."

Dad Everett kicked Doc as hard as he could beneath the table.

"What was that for?" Doc whispered.

"Well, you just put the noose around our necks. Might as well kick the stool out from under us too. I thought that drunken fool Humason was an idiot; the man was a savant compared to you!"

The Widow Simms, however, adjusted her spectacles and held the letter more at arm's length. The words, which she now read aloud, were piercing her heart as well.

"But in our brief time together," she said, wetting her lips and swallowing, "believe me when I say, to my surprise, I found life's true treasure. I have, at last, found oil. But it does not equal the wealth I found in your embrace, and were it in my power…." She paused and looked up at Doc now, as if she could not believe what she was reading, then continued. "I would not trade that for a hundred kings' ransoms. Not for all the oil beneath the earth, nor all its diamonds and rubies, would I trade the sweet warmth of the touch of your hand upon my arm." Despite herself, there was a cry of emotion welling up in her throat, which she fought hard to control. She had, indeed, come to bury Caesar, not to praise him. Here and there, some of the women in the gallery dabbed a hankie at a tearful eye.

And now, Flora May read not only as one touched by the words but also with the warm glow of nostalgia for a shared memory that once had been one of life's sweetest.

"I remember that touch as it was on that glorious morn when we walked alongside the fence beside your meadow, with the sun golden upon your sweet skin…." Her voice now broke audibly, and tears welled in her eyes as she said, "And the touch of your hand in mine."

She had to pause once again to get ahold of her emotions. And, despite himself, Circuit Judge J. J. Watson dabbed a tear from his own eye with the edge of his robe.

"In the words of the orphaned child, David Copperfield," Flora May read aloud in a trembling voice, "'I wish I had died then, with that feeling in my heart. I should have been more fit for heaven than I ever have been since.'"

Flora May looked up from the letter and locked eyes with Doc. There was no courtroom now, no reporters—though many of the photographers flashed lightning with their cameras at this amazing turn of events. There was no judge, no jury, no prosecutor. There were only Flora May and her Horatio as she tearfully read.

"For you are the flower of my heart and the master of my soul."

She carefully folded the letter and tried, in vain, to keep her own tears from falling upon it.

Throughout the courtroom, there was the sound of weeping; some of it from the widows who had been swindled, some of it from women who had never had such words of love directed toward them in all their days and wept with longing, wishing, even if it were an illusion, that someone, sometime, had opened their hearts so purely to them.

Flora May gazed lovingly at Doc Boyd as the flashbulbs popped.

As for Doc, he looked at her in wonder that she bore him no ill will but returned his love with hers.

"Your Honor!" Mr. Grimm shouted, leaping to his feet. "Your Honor, I object!"

"You can't object to your own witness," the judge sniffled, wiping away his own tears.

"Then," Grimm said, in his frustration at his own best plans running amok, foundering on the shore of this addle-headed woman, who had promised to be the witness that would drive a stake through the defense's heart and had scuttled him instead, "I object to all this…sniffling!"

At that declaration, some folks booed, and others hissed aloud at this hard-hearted mortician who mocked their emotions.

"Your Honor," said the Widow Simms. "May I say something?"

The judge turned to her like a father or older brother consoling a bereaved loved one.

"You go right ahead, Mrs. Simms."

Flora May looked from the judge to the jury and then to the gallery, including some of the other widows, entreating them with every fiber of her being to hearken to the better angels of themselves.

"Your Honor, I had a feeling that Horatio was a scalawag."

At the mere mention of his name, "Horatio," she had not only humanized the defendant but identified him as her beloved as well.

"But I *wanted* to believe." She pronounced the words with such longing, such naked honesty, as she said, "And perhaps I'm a fool as well." She turned to Doc and said, directly to him and him alone, though it was said aloud for all the world to hear, "But I still do!"

There it was. A declaration of her love. And she was not ashamed but proud to say it and defiant of anyone who would judge her for it.

"And despite what Mr. Grimm here says, I'm not some helpless, silver-haired, wrinkled-browed plaster saint!"

There was steel in her voice as she straightened herself up and looked intently at Grimm and then to the gallery, as if to tell the whole world she was, unapologetically, a woman in love.

"I've been to a rodeo," she said, "a county fair, and a church picnic or two. But the only real poetry and beauty I've ever known was in the few months that Horatio and I had together and in this bundle of love letters."

She paused and caressed the bundle of letters in her lap just as she had once brushed a lock of hair from his forehead. "These," she continued, "are the remembered words of tender mercies."

And once again she looked at Grimm to put him in *his* place. "And though I'll speak no ill of the dead, it was a tad more than I ever knew with that lazy good-fer-nothin' I put in the grave after thirty-five years of marriage!"

Laughter echoed throughout the courtroom, not in derision but embracing the spunk of this frontier woman. She rode the wave of that laughter and crested it as she rose halfway from her seat and proclaimed aloud for one and all to hear, "And truth be told, it was worth every penny. And I'd pay it all over again. And more to boot!"

Seemingly all the widows, each and every one who had been flimflammed by Dad and Doc, nodded their heads in fervent agreement, some even clapping their hands as if at a revival meeting.

"But more than that," Flora May said, her voice rising up over the laughter and shouts of encouragement of the women in the court, some of whom poked their own spouses as if to say, *Why couldn't you have ever wooed* me *with such fervor?* "But more than that," Flora May said again, raising her right hand as if testifying in church, "I know that with God's sweet grace, these men can be saved. The law might say they deserve prison."

Here she looked at the jury, each one of them, one at a time. "But I'm supposedly the one they wronged. And I'd ask you…" Now she looked from the jury to the judge. "I'd ask *you* to set them free."

Chapter 24

Half the widows leapt from their seats to shout, "Amen!" Some of the men, shamed at the inadequacy of their eloquence when compared to that of Doc Boyd, stood up and demanded vengeance, disguised in the robes of Texas justice. The members of the jury were clearly shaken. Grimm was on his feet, objecting.

Wimple had leapt to his feet, saying, "We would accept that, Your Honor! We would accept a summary judgment!"

It was chaos as flashbulbs exploded and reporters scribbled furiously in their notebooks.

"Order!" said Judge Watson, banging his gavel on the table as if he were Thor himself spitting thunderbolts. "Order in this court!"

"I object, Your Honor!" Grimm shouted. "I *strenuously* object!"

Judge Watson pointed at the prosecutor, moving his arm with such furious speed that it made his robe snap like a banner held aloft in an angry wind. "Oh, shut up!" he said. "And sit down, or you'll wind up in the clink for contempt!" This threat of incarceration silenced the unruly crowd as Watson added, "I *will* have order in this court!"

The amens and laughter and shouted calls for justice subsided as Judge Watson stroked his beard like an Old Testament Solomon presented with a baby claimed by two mothers. He looked from the jury to Dad and Doc, to the spectators, and, finally, to the widows, then seemed to contemplate aloud his own heartfelt feelings.

"All of us here know, especially in tough times like these, what the prospector or the wildcatter feels, hoping that this time, finally, their lucky number will come up."

Not a few men with callused hands in the courtroom nodded their heads in agreement and approval.

"These two could have capped that well," the judge continued, "said it was a dry hole, and made their getaway, as they had before, and no one would have been the wiser."

Doc poked Dad in the ribs, as though the judge had just vindicated the sound advice he'd given on that fateful night when they had discovered the Woodbine sand in the cuttings bucket.

"But they didn't do that," Judge Watson mused, "and I scratch my head in wonder, because it couldn't have been greed that made them do it. They had to have known they would be caught and their scheme discovered. But because they brought that well in, this whole part of the state may see better days."

There was absolutely no denying the wisdom of the judge's words. There wasn't a soul in that court, including the jury, who hadn't benefited from the town's new prosperity, whether they had found employment on a rig or profited in their stores or had sold mineral rights themselves or had family members who did. They all knew that, but for Doc and Dad, their futures would be appreciably dimmer than they were now.

"And," said Judge Watson, "a witness who came into this court bent, I daresay, *bent* on vengeance, with righteous indignation for the wrong committed against her, has now, instead, asked this court for tender mercy. I scratch my head in wonder. So I'll tell you what."

Now he scanned the crowd with his steely blue-eyed gaze.

"Before some of y'all start lookin' for a rope and a tree, I'm going fishing to try to deal with the bewilderment that I myself feel. This court is in recess for one week." The judge thoughtfully reconsidered. "Maybe two. Depends on the fish."

He banged the gavel and rose. "The defendants shall remain in custody without bail."

He exited the courtroom, which erupted in pandemonium.

The widows and other well-wishers crowded around Doc and Dad, pounding their backs in triumph and rejoicing at the turn of events.

Wimple turned to his clients and said with unrestrained pride, "Told you I'd handle it!"

As for Doc, he ignored the well-wishers, the glad-handers, and his puffed-up attorney. His eyes were now locked, instead, with those of Flora May Simms.

Chapter 25

The Cornville County Jail was a grandiose title for the local hoosegow, which contained but two cells, one of which was occupied by Dad Everett and the other by Doc Boyd. Acting Chief of Police Donnie Joe Durban had allotted the two aging con men the two cells, which normally held two to three prisoners apiece. They were, after all, the biggest celebrities ever to have been incarcerated in his jail.

With the trial in recess, the Widow Simms had asked to pass a note to Doc Boyd. She was too embarrassed to visit him in a place where she knew there would be no privacy. It was not in her nature to publicly share her emotions, and she had just done so in front of the entire world and was shaken by the experience. She had determined to return that day to Lathrope, Oklahoma, but first she penned the note to Doc.

He never revealed to another soul what words it contained, but as he read them, he choked back tears and then unabashedly let them fall. That note would be his dearest physical possession to the end of his days.

He knew, despite the widow's entreaty and the judge's acknowledged befuddlement, that the odds were that he and Dad would, barring some miracle, be convicted and sentenced to prison. The sentence would be up to the judge, but regardless of his feelings, Doc knew he was a strictly by-the-book interpreter of the law. He might show mercy, but either way Doc felt sure that his fate was sealed. His address for the foreseeable future would be behind one set of bars or another.

Food was delivered daily from New Dugan's, as were competing pecan pies and at least two shoofly pies, which were sent by the various widows whom Doc and Dad had swindled and not a few who'd wished they had. Since they could not possibly consume all that poured in, they shared their delicacies with Donnie Joe Durban, Jimmy Q., and the other two deputies, Lyle Voss and Kenny Cunningham.

All of them agreed that the pecan and shoofly pies baked by the Widow Martha Jean Tyler surpassed all the others.

Two days after court was put into recess and Judge Watson had gone fishing, Deputy Quattrochi opened the door to a dapper man in a double-breasted, gray pinstripe suit with a handsome maroon tie and matching pocket square. He had slicked-back hair and a well-groomed mustache, and he walked with the ease and careless grace of a man of wealth, influence, and power. There was about him, however, something that belied his well-tailored, sartorial splendor. Doc had a keen eye, and there was something in the stranger's appearance that made Doc certain he hadn't inherited his money; he had come up the hard way. What he was doing there, however, was a mystery.

That mystery was not cleared up by Deputy Quattrochi, who simply said, "You got a visitor, boys."

The visitor in question turned politely to Jimmy Q. and said, "Thank you, Deputy. Now, if you'll be so kind…" Which was, of course, a rich and powerful man's way of saying, "Get lost, pal."

Doc did not doubt that the stranger had tipped Jimmy Q. handsomely for the private audience that was about to take place with the two con men.

The stranger pulled a chair up from behind the deputy's desk and set it between the two cells so he could speak to both Doc and Dad simultaneously with unobstructed views of each. The man carried a leather briefcase and sat it down next to the chair, crossed his legs, and hung his straw boater, with a graceful gesture, on the back of his chair.

"If you're a lawyer," Doc said, "we already got one. He's not worth a bucket of spit, but we can't afford another."

Dad leaned back against the wall of his cell, sitting on his bunk, ignoring the stranger. For his part, the stranger kicked back in the chair, balancing it on its back legs and up against the wall. This confirmed, for Doc, that the stranger had not been educated at Harvard but in the school of hard knocks.

"I've been called a lot of insulting names in my life," said the stranger. "But lawyer isn't one of them."

Dad belched from the hearty lunch of T-bone steak and frijoles supplied by Timothy O'Sullivan and said, "Then what are you tryin' to sell? Because whatever it is, we're not buyin'."

"Gentlemen," said the stranger in a Louisiana accent that did not bespeak inherited wealth, "I began life as a penniless, fifteen-year-old runaway and developed only one talent." He leaned forward, letting the front legs of the chair hit the floor like the judge's gavel ringing out justice. "I took a deck of cards," he said, "and I practiced with each one. Over and over again. Tossin' 'em against a slat-board wall. I musta done it straight for three months, till finally, I could take any card in that deck, toss it from fifteen feet away, and make it stick in any slat I wanted to."

The stranger looked from Doc to Dad.

"Now, you might say that's not much of a talent, but it's the only one I had. And I was awful good at it. Fifteen years old, penniless, hungry as a scrawny alley cat with not a mouse in sight. Now, you wouldn't think that's much of an advantage in life, and the truth is, it wasn't. The advantage that I did have, however, was in the number of people willing to bet I couldn't do it! I parlayed that mild talent, takin' the money of suckers and bumpkins and a few city slickers who thought I was the bumpkin, and I used that to buy my first oil lease."

The stranger took a dramatic pause, looked to both men again, smiled beguilingly, then said, "My name is Heinz. L. D. Heinz."

"Heinz? Of Heinz Petroleum?" Doc sat up, finally taking notice of the owner of the largest privately owned petroleum company in the state. The man was no John D. Rockefeller, but he clearly had ambitions to equal or surpass him. The stranger extended his hand to both men and said, "You can call me L. D."

"Well, howdy, L. D.!" said Doc Boyd, shaking his hand heartily and knowing, whatever the outcome of the trial, or whatever anyone else might say or think, he and L. D. were on equal footing. "Pleased to meet ya! I guess you might have heard about our well comin' in."

"Congratulations," L. D. said to both men. "It's a beaut. Heck of an achievement."

"I predicted we'd hit Woodbine sand at thirty-five hundred feet. And we did!" said Doc.

"And I brought her in!" Dad quickly added.

L. D. graciously nodded to both men. "Well, it's an honor and a pleasure to meet the oilmen that brought in the Junipera Sue Number One."

And that's all Dad Everett needed to think it all worthwhile. Over half a century of bein' a joke, and here was one of the biggest independent petroleum magnates in the country calling David Henry Everett an oilman. Not a con man, not a huckster or snake oil salesman or flimflam man. Not even a wildcatter and sure as heck not *Dry Hole Everett*—but a title reserved only for those who had played with all their hearts, gambled everything they had, and won. You couldn't be an oilman unless you'd *brought in* oil.

Dad had to turn away to fight back his emotion, which, of course, is exactly why L. D. had used the phrase. All oilmen, at one time or another, were lease hounds. And all lease hounds, almost by definition, were con men. L. D. was no different.

"I admire you boys," L. D. said with genuine appreciation. "Because, like me, you possessed only a mild talent, and it had nothin' to do with geology. It had to do with romance. Not swindlin' little old ladies but offering them a chance to buy a commodity which, Lord only knows, must've run mighty scarce in the dry desert of their lives."

Doc, however, was insulted. There was no professor of geology on the face of the earth who could have been more precise in his calculations. "What're you talkin' about? I predicted we'd hit the Woodbine sand at thirty-five hundred feet, and we did!"

L. D. could ill afford to allow Doc and Dad the comfort of illusion. He had come here this day to make them face facts and then take action. "You predicted exactly the same thing to every widow in Oklahoma and nearly half the ones in Texas. Even a broken clock is right two times a day."

"I take umbrage at your remarks, sir!" said Doc.

Chapter 25

L. D. looked at him with one eyebrow raised and asked, "Do you deny 'em?"

"No," said Doc, mustering all the dignity remaining in his arsenal. "But a fellow's got a right to take a little umbrage, and I just took mine."

L. D. could not allow this conversation to get off track because of bruised egos. "Boys, this is the greatest country on earth because we're free to make our own choices. Free to gamble on nothin' but the mildest talent in the world. Free to bust our humps, get our hearts broke, dust ourselves off, and do it all over again. You might not think so, but I admire you boys. I know that con of yours as well as I know that slat-board wall of mine, and I'm not ashamed to say it. You could have capped that well and got away clean. But you couldn't walk away from it. And I don't believe it was the money. I believe it was about *respect*. And for what it's worth, you've earned mine."

There was no guile in the way L. D. said it. It was a statement of fact.

"That means a lot," Dad said, "comin' from a man like you."

The trap was baited, and now it was time for L. D. to spring it. And the only way it could work was if they didn't see it coming until it was too late.

"You boys pulled somethin' off that even *I* could not do. Either by blind luck—in which I do not believe—or through the grace of God, which I do not pretend to understand, you brought in the greatest sea of black crude the world has ever known. But you boys are sinking fast in it, and I've got the only life vest in sight."

Doc was pleased to see the con man coming out in L. D. They were back on equal footing once again. "Well, I sense there's a deal to be made," Doc said, smiling.

"There is," said L. D. "And you're gonna take it, too, but you won't like it. I'm willing to go and buy up all the widows' worthless shares, every certificate you issued. I'll buy 'em all. From the widows, from the Dials, even from Tanner Irving. I know about him too. I will risk my capital in the belief that I can convince every one of them to sign over their shares. That's the American way. Work hard, risk when you think it's justified, and reap your reward. And I intend to do all three. I will issue all the widows new stock in the new company I create. That will then, effectively, let you off the hook."

"Sounds good so far," Dad said. Off the hook meant out of jail.

"And what percentage do we get?" Doc asked, ready to get down to brass tacks.

"You get to walk out of jail, boys. That's it. That's all."

There is an old salesman's rule. He who speaks first after the deal has been broached loses.

All was silent as L. D. said not another word. Finally it was Dad who shouted out in frustration.

"But we're the ones who brought this thing in!"

"We're the ones who discovered it!" Doc added.

"For which I am truly grateful," L. D. said, knowing he had already won. "But discoverin' and bringin' it in is only half the trick, boys. Keepin' it is what counts. That's the American way too." So saying, he opened up his beautifully hand-tooled leather briefcase and brought out a contract at the bottom of which was room for three signatures: his, Dad's, and Doc's.

"That's the deal. Take it or leave it. It won't come again."

Now, if there's one thing any oilman knows, it's that once you've struck the oil and are negotiating with a buyer, you have to be prepared to get up from the table and walk away. Otherwise you got no right takin' a seat at it in the first place.

Once again, L. D. was silent.

Once again, whoever spoke first lost.

"We'll be broke!" Doc said.

"You'll be free," said L. D. "And you can't put a price on freedom. But the one thing you *can* say about freedom is that it ain't free."

So saying, he proffered the contract and a pen to Dad first. Being an older man, Dad realized that time as a free man was worth more than money. Dad put the contract on the little table by his bunk and affixed his signature, unable to resist one flourish. He signed his name D. H. "Gusher" Everett.

"I'll sign, on one condition," Doc said.

L. D. smiled. "You don't have many cards to play, sir."

"I don't sign it as Heinrich Bumstetter. I get to sign it as Horatio Daedalus Boyd, PhD in petroleum engineering, geology, and all matters petroliferous."

L. D. looked at Doc with the greatest respect and said, "Sign here, Dr. Boyd." It would be the last time that Heinrich Bumstetter ever used that alias.

And that was how L. D. Heinz became the richest oilman in the history of the world.

As for the widows, all of them—even the ones Dad and Doc had swindled in Oklahoma, to whom Heinz had issued shares as well, just to be on the safe side—lived out their years in comfort beyond their dreams.

When Junipera Sue and Thurman Dial were issued their shares by L. D. Heinz, they called in all the farmers to whom they had extended credit over the years. There were literally hundreds of them—the same folks who had stripped the tires off their automobiles when there was no more wood left to burn because *all* of them had a stake in whether that well came in. Now was the Dials' day to collect. Thurman and Junipera Sue took great delight in taking out a box of credit slips, tearing them up, and scattering them to the winds like a New York ticker-tape parade or a gusher raining down black gold.

The members of the Beth El Baptist Church became millionaires and sent their children to college and taught them all to be regular churchgoers and give their thanks to the Lord.

"And," said Tanner Irving Jr. to Matt and Denise, coming back from the depths of his tale, "I was one of 'em. Got my bachelor's degree from LSU and my master's and PhD in petroleum engineering from the University of Texas.

"As for Dad and Doc," he continued, stretching a little in his rocking chair and tapping his pipe against the palm of his hand, "they had not only seen the light. They were saved by it. Doc was baptized in the newly rebuilt Beth El Baptist Church, and he entered the ministry as well: the Reverend Heinrich Bumstetter! I was there in the pews when he officiated at his first wedding.

"'Only a crazy man,' Bumstetter said, 'would get slapped in the face by genuine miracles and refuse to see them for what they are. I may have been accused of being many things in life, but crazy isn't one of them. When I get slapped upside the head by ten miracles, not one, I know a good thing when I see it. Of course the real miracle was that every lie I told turned out to be the truth. Not by *my* design but by that of a higher power. I have been to the nadir of the nadir and the apex of the apex and have known the redeeming warmth and affection of my beloved wife, Flora May. I have seen the light of my Lord and Savior, Jesus Christ, who, in spite of my best efforts to backslide, led me into the true treasure in life. He led me not only into matrimonial bliss but into the ministry as well. And one of the greatest blessings I have been granted is to have my beloved Flora May act as matron of honor as I preside over the wedding of my dear friend Gusher Everett and his beloved Martha Jean.'

"I remember," said Tanner Irving Jr., leaning back in his rocker, "that Sister Rosetta Nubin was there on that guitar, and Mother Katie Bell played the 'Wedding March' on the magnificent new pipe organ that Dad and Doc donated to the new church. The Reverend Bumstetter now used all the gifts the good Lord gave him not to sell snake oil or worthless oil leases but to be a fisher of men and save souls for the Lord. And every day, until the end of his days, Heinrich Bumstetter wrote a love letter to his beloved Flora May. She lived another five years after his passing, and when she died, she asked to be buried beneath the mountain of his love letters.

"Truth is, people who met the Reverend Bumstetter and Gusher Everett in the later years of their lives said that no two finer Christian gentlemen had ever existed on the face of God's good earth."

About the Author

Miracle in East Texas is Dan Gordon's tenth published novel. Gordon is also the screenwriter of twenty produced feature films, including *The Hurricane* (starring Denzel Washington, who received an Academy Award nomination), *Wyatt Earp* (starring Kevin Costner), and the 2017 faith-based film *Let There Be Light* (starring Kevin Sorbo). Gordon was also the head writer of Michael Landon's *Highway to Heaven*. Together, Gordon and Jerry Falwell Jr. cofounded the Zaki Gordon Cinematic Arts Center at Liberty University.